A COLD, COLD WORLD

A COLD, COLD WORLD

Elena Taylor

SEVERN
HOUSE

First world edition published in Great Britain and the USA in 2024
by Severn House, an imprint of Canongate Books Ltd,
14 High Street, Edinburgh EH1 1TE.

severnhouse.com

British Library Cataloguing-in-Publication Data
A CIP catalogue record for this title is available from the British Library.

ISBN-13: 978-1-4483-1406-5 (cased)
ISBN-13: 978-1-4483-1407-2 (e-book)

All Severn House titles are printed on acid-free paper.

MIX
Paper from
responsible sources
FSC® C013056

Typeset by Palimpsest Book Production Ltd.,
Falkirk, Stirlingshire, Scotland.
Printed and bound in Great Britain by
TJ Books, Padstow, Cornwall.

Praise for the Sheriff Bet Rivers Mystery series

"Taylor perfectly captures the tension and determination of a small town sheriff facing down an isolating blizzard while racing against the clock to solve a murder and save a missing child. Sheriff Bet Rivers will be your new favorite character"
Lisa Gardner, #1 *New York Times* bestselling author

"A terrific ensemble cast in a total immersion setting! Fans of CJ Box and Julia Spencer-Fleming will adore this novel – it's whipsmart, completely cinematic, and full of heart.
Not to be missed!"
Hank Phillippi Ryan, *USA Today* bestselling author of
One Wrong Word

"Sheriff Bet Rivers is back with a suspenseful and shrewdly plotted story of deadly small town secrets . . . Think *Longmire* meets *Yellowstone*"
James L'Etoile, award winning author of *Dead Drop* and
Face of Greed

"Tense and divinely atmospheric, this is the perfect book to curl up with on a cold winter's day"
J.L. Delozier, author of the multi-award-winning mystery
The Photo Thief

"Taylor skillfully sets the scene, [while] the introspective, conflicted Bet proves her mettle. Readers will look forward to her next outing"
Publishers Weekly on *All We Buried*

"At the forefront of this haunting, impeccably plotted mystery by Elena Taylor is a sharp new heroine, Sheriff Bet Rivers, that crime fiction fans are sure to fall in love with"
Sheena Kamal, author of *The Lost Ones,* on *All We Buried*

About the author

Elena Taylor worked in theater before turning her storytelling skills to novels. The Sheriff Bet Rivers series draws on her dramatic roots. As Elena Hartwell, she writes the quirky Eddie Shoes Mysteries. Elena is a developmental editor with Allegory Editing, where she works one-on-one with writers to shape and polish their manuscripts. She also writes the Wait, Wait, Don't Query (Yet!) series.

Her favorite place to be is home at Paradise, near Spokane, Washington. She lives with her hubby, three horses, two dogs, and two cats. Elena holds degrees from the University of San Diego, the University of Washington, and the University of Georgia.

www.elenataylorauthor.com

To Sheila Sobel—my life raft through all the storms.

The cold earth slept below;
Above the cold sky shone;
And all around,
With a chilling sound,
From caves of ice and fields of snow
The breath of night like death did flow
Beneath the sinking moon.
—Percy Bysshe Shelley

Cold, Cold World
—Blaze Foley

Acknowledgements

It takes a lot of people to make a book happen, and I'm thankful for everyone who helped bring A Cold, Cold World to life.

First and foremost, to my brilliant agent Madelyn Burt at Stonesong. I can't imagine trying to navigate writing and publishing without you. Thank you for your unflagging support.

Much gratitude to my editor Victoria "Vic" Britton and everyone at Severn House. I'm so thrilled that Bet Rivers found a home with you.

Diego Zanella, former Italian Special Forces, major crimes task force officer, current lieutenant with the Lake Forest Park police department, and my longtime partner in crime. I would fail without your expertise in law enforcement and insights into cops and criminals. Any errors of procedure are solely mine.

Elyse Hammerly Filer and Dan Filer, who fill in blanks for me in so many areas that I know nothing about. Curtis Bingham, Jason Lewis, and Adventure Protection for teaching me how to fire a weapon and always being up for my crazy questions about firearms.

Shawna Comber, Mario Garcia, and Tamara Garcia. Thank you for helping me with current teen lingo. I would have been lost without your insights. Patric Ryan for helping me get additional language right. It's an honor to call you my friend.

Gratitude for my beta readers, Sheila Sobel and Sherry Hartwell, and especially to Amy Cecil Holm—your eagle eye makes everything I write so much better.

To my hubby JD Hammerly and our crazy menagerie out on the prairie. I love you, all the babies, and Paradise.

Courtenay Schurman, for all your encouragement, check-ins, and support. You are a rock star.

And last, but not least, to all my readers, who have supported Bet Rivers and my other work over the years, I couldn't do this without each of you.

A note about horses. Cyd and Sire are named for real horses.

We held a White Elephant Gift Exchange for the holidays at the stables where I boarded. My gift was to name a horse in a novel for one of the other horse owners. Kristen Eldredge Lindsey won for her horse Cyd. But it was so much fun, I offered up one more, which was won by Donna Barnes for her horse Sire. For photos and more information about the real Cyd and Sire, please visit my website at www.ElenaTaylorAuthor.com

ONE

Bet Rivers sat in the sheriff's station and watched the radar on her computer screen turn a darker and darker blue. Snow headed for the little town of Collier and keeping everyone safe was her responsibility. Bet's advancement to sheriff had taken place less than a year ago, but the name Rivers had followed 'Sheriff' all the way back to the founding of the town. None of the previous Sheriff Rivers, her father included, ever failed the community, and she didn't plan to be the first. With her father's death last fall, Collier residents were the closest thing she had to family.

The valley Bet protected sat high in the Cascade Mountain Range of Washington State. Winter storms often dropped a couple inches of snow at once, a situation Collier could handle, and winter had been relatively mild so far. February, however, was shaping up into something else.

This morning, nearby Lake Collier – a dark and dangerous body of water the locals respected from a safe distance – started freezing completely over for the first time in years.

Bet couldn't remember such a large storm ever bearing down on the valley. The weather was determined to test her in ways that patrolling the streets of Los Angeles and her short stint as sheriff had not yet done.

Clicking off the weather radar screen and opening another file, Bet read over her severe winter storm checklist. Snowplow – ready to go. Volunteers with tractors and trucks with snowplow attachments – set. The community center would be open twenty-four hours a day in case the town's power went out and people needed a warm place to go. Donna, the elementary school nurse, was on hand for minor health emergencies. She would be staying at the center twenty-four seven until the storm passed.

Most residents owned generators and a lot of people used fireplaces for heat, but the community center provided a central location for anyone in trouble.

Nothing like living in an isolated mountain valley to make

folks respect what Mother Nature hurled at them – and rely on each other, rather than the outside world. A lot of people would look to the sheriff as a leader. She couldn't let them down.

Bet turned her attention to the pile of pink 'while you were out' notes that Alma still loved to use rather than sending information to Bet digitally. Alma was much more than an office manager, but she also fought certain modern conveniences.

Most of the notes were mundane issues that Alma could handle, but the last in the pile was a call from Jamie Garcia, a local reporter trying to get back into Bet's good graces after an incident a few months ago had cost her Bet's trust.

Wants to chat about the possibility of an increase in drug use in the area, the note read. *Specifically – meth.*

That would definitely have to wait. It crossed Bet's mind that Jamie might exaggerate the situation just to have reason to touch base with her, but Bet taped it to the computer monitor to follow up on after the storm passed. Her valley didn't have the kind of drug problems as many other communities, and Bet wanted to see it stay that way. If Jamie had any information on a rise in illegal activity, that could be useful.

The rest of the notes she would return to Alma to deal with. Right now, weathering the tempest would take all of Bet's resources.

Bringing up the radar one more time, Bet's stomach clenched as she tracked the monster storm. What if she made a decision during this event that hurt her entire community? Confidence didn't make responsibility lighter to bear, and the hot, sunny streets of Los Angeles hadn't prepared her for one thousand residents slowly buried under several feet of snow. They were a long way from the plowed highways and larger cities with fully functional hospitals.

Bet was the first line of defense against disaster.

She was also likely the last line of defense. Once they were snowed in, she couldn't bring help in from the outside.

A year ago, she had been poised to take the detective's exam in Los Angeles. Her goal was a long and successful career in the nation's largest police force. But events outside her control got in the way, and now she was back in Collier, trying to fill her father's large, all-too-recently vacated shoes.

She faced a once-in-a-century storm with her lone deputy, a septuagenarian secretary, and one very big dog.

Her first instinct was to talk to her father, but his death prevented her from ever gaining new insight into his expertise. Her second instinct was to contact Sergeant Magdalena Carrera. Maggie had mentored Bet during her time at the LAPD.

'We *chicas* need to stick together,' she'd said to Bet early on in her career, back when Bet still called her Sergeant.

But as good as Maggie was at her job, Bet doubted she'd have much advice about facing a blizzard.

'It's up to us, Schweitzer,' Bet said to the Anatolian shepherd sitting in her doorway. 'As long as no one has a heart attack after the storm hits, we'll be fine.' Schweitzer had a look on his face like he knew what was coming. He always could read her mood, not to mention the weather, and he'd been edgy all morning.

She had learned to read his mood too, and right now it wasn't good.

'It's going to be all right, Schweitz.' It surprised her to realize she believed her own words. She could handle this.

Lakers – residents proudly took the nickname from their mysterious lake – could hunker down in their valley and survive on their own. Everyone in town knew that if snow blocked them in and a helicopter couldn't fly, they had no access to a hospital. But Donna was good at her job too. Plus, it would only be for a couple of days.

The phone on her desk rang, jarring her from her thoughts.

As long as the ring didn't herald an emergency, everything would be fine.

Bet rolled out in her black and white on the long teardrop of road that circled the valley. She didn't turn on her siren; there wasn't anyone on the loop to warn of her approach and the sound felt too loud, like a scream into the colorless void. The emergency lights on top of her SUV stained the white unmarked fields of snow on either side red, then blue, then red again, like blood streaking the ground. Her studded tires roared on the hard-packed snow, the surface easy to navigate – at least for now.

The drive to Jeb Pearson's place took less than twenty minutes, even with the worsening conditions. Pearson's Ranch sat at the end of the valley farthest from the lake and the town center. The ranch occupied an area the locals called the 'Train Yard', though that name didn't show up on any official maps.

Long ago, the roundhouse for the Colliers' private railway perched there at the end of the tracks. The roundhouse was a huge, wedge-shaped brick structure, like one third of a pie with the tips of the slices bitten off. It was built to house the big steam engines owned by the Colliers. The facility could hold five engines, each pulled inside through giant glass and iron doors. Engines could be parked and serviced inside the roundhouse, while an enormous turntable sat out front to spin the engines around, sending them down different tracks in order to pass each other in opposite directions.

It was unlikely the Colliers ever housed five engines up here all at once, but they owned other mines around the state and had used engines in other places. It must have been reassuring to know that if they ever needed to, they could bring their assets up here, protected in their high-elevation fiefdom.

Jeb used the property as a summer camp for boys who struggled with drug and alcohol addictions, and guesthouses for snow adventure enthusiasts during the winter. Jeb lived there yearround, with a giant Newfoundland dog named Grizzly, a half a dozen horses, and one mini donkey named Dolly that helped him rehabilitate the boys.

Bet pulled up in front of the roundhouse. The cabins and other outbuildings stretched away from where she parked, with the barn the farthest from the road. The pastures were empty with the storm bearing down, the animals all safely tucked away in their stalls. Jeb stood out front with two bundled figures that must have been the father and son who were currently staying at his place. A third member of their party, the mother, was nowhere to be seen.

Bet got out of her vehicle and walked over to where two of Jeb's snowmobiles were parked, running and ready to go. Layers of winter clothing padded Jeb's wiry form, his face ruddy in the arctic wind.

'What have we got, Jeb?'

'Mark and Julia Crews and their son Jeremy came across what looks to be a solo wreck up on Iron Horse Ridge. They didn't have any details about the driver's condition, so I'm not sure what we're looking at. The parents wanted to protect their son and got him out of there before he could see anything gruesome. These two came down to get me while Mrs Crews stayed with the injured rider.'

Bet nodded to the man standing a few feet away. Only part of his face was visible through the balaclava he wore. His eyes looked haunted.

'You did the right thing,' she said to him. 'If the driver's got a spinal injury, you could have done more damage than good trying to bring them down.' She didn't add that if the driver was dead there was nothing to be done except locate the next of kin.

'Thanks, Sheriff,' Mark Crews said, his voice shaky. 'That was—'

Emotion cut off the man's words. He reached for his son and pulled him close. The boy didn't resist, but he also didn't hug his father back. Bet considered checking the boy for shock, but guessed he was just a teen being a teen.

She gave Mark a nod and hoped the accident victim survived the wait – otherwise Mark Crews would always wonder if he should have made a different choice.

The father got his emotions under control and turned his attention back to Bet. 'Please get my wife Julia down safely.'

Jeremy might be shocky, but the two people up on the ridge were her priority.

'Always prioritize,' Maggie said to Bet on a regular basis. 'Don't get caught up trying to fix everything at once. Fix the big things first.'

Her father would have agreed. His voice no longer took precedence in her mind, but his teachings never left her.

Bet promised to take care of Julia Crews and walked over to straddle the closest snowmobile. Pulling on the helmet she'd brought, she tucked her auburn curls out of the way before closing the face shield. Bet admired the Crews family for helping a stranger as the ominous storm bore down on the area. It must be terrifying to know Mrs Crews waited up on the ridge as the weather closed in. Bet was impressed the family put their own safety in jeopardy for someone they didn't know. Not everyone would do that. It would have been easy enough to pretend they never found the accident, leaving the driver alone in the snow.

Jeb hopped on the other snowmobile, which was already set up to tow the Snowbulance – a small, enclosed trailer with a stretcher mounted inside. Bet made eye contact with Jeb to confirm she was ready, and they took off with him in the lead. Search-and-rescue was Jeb's specialty, and he knew the terrain better than she did.

Her father Earle always said a good leader knew when to follow. Like most of her father's advice, Bet knew it was true even if her instinct was never to admit someone else was the right person for a job she could do. In her defense, her father never faced life in law enforcement as a woman.

Maggie always said, 'Never let a man think he's got control. If you hand control over, he'll never give it up.'

Bet wasn't her father, but she wasn't a patrol officer in LA, either. Sometimes neither Maggie's nor her father's advice was any help to her at all.

Not far from the ranch, Jeb turned off the main road and started up a forest service road that went west and north into the mountains. The turnoff wasn't obvious, so it was interesting that the Crews had found that particular trail.

Snowmobiling was a popular sport in Collier and a lot of people used these forest service roads for trails, even the ones that were officially closed to traffic because there were no funds for maintenance. Without anyone to police the extensive system, the locals used them as their own private playground.

The roads connected in a complex web throughout the area. The injured teen could have arrived at the ridge from any direction. The forest was riddled with paths that the forest service no longer had the money or workforce to keep up, but people and animals kept cleared. In a lot of ways, the community benefited from the interlopers who cleared the roads, because that provided fire access into their local forest, which would otherwise become impassable through neglect.

If the brunt of the storm held off long enough for them to locate the scene of the accident and get the injured teen down the mountain before the conditions worsened, everything should still be all right.

Bet kept her focus on Jeb's sled as they rode up the hill. The road turned dark as they got farther into the trees and the cloud cover grew almost black. She was glad for the headlight and someone she trusted to follow. At least in this moment, her father's advice was right.

If only the injured rider survived the wait.

TWO

T hirty minutes later, they reached the top of Iron Horse Ridge, a spine of rock stretched between mountaintops. Trees grew sparse, and the ground fell away on either side of the trail. A figure waved to them at the sound of their approach. Julia Crews. Her bright orange safety vest made it easy to spot her against the snow.

Bet and Jeb parked and forced their way through the drifts to reach the prone figure on the ground. A bent and twisted snow-mobile lay smashed against a nearby tree. The Crews had covered the victim with an emergency Mylar blanket, which Bet and Jeb peeled away. Underneath, the boy was still and cold.

Recognition jolted through Bet. Grant Marsden was a local teen she knew on sight. His father, Doug, was a contractor who lived in the valley; he'd done some work on Bet's house in the past but also worked out of town on bigger jobs. She bit her lip to push her emotional reaction aside and shucked her gloves to search for a pulse in his neck.

Finding nothing, she leaned over and got her face close to his mouth, hoping for any sign of life. She sat back on her heels and looked at Jeb with the slightest shake of her head. Jeb repeated her actions – first the neck, then the mouth. He failed to find a heartbeat as well. Both of them grabbed an arm, resting their fingers on the pulse point in his wrists. Bet considered what lifesaving measures she and Jeb could do out here in the middle of the wilderness with the storm of the century on its way.

Cold sometimes slowed death to a crawl. It could keep a person's brain alive. Bet looked at Jeb. 'Should we try CPR? And hope the cold . . .'

Jeb was already shaking his head. 'He's stiff. Too far gone. There's nothing we can do.'

Bet knew it too, even before the words left Jeb's mouth. It would be different if he was just cold, but the onset of rigor showed it was too late to try to revive him.

When Bet didn't move, Jeb touched her lightly on the shoulder. 'I'm sorry, Bet, but we have to go.'

'He can't be dead.' Julia Crews stood a few feet away. Her voice quivered, and it wasn't from the cold. 'We covered him up. He can't be dead. I thought maybe . . .'

Julia Crews could go into shock over the trauma of the experience and exposure to the elements. Bet sprang into action at the reminder there were living people who needed her help. She asked the woman to sit down on her own snowmobile, parked not far away, and take a few deep breaths. Julia followed Bet's request, and her breathing evened out.

'Mrs Crews, we need to bring him down to the valley now.' Bet carefully avoided any comment on Grant's condition. 'But I need to make sure you are going to be able to ride your own machine down. How experienced a driver are you?'

The last thing Bet wanted was for this out-of-towner to drive into a tree and become another casualty. They all needed to get off this ridge before the storm hit.

'Julia,' the woman said. 'You can call me Julia.'

'Thank you, Julia. My name is Bet.' Bet reached out and took Julia's wrist as they continued talking. She checked the woman's pulse and respiration.

'I'm OK,' Julia said, though she let Bet tend to her. 'Really. It's just so awful.'

Bet understood her reaction. Julia's son Jeremy looked about the same age as Grant. The mother no doubt made a comparison to her own child. The thought that Julia might not want Jeremy on a snowmobile again after Grant Marsden's death crossed Bet's mind. The fears of the mother transferred to the son. Bet understood the impulse, even if she didn't have a child. She had an entire valley of dependants who were her responsibility.

Julia's pulse was steady, and her breathing continued to slow as they spoke. After confirming Julia was experienced driving a sled and wasn't going to faint, Bet and Jeb wrapped Grant back up in the Mylar emergency blanket and strapped the boy down in the Snowbulance, a struggle because of the stiffness of Grant's limbs.

Cold slowed rigor; it didn't speed it up. Why was rigor so far advanced? The boy must have been dead when the Crews found him. It was possible Julia never actually checked his condition and Mark and Jeremy had reportedly left the scene before Jeremy could see it too closely.

But wouldn't Julia have checked when she covered Grant?

Bet felt a shiver that the weather couldn't account for. Something was off up here on the ridge.

Bet waited for her instincts to show her something useful. There were other snowmobile tracks, but both Mark and Jeremy had used the trail too, so that didn't prove anyone else was involved in the accident.

Deciding it would be helpful to get the registration from the snowmobile, she walked over to the kid's ruined machine. Doug had worked at Bet's house, but she didn't know his home address. Besides, it would help to have that registration in her hand when she contacted the boy's father to tell him that his son was dead. She'd have to explain to Doug that he would need to identify the body with the medical examiner at the morgue in Ellensburg.

The coroner would pick Grant up and take him to the morgue for the ME to confirm cause and manner of death. It wasn't Bet's job to show Doug the body for the formal identification.

Without seeing the body, it might be hard for Doug to accept Grant's sudden death. The registration would provide tangible proof it really was Grant in the accident and keep Doug from holding out hope there had been a mistake with his son's identity.

Leaning over the sled – it was tilted on its side – Bet opened the glove box and dug out the document. It wasn't a surprise to see Doug Marsden's name on the paperwork with an address not far from Jeb Pearson's ranch. She also found Grant's wallet, but no cell phone. As Bet stood back up, she saw a flash of red against the snow. Something was trapped underneath the machine.

The bright red fletch of an arrow embedded in the sled's fuel tank.

Had someone shot at Grant, hitting the sled and sending him off course into the tree? Deliberate? Or a bizarre accident?

Hunting season was long over. But someone could have been out bow-hunting illegally.

Except a snowmobile couldn't be mistaken for a deer.

'Bet?' Jeb's voice called out from the Snowbulance. He gestured he was ready to go. She held up a hand to show him that she needed a moment. This was now a crime scene, and all her evidence would soon get buried from the storm. Should she document everything before heading off the ridge? Try to get the arrow out from under the sled? Or would that do even more damage to her evidence than coming back later and taking her time?

Maggie's voice popped into Bet's mind, reminding her that getting her living witness off the ridge safely was her priority, along with transporting Grant to the morgue in Ellensburg. At some point, she needed to notify Doug as Grant's next of kin.

But whatever crime had happened here mattered too.

Sending Jeb back down the mountain by himself with a dead boy and the traumatized woman felt like a bad idea. Bet would have to ride back out later to gather evidence. At least she knew her crime scene wasn't going anywhere and no one else would find it.

Snow began to fall as Bet pulled out her cell for a few quick photos of the snowmobile and the arrow.

As she climbed on to her own sled, snowfall obscured the scene of the accident in a swirl of white. It would make their trip down all the more dangerous, but Bet felt exhilarated by the conditions. The world felt pure. Nature made the location pristine again, hiding the scene from prying eyes.

As if no one had died there at all.

Bet signaled to Jeb she was ready to go, and they – the living and the dead – started Grant's final voyage out of the mountains. They drove at a slow pace. Beating the worst of the weather down to Jeb's was important, but visibility was already limited. They couldn't afford another wreck.

Reaching the southeast end of the ridge and a return into the denser forest, Bet could barely make out the back of the Snowbulance behind Jeb's sled, with Julia driving slowly but steadily after him.

Just before Bet plunged into the trees after the other two, she took a brief pause to look back in the direction of the ridge.

What had brought Grant out there by himself this morning? Or had he been with someone else, someone who caused the accident? Or was someone else stuck out here as well, too injured to call for help?

Should Bet have done a bigger search of the area before getting Julia and Grant back down to the valley floor? Or sent Jeb down with them alone?

Snow obscured the ridge as the storm descended on Collier, reminding her that her life was at risk, too.

Gunning her engine, Bet followed Julia. She had to get back down to the valley floor and find out if anyone else had gone out with Grant.

Though if anyone else was alive on that ridge, they wouldn't be for long. Bet would have to live with the choice she'd made as the snow worsened.

Had she just made her first mistake of the storm?

THREE

The storm's power had ramped up by the time they reached the spot where the forest service road met the loop road. Once out of the trees, the wind pushed the snowmobiles sideways and near whiteout conditions shortened their visibility to a few feet. Bet could no longer see Jeb and the Snowbulance, but Julia's constant forward motion meant he must still be out front leading the way.

They finally arrived at the roundhouse without incident, and Bet's cell phone came alive with vibrations and dings and message notifications. She explained to Jeb that she needed to call the station to update Alma, and for him to get Julia Crews inside and out of the cold.

'Ask the family to stay at their cabin for now. I'm going to have to ask them a few questions.'

She didn't want an audience while she and Jeb unloaded Grant Marsden's corpse.

Fresh snow had already covered the SUV, turning it into a

shapeless mound. Bet reached out and cleared the door handle before climbing inside.

She started up the engine and called Alma, the glue who kept the sheriff's station together. Bet could use the radio, but she always had to assume someone else could listen in, so she preferred her cell whenever possible.

'We've got a problem.' Alma answered the phone on the first ring. 'There's a power line down with a couple trees across the road at mile marker three.' Bet didn't have to ask which road. With only one main road in and out of the valley, it was the only road that mattered in a storm. 'The county crews can't clear the snow on the road until the trees are cleared, and the trees can't be cleared until the power line is dealt with. The power company is sending out a team from Ellensburg.'

That also meant power was out for the entire valley. Collier had a substation, but if the high-voltage line that ran to it from E'burg went down, everything was out.

'How long are we looking at?'

'At least a couple of hours.'

'Crap. I need to get the coroner out here.' She heard the hitch in Alma's breath as she took in the fact that the accident was a fatality and not just an injury.

'Not today you don't.'

Bet waited, knowing what Alma would ask next.

'Who needs the coroner?'

'I'll fill you in later.'

The two women sat quiet. Bet's windshield got darker under its deepening layer of snow. She would have to scrape it – the snow was too thick for the wipers to work against the heavy pile.

Her mind wanted to focus on Grant, but she had an entire town's welfare to worry about. He had to take a back seat to the living. With no evidence, there was little she could do in the moment. She had to get over to talk to Doug and find out if his son rode out with anyone else. It could even be Doug himself out lost in the snow.

'Where's Clayton?' Bet finally broke the silence.

Bet's full-time deputy lived down near Cle Elum – a slightly larger small town a thirty-minute drive away. Cle Elum sat near the state's largest east–west interstate and didn't share the isolation of Collier, but it too would be impacted by this heavy onslaught of winter.

Clayton had been in the valley before Bet headed out to Jeb's and she knew he wouldn't leave her alone at a time like this, even with a pregnant wife at home. Now he couldn't go home. Bet hoped Kathy didn't go into labor until after the roads were passable again.

'He's gone out to do a sweep of the folks without generators to make sure they'll be warm enough. He's also checking on some of the older residents.' Alma would never include herself in that group, no matter that she was closing in on her eighth decade.

'OK. Let me sort out what I've got here. Have Jack and Sally started down the main road?' Jack and Sally Stenley ran a landscaping company during the warmer months and a private snow-plow company in the wintertime. The sheriff's station maintained a contract with them for emergencies.

Alma assured Bet that the Stenleys had already plowed the circuit of Collier's tiny downtown and were headed as far as they could go toward the highway before the fallen trees blocked their way.

'They'll keep Lake Collier Road cleared on our end while the power company does their work.'

Lake Collier Road was also the name of the road that ringed the valley, but locals called the section outside of downtown 'the loop', so Bet knew Alma only referred to the section closest to the town center. With the Stenleys keeping the town proper and the road out of the mountains cleared, Bet would have to rely on the people with plows on their trucks and tractors to keep the loop passable.

'I'll be back in soon.' Bet finished the call and looked up Doug Marsden's landline on her smart phone. She thought it was going to go to voicemail when someone finally answered.

The speaker was male but didn't identify himself, and there was enough noise in the background to make it hard to hear.

'I'm looking for Doug Marsden.'

Was he having a party?

'Sorry. He's not here right now.'

Was that because he'd been out on a snowmobile with his son?

'Do you know when he'll be back?'

'He's out of town for a couple days. Who is this?'

'I'll call back.' Bet hung up, glad that her cell number wouldn't display on the caller ID. At least she knew Doug wasn't out with his son and missing in the storm, unless the person who answered had lied. Regardless, she'd have to track him down later. Bet couldn't go back up on the ridge now even if there was another snowmobiler lost out there, and she really didn't want a distraught family member going up there in her place.

Tucking her cell away, she tramped back through the snow to the snowmobiles. The hum of Jeb's generator droned a bass note under the sound of the wind. Jeb stood waiting near the Snowbulance, and she explained the situation.

'I can't get the coroner in or the body out to the medical examiner,' Bet said. 'I hate to ask you this but—'

'My walk-in cooler is your walk-in cooler.'

The two got the stretcher out of the Snowbulance and carried Grant into the roundhouse. They went through the front room, which had a scattering of sofas and comfortable chairs along with a big-screen TV Jeb had put in a few years ago to watch sports and hold movie nights.

They went down the hallway toward the kitchen and the storage rooms. Reaching the kitchen, they continued to the back wall, where doors led to the walk-in coolers.

'Are your guests in their cabin?' Bet asked as they set Grant on the floor of the last walk-in. 'I'd hate for them to know there's a body in with their dinner.'

'They are. But I only use this walk-in during the summer when I have a full complement of kids staying here.' Jeb made a gesture at the half-empty shelves. 'All the food in here is elk and venison I dressed for my own use.'

'Does Grizzly get some of that?' Jeb's Newfie sat in the doorway, curious about what the humans were up to and checking on his meat supply.

Jeb reached out and rubbed his dog's head, roughly the size of a watermelon. 'He does at that.'

As they handled the body, Bet thought again about how the corpse was much stiffer than a recent death could explain. Bet was confident she was correct that cold slowed rigor mortis – it didn't speed it up. Grant wore several layers of clothing, plus the Crews had covered him. If he had died recently, he shouldn't already be stiff, or so cold. Algor mortis, the phase of death during which the body matches the ambient temperature, wouldn't have happened so fast. Even in the elements as Grant had been, he was too wrapped up for that.

Curious.

'Can you put the temp at thirty-six?' Bet asked before they left the freezer.

Jeb fiddled with a temperature control mounted on the wall. 'Got it.'

Thirty-six was the optimal temperature to preserve a corpse, but not Jeb's meat, which would do better several degrees colder. Random details about forensics stuck in Bet's mind from her training in Los Angeles. 'Sorry about your steaks.'

Packages neatly wrapped in white butcher paper filled a few of the stainless-steel shelves.

'It's only about two hundred pounds,' Jeb said. 'I can move it into another walk-in if I need to.'

Jeb started to leave when Bet stopped him. 'Hold on a sec, would you? I want to ask you a few questions.'

Jeb looked at her expectantly.

'Any thoughts about the family who found Grant?'

Jeb's expression changed to one of surprise. 'Do you suspect them of something?'

The red fletch of an arrow trapped beneath the snowmobile.

'I need to go back up and take a better look at the scene of the wreck.'

Jeb started shaking his head even before the words left Bet's mouth. 'No way, Rivers. With this storm coming in, it's too dangerous. I'd end up having to go back out to look for you.' He didn't have to add, 'and you have responsibilities here in town.'

Bet weighed her options. She could choose to go anyway. No matter what Jeb said, it wasn't his decision.

She had a responsibility to Grant's family and to Grant. Someone shot that arrow into Grant's sled, and it was up to her to figure out who and why. She was elected to her position as sheriff when her opponent dropped out at the last minute, and she ran unopposed. So, it wasn't a true mark of the community's support. She needed to prove she was worthy of the position that had been handed to her because of circumstances of birth and another person's misfortune.

'I have to investigate how Grant died.' She considered the things she could do rather than the things she couldn't. 'I better try to establish time of death. I also need to check in with his family and determine if he was out there alone.'

Jeb looked troubled. 'The Crews didn't see any signs of another sled wrecked nearby and neither did we.'

Bet still didn't mention the arrow. Without any further information, there wasn't any use in involving Jeb who, despite his abilities, was still a civilian.

'I know, but we didn't look that hard, and what if someone was riding on the back of his sled and was thrown farther away?'

'It seems unlikely—' Jeb cut himself off and looked back down at Grant. 'What's your plan to figure out time of death?'

Bet steeled herself to say the words out loud. 'Got a meat thermometer?'

FOUR

Before doing anything to the corpse, Bet called down to the medical examiner in E'burg. She had known Dr Carolyn Pak for years from tagging along with her father on trips to the morgue for his job. They'd reconnected back in September during Bet's first homicide investigation as sheriff. Carolyn had also performed the autopsy on Bet's father. The accident that had left her an orphan, albeit an adult one, and solidified Bet's decision to stay in Collier.

Jeb leaned against the wall, pretending not to listen in.

'What's up, Red?' Carolyn employed her usual greeting for the auburn-haired sheriff.

'I've got a rather dicey request to make.'

'Oka-a-ay.' Carolyn drew the word out, clearly not excited to know what Bet had in mind.

'We're getting hit hard by this storm. Our road out is blocked. And I have a body I need a time of death for.'

'Are you at a crime scene?'

'That's part why this is dicey. We just brought the body down off Iron Horse Ridge. He was a victim of a snowmobile accident. The spot where he died is currently getting buried under a couple feet of snow.'

Carolyn paused a moment. Bet guessed she was contemplating the difference between expediency and protocol.

'Why do you need TOD? If you want to know if he was drinking or under the influence of drugs, blood tests will do it. I can do those in a few days when the coroner brings him in.'

'I don't think the driver made a mistake.'

Jeb looked at her sharply but said nothing. He knew better than to ask Bet about an ongoing investigation, even if he did help recover the body.

Carolyn sighed, not yet giving in, so Bet took a different tack. 'Let's just say I want to make sure I've done what I can to show the father of a dead kid that I took his son's death seriously.'

Carolyn's slow exhale told Bet that sentiment got through to her.

'OK. I can walk you through a couple tests.'

Jeb held the phone up for a video call, and the three of them got to work.

As Bet expected, getting a body temperature came first. Using the meat thermometer, Carolyn directed her where to place the spike in the chest cavity. Bet had a moment of paralysis just before she pushed the metal skewer into the corpse, but she managed to disconnect from the idea that the victim was someone she knew. It helped to do as Carolyn suggested and cover his face with a clean towel.

Next Carolyn walked her through methods to assess rigor mortis and eye condition. Pupils relaxed and dilated when a person died, but that changed over time. The degree to which the body showed rigor mortis was an indicator for time of death, though Carolyn reminded her that if Grant had been out in the snow a long time, the freezing temperatures could make determining TOD next to impossible.

After Bet finished, Carolyn did some calculations. 'Based on all your findings, I'd put the time of death sometime yesterday afternoon.'

Bet looked at Jeb, who pursed his lips.

Had the Crews even checked to see if Grant was still breathing?

'What? That doesn't jibe with what else you know?' Carolyn's voice pulled Bet back to her cell phone screen.

'That means this kid was missing overnight,' Bet said. 'The people who found him led us to believe he was still alive, though they didn't actually say it in those words.'

Bet looked to Jeb, who shrugged. 'I might have misunderstood them,' he said. 'Mr Crews was pretty shaken up, and Jeremy didn't say anything at all.'

Carolyn's voice turned cautious. 'Keep in mind nothing you did today is remotely as accurate as what I could do in the lab, but I can't imagine his rigor would be this far advanced in such a short amount of time. I don't suppose your victim was wearing a watch that was smashed at the time of the accident?'

Bet laughed without mirth. 'No watch, no cell phone. I think that only happens on TV.'

'It was worth a shot,' Carolyn said.

Bet promised to have Grant Marsden brought down to Carolyn in the morgue as soon as the road cleared. She would locate Doug and send the father down to Carolyn after that. Bet thanked the medical examiner and ended the call.

'So . . . what does this tell us?' Jeb asked as they cleaned up and wrapped Grant's body in the Mylar sheeting.

Bet wished she could do the other procedures a medical examiner performed on a corpse to verify time of death, but inserting the thermometer was as far as she could go beyond checking external signs. Regardless, Carolyn's instincts affirmed Bet's. The rigor was too far advanced for Grant to have been alive even a few hours ago.

'I'm not sure. Did the Crews go out on their snowmobiles yesterday?'

Jeb shifted his weight as if uncomfortable. 'They were out most of the day.'

'And what time did they go out this morning?'

Jeb glanced at his watch as if that would give him answers. 'Just after breakfast, which I served at seven, so around eight, eight thirty. They knew the storm was coming in and wanted one last ride before they had to pack it in for the weekend.'

'And they said they found him at roughly ten o'clock.'

Jeb looked troubled.

'Tell me again exactly what Mr Crews said to you about finding Grant.'

Silence fell as Jeb tried to recall the exact words. After a moment, he shook his head. 'I'm sorry, Bet. Mr Crews said they found an accident victim who needed to be brought down from the ridge. I don't recall him actually saying they'd confirmed he was still alive. The way he said it, I just thought . . .'

'It doesn't matter now.' Bet wanted to reassure him. 'They didn't say they'd found someone who *died* in an accident. It was an easy mistake to make.'

Jeb looked away.

Bet's words likely wouldn't make him feel any better, but she gave it a try. 'We couldn't have done anything differently. The parents wanted their son out of the situation. Mr Crews might not have even gone near the accident, just turned around with his son and came down here to find you.'

Julia had been left alone with an accident victim, far from anyone else, the storm coming in. It would have been a terrifying situation. She could easily have thrown the emergency blanket over Grant and not checked on him at all.

The thought of Grant alone on the ridge overnight felt tragic. Was no one looking for him? Why hadn't someone contacted her when he didn't come home? He was barely sixteen. Though if his father was out of town, it was possible no one was keeping track of him. Doug was a single father.

There were a lot of trails the Crews could have ridden today. What were the chances they would take the trail where Grant died?

Bet considered the Crews family. 'And they all went out together yesterday?'

'As far as I know. This morning they had breakfast together and disappeared as a group.'

Bet had no reason to suspect the Crews of anything. But someone shot an arrow at Grant.

'Have you ever had them stay with you before?'

'Nope. First time.'

Bet's phone rang. She could hear the tension in Alma's voice. 'You better get back to the station.'

Bet fought the urge to say, 'What now?' and took one last look at the shrouded body on the floor of the walk-in freezer. The living came first.

'On my way.'

FIVE

Through the glass of the station's front door, Bet could see Alma at her desk, her eyes scanning the street out front, waiting for Bet to appear. Between the vantage point of her desk, extensive phone tree, and sharp mind, Alma missed very little in the community, something for which Bet was grateful – most of the time.

Schweitzer came out from underneath Alma's desk as he heard Bet step inside, bringing a blast of snow in with her. She pulled off her gloves as she came into the warmth, scratched the dog's head, and looked at their visitor.

George Stand, the caretaker for the Collier estate and all of the buildings the family owned in the valley except the Train Yard, sat in one of the visitor chairs sipping a cup of coffee. The Colliers had founded the town and the mine that supported the local economy until the mine closed in 1910. Robert Collier senior and his son had both left the area years ago. Then the son – Rob – had turned back up in September, complicating Bet's life in more ways than one. She pushed away thoughts of kissing him to focus on the here and now.

'Howdy, Younger.'

George had greeted her as *the Younger* ever since she was a child and she spent so much time as her father's shadow. Her father Earle was *the Elder* and, unless Bet had a child, he always would be.

'You had a break-in?' Bet asked after she greeted him in return, his hand warm in hers as they shook.

'I did. At one of the summer-rental properties. I had it closed up for winter, so I'm guessing whoever broke in thought it would be a safe place to squat.'

'It looked like they were squatting? This wasn't just a burglary?'

'I don't think anything was stolen,' George said. 'But I'm worried someone is hurt or dead.'

George went on to explain he had been doing rounds on all the buildings he maintained before the storm hit. It was the first time he'd visited the house since he closed it up at the end of September. He went inside and found a bloody sleeping bag on the table in the dining room.

'The blood is fresh, Rivers.' Bet heard the concern in George's voice and knew it was from his fears for another person's safety, not the mess they left behind. 'Blood will come clean,' he said at the end of his description. 'But this storm is no time to wander around injured.'

'Did you see signs of anyone still in the house?'

George shook his head. 'I walked through after I found the blood, thinking someone might need my help. But no one was there.'

'Did you touch the sleeping bag?' George wasn't a squeamish man.

'I didn't touch anything except the doorknob going in and the doorknob coming out. The dining-room table is visible from the front door. I knew right away something was wrong.'

It was a strange event, with several possible scenarios. Bet stopped herself from spinning a narrative that might fit.

'Do you keep camping supplies there?'

'No. Someone must have brought the sleeping bag in.'

Bet considered what else to ask before she drove to the property. Everyone's memory was faulty, and George was already forgetting what he saw when he first arrived on the scene.

'See any tracks? Either from a vehicle in the driveway or footprints in and out of the house?' A house currently getting buried under heavy snow.

'Nope. But we had enough snow fall last night that it could have obscured anything left behind before morning.'

'OK, let's go.'

Hopefully George was wrong about the amount of blood, though as an avid hunter who dressed his own meat, she didn't think so. If George said it was soaked in blood, it was soaked

in blood. The question was how much, whose, and why were
they bleeding? And most importantly, was it even human?

Bet decided to bring Schweitzer along, even though the current
weather conditions would make it hard to track anyone. Tracks
left behind in the snow were relatively easy to follow, both visu-
ally and by scent, but new snow obscured old tracks and the
smells they left behind. If the person or persons had been in the
house more than twenty-four hours ago, there was already too
much new snow on top of any clues left for Schweitzer to find.

George gave Alma the address for the report they would file
for both Bet's investigation and the Colliers' insurance.

'Don't forget to eat lunch,' Alma said as Bet stood to follow
George out the door.

'Will do.'

Bet just hoped it wouldn't be at midnight.

She fell in behind George as he drove out of town toward the
cemetery. Even with her windshield wipers on full, snow blocked
her view. Bet leaned forward, as if getting closer to the glass
would help her see. She gripped the steering wheel, relieved that
spending a few years in Los Angeles hadn't counteracted more
than a decade of experience she had driving in winter weather.
Her father had started having her drive if they went out in a
storm as soon as she secured a driver's permit – though he also
had her drive on snow-covered forest service roads as soon as
she could reach the pedals.

'Better to practice now instead of in the middle of an emergency,' he would say when he handed her the keys. 'Driving
successfully in snow and ice is a combination of muscle memory
and not overreacting if something goes wrong.' His assumption
was that she would one day take the reins as the sheriff of Collier
and face emergencies on a regular basis.

At least his somewhat unusual parenting style had prepared
her for an event like this storm. He might not have taught her to
trust in things like love, but she did trust her physical abilities
in a crisis.

Fifteen minutes later, she pulled into the driveway at the rental
house. Set back from the loop down a narrow lane, it was a
perfect residence for squatting. Like many of the properties in
the valley, the house wasn't visible from the road, and no curious

neighbors lived near enough to see anything. Plus, people living in the vicinity might not think twice about strange vehicles coming and going from a rental.

There certainly were no signs of tracks on the driveway now. Even the tread marks from George's earlier visit had been covered. Bet was in awe from the volume of snow coming down. Though snow on the ground was common in the winter, at most it was usually only a few inches at a time. This was an entire winter's snowfall dropped in less than an hour. It was a good thing she had the community prepared for a severe storm.

She parked next to George's truck in front of the garage and got out, leaving Schweitzer in the back while she looked things over.

'I won't be gone too long, buddy,' she said to her dog. He gave her a woof and pressed his nose against the glass. Bet knew from visiting her father over the past few years that there were few things Schweitzer liked better than playing in the snow, the fresher and deeper the better. But this year, she would get to be the one to tussle with him all winter long. The whole world had magically become a playground, and he could barely contain his delight.

She peeked into the garage, but the space was empty. The lack of fresh footprints led Bet to believe no one had returned after George checked on the property. The heavy snowfall might cover footprints on the ground, but if someone had come back there would be footprints on the porch, which was covered with only a light drift of snow.

Bet nodded for George to unlock the door. She trusted George that the house was empty, but she needed to check every room and closet. The house would have to be processed, and she had protocol to follow.

Pulling on the gloves and booties she'd brought with her, she would treat this as a crime scene which, since someone had broken in, would be true even if there wasn't all the blood. 'Sorry, George, you're going to have to stay outside.'

'Sure thing, Younger.'

With George's permission and evidence of a crime, she had exigent circumstances to do the walk-through without a warrant. An individual could need help, or evidence might be in danger of destruction. If nothing else, the bloody sleeping bag gave her the right to enter.

Bet clicked on the light by the front door, but the power was still out. She shined her flashlight around from where she stood. As George reported, the sleeping bag lay on the table in front of her. The house had that musty smell a place got when it was closed up for a long period of time, overlaid with the distinctive scent of blood.

Indentations in the white furniture covers on the living-room sofa and easy chair showed signs that someone had sat there, just as George had described. As she stepped past the dining-room table – and its gruesome piece of evidence – the air turned colder, and the smell dissipated. Shards of glass lay scattered across the floor by the back door, glittering in the diffuse light that filtered through the storm.

A small window in the door had provided the intruders access to the lock on the inside. A bitter wind blew through the opening as the temperature outside continued to drop. She resumed her quick survey of the premises. The bedrooms at the back of the house showed no sign of intruders, but the shower curtain was missing from the master bathroom.

The rest of the house was just as George said it would be. Empty.

Walking into the dining room again for a closer look, Bet found the dark green sleeping bag soaked in so much blood that it had not yet dried. It could potentially be more blood than an individual could lose and live, though at this point Bet had no way to know if it was only one person's or even human. She couldn't jump to conclusions just because of instinct or what appeared to be a likely scenario. She reminded herself to be methodical.

When Bet had studied for her detective's exam, Maggie hammered that point home the most. 'Patrol officers have to respond quickly,' she would say. 'But detectives have to move slow. Methodical. You need to be a different kind of cop if you want to be a detective.'

The problem now was Bet had to take on the role of both patrol officer and detective.

Bet focused on the evidence at hand. Nothing else was disturbed, so a struggle probably hadn't taken place. Was someone killed in their sleep? Why on the table? Or had they died so fast they didn't see what was coming? Bleeding to death would likely send spatter around the room. Arterial spray would be visible on the ground, even if the person couldn't move. There were no obvious signs of that.

Had someone dressed a deer? Perhaps one illegally poached up on the ridge with another bright red arrow. She dismissed the thought. The ridge was miles away from this house, and other than just finding Grant – so his death weighed on her mind – there was absolutely no reason to think his death was related to the break-in here.

'Crap.' Her gut said she was looking at the scene of a violent crime, but where was the victim? Why dispose of the body and leave the sleeping bag behind? If someone used the shower curtain to wrap up a body, why take the body out of the sleeping bag?

She couldn't come up with a narrative for what was laid out in front of her.

First things first, the house had to be processed. Evidence like fingerprints could point to whoever broke into the house, giving her a place to start in her investigation.

Bet went back outside to find George waiting in his old Willys truck, the windshield wipers *almost* keeping his view clear. At least the vintage vehicle had four-wheel drive and did fine in the snow. She gestured for him to unlock the passenger door so she could join him out of the weather. Once inside, she pulled out her notebook and a pen.

'Did you remove a shower curtain from the master bathroom?'

George looked startled. 'It was missing?'

Bet told him it was.

'I'm sorry, Younger, I didn't notice that when I searched the house. It should have been there. I always make sure everything is set up for summer when I close a house up in the fall. I was so worried I was going to find someone dead after seeing all that blood, it must not have registered that it was gone.'

'That's OK, George. The sight of all that blood would have thrown me off too.' Bet made a note that the shower curtain was confirmed missing from the bathroom. 'Was there anything valuable in the house?'

'Not much. There's a TV, a DVD and a CD player, but nothing high end. We don't keep computers or other electronics in these places. If people want those, they have to bring their own. I didn't notice anything missing.' He made a sound that might have been a laugh. 'But then I didn't catch the missing shower curtain either.'

'Don't worry, George. We'll figure out if anything else is gone.' Bet didn't think a robbery was the motive. Nothing looked disturbed during her walk-through. No gaping holes where a DVD player or a TV used to be. Nothing broken or moved as if someone searched for valuables. Not even drawers left open from a search. She confirmed with George there wasn't a safe.

Bet made another note, her thoughts on how impossible it might be to track down the intruder. Statistics for clearing burglaries were dismal across the US. She had to hope they not only left fingerprints, but that their fingerprints showed up in a database somewhere. Fingerprints were useless if they didn't; without a comparison they would tell her nothing.

'And you don't have alarms on the rental properties, correct?'

George shook his head. 'Only the commercial properties in town. We tried it on some of the rental houses a few years ago, but we ended up with so many false alarms it wasn't worth the expense to Mr Collier or the time I spent coming out to find a renter had accidentally set it off.'

Bet knew George referenced Robert senior when he said 'Mr Collier'. Rob owned the original Collier estate, willed to him by his grandfather, but it was Robert senior who owned all the properties around the valley, including this rental house. At least until he died. Then she guessed it would all go to Rob. She tried not to think about how much the man was worth. The difference in their financial situations shouldn't matter for whatever future they might have, but deep down, it did. He moved in circles she couldn't imagine and wasn't sure she wanted to know.

Bet nodded to show George she was listening. With minimal property crimes in the valley, alarms weren't something very many residences invested in.

'Once,' George said with a chuckle, 'I went out in the middle of the night to find the intruder was a raccoon.'

Bet laughed at the image. Raccoons were a common sight

around the valley – tricksters, the lot of them, with nimble little hands that looked vaguely human.

She sobered up and returned to the current problem. 'OK, George. Now that I've confirmed there's no one holed up or injured on the premises, I need to get a warrant before I process the house.'

'You've got my permission,' George said. 'I know Mr Collier would want this done as fast as possible, storm or no storm.'

Bet wished it was that simple.

'I appreciate that, and I'll take your key so I can get back in, but having a warrant is one of the steps I'm required by law to follow.'

George nodded. He was a man who appreciated rules and regulations, even if he didn't always follow them. 'At least let me cover that broken glass with plastic so snow doesn't fill the kitchen.'

The snow coming in could potentially damage evidence as well. Bet agreed to patch the door but made George wait in the truck. She took photos of the outside and the broken window for her records, then covered it with a piece of tarp and duct tape George kept handy, protecting the areas she would fingerprint.

'I 'preciate that, Younger,' he said when she showed him the photo of her work. 'Looks almost as good as I could do.'

High praise from the man.

'I'll let you know when I can release the property back to you,' she said.

Bet asked a few more questions about when George last visited the property, then explained she was going to get Schweitzer to nose around. He was free to leave.

'Call me immediately if you see anything odd at your other buildings, OK? Do not go inside. If someone is staying in empty houses in the valley, the intruder could be holed up elsewhere, and all this blood indicates that person could be violent. It's possible whoever was here broke in elsewhere to wait out the storm.'

'Will do, Younger.'

Walking toward the SUV, she could see Schweitzer wagging his tail, eager to get out of the vehicle even with the snow coming down hard. Bet gave him a good scratch but told him it wasn't playtime and signaled him to fall in at her side before the two walked around behind the house. She gave him the command to follow any scent he found at the back door where the break-in occurred. After a few minutes of him digging his nose in the snow, he finally sat down and looked at her with his 'nothing-I-can-do' look, so she stopped asking.

'Good dog,' she said as she rubbed his face. He showed distress if he couldn't do what she asked.

And she loved how hard he tried.

Glancing around from her perch on the back step, a flash of light off to the right captured Bet's attention. Squinting through the swirls of snow, she could just make out lights in an upstairs window next door.

With the deciduous trees shedding their leaves for the season, the shape of the neighbor's house showed through the trunks. Maybe someone had noticed people in the vicinity or could at least remember a vehicle in the driveway over the last few days.

'First things first.'

She loaded Schweitzer into his spot in the back of the vehicle, where he got to work on a chew toy, and she pulled out the crime scene tape.

The bright yellow felt far too cheerful.

SIX

Bet completed the tasks of marking and sealing the crime scene before walking past her SUV to visit the neighbors. Schweitzer's bright face watched her from the back window as she made her way through the deep snow to the trees. The best partner she could ask for, he'd rather be at her side no matter the weather, but she didn't want his size to intimidate whoever answered the door.

'Use being a woman to your advantage,' Maggie had said. 'People think we are more empathetic and less likely to get aggressive. It's easier for people to trust us than our male coun-terparts. That can make them more likely to talk to us and tell us the truth.'

Earle always said there *shouldn't* be differences between male and female officers, so Bet never questioned the complexities of gender in policing until she started working with Maggie. She'd just begun to realize she couldn't be sheriff the same way as her father, nor did she have to be.

Winding around through the forest, she reached the neighbor's yard without stumbling over anything lurking under the thick blanket of white. The thought that one of the mounds of snow covered a corpse didn't escape her imagination, but she found no footprints, indentations, or other evidence that someone had traveled between the two houses, and she didn't have the time to poke at every lump under the trees.

She arrived at the edge of the neighbor's property and skirted the open yard in front of her. The snow wasn't as deep in the tree line as it was in the open area and she stayed under their protection to make her way around to the front door. The grumble of a generator ran in the background, but not enough to block out the sound of the doorbell when she gave it a ring. A moment later, a curtain twitched, and a face peeked out at her from a window near the door. Bet gave a wave and produced her most benign smile.

'Hello, Sheriff,' the woman said as she opened the door. 'Checkin' in on folks?'

She wore the kind of turban Bet associated with cancer patients. Her black eyes were sunken but had an intensity that indicated she didn't miss a thing.

'Are you doing all right?' Bet asked.

'Chemotherapy sucks, but other than that I'm OK.' Her dry chuckle matched the light in her eyes. Bet felt a tug. The woman held on to her sense of humor while facing a devastating situation; Bet wasn't sure she could stay upbeat in similar circumstances. Her own father had cancer at the end of his life, though it wasn't the disease that had killed him.

'We'll be getting more snow, and the power will be out for a while. Maybe you should come into town?'

The woman didn't even pause to consider Bet's suggestion. 'No. But thank you for the concern. I have my generator. I'll be all right. The last thing I need right now is to be exposed to a crowd of people. I'm much better off here, even if I do end up in the dark.'

Bet understood her fears. The community center would be crowded with kids, who carried germs around like little sponges, not to mention a lot of people with colds and other more serious winter ailments. The woman assured her she was used to being alone. 'I was a nurse all my life. I can take care of myself.'

'I'm Bet Rivers – I don't think we've formally met.' Bet started to reach out her hand but caught herself. 'Sorry, I probably shouldn't shake your hand.'

'That's all right, Sheriff. My situation takes time for people to get used to. I'm Wanda Dupree. It's a pleasure to meet you in person.' She gave a nod of her head in place of shaking hands. 'I voted for you.' She gave a shy smile. 'Even though you didn't have anyone running against you. It was pure pleasure to check the box next to a woman's name, even if you were guaranteed a win.'

Bet laughed. 'Thank you for that. How am I doing so far?'

Now it was Wanda's turn to chuckle. 'Ask me that again after the storm is over.'

Her comment earned her another quick laugh from Bet, who wanted to keep the conversation light. 'Fair enough.'

Wanda looked over Bet's shoulder. 'Lose your car?'

'I was over at the house next door. There was a break-in.'

'Oh no. When?' A flash of fear crossed Wanda's eyes. Bet wasn't surprised. Crime in a person's neighborhood, especially one as quiet as this, could make someone feel vulnerable in the best of times.

'Recently, though I'm not sure when.'

'I'm not in any danger, am I?' Her face creased in concern. Bet felt bad for adding to the woman's stress level, so she did her best to allay her anxiety.

'No reason to think so.' Bet didn't want her afraid of being alone. The danger of exposure to germs in a crowd was more serious and immediate than events next door. 'Whoever stayed there probably broke in knowing the house was empty. Yours is clearly lived in. Did you happen to notice anything going on over there in the last couple of days? Someone driving in and out? Lights on? Voices?'

Wanda peered over at the house for a moment as if looking that way would jog her memory.

'You know, there was a vehicle over there last night, late, maybe one or two in the morning. I don't sleep well, and I tend to pace the house at odd hours.'

'It must have been loud if you could hear it from here with all your windows closed.' Bet eyed the distance between the buildings. 'Could you see the make and model?'

Wanda stood a moment in thought, lips pursed as she recalled the scene.

'You know,' she said. 'I didn't think about it at the time. But it sounded like a snowmobile. That would explain why it was so loud.'

Wanda didn't remember anything else out of the ordinary from the last couple days, but she promised to keep an eye out and contact Bet if anyone appeared in the woods or at the house next door. 'I know George's truck. I assume he's not a suspect.' She raised one eyebrow in a question.

At this point, everyone was a suspect. But Bet had known George her entire life and thought it unlikely. George might be capable of murder, but not of leaving a messy crime scene. He would have tidied up.

'George can't go in either until I process the house for evidence. Give me a call if anyone shows up.' Bet pulled out one of her cards and handed it over. 'Or if you need anything during the storm.'

'Will do. I'll get out my binoculars. It will give me something to do.'

As Bet trudged through the snow to her SUV, she made a mental note to check on Wanda later if the power wasn't back on.

She'd no sooner got into her car and started the vehicle when her phone rang through the Bluetooth. She recognized her deputy's number.

'Everything OK?' she asked.

'We have a problem,' Clayton said.

Of course we do.

She just hoped it didn't involve another crime scene. The crew at the Collier Sheriff Station was stretched thin enough already, and the storm had barely started.

SEVEN

B et didn't hear any sounds in the background, so she guessed Clayton called from inside his patrol vehicle. She sat in the driveway with the heat cranked and watched her windshield wipers fight with the falling snow. It wasn't clear who was going to win, the snow or the thin rubber strips.

'What's up?' Bet held her breath. Had Clayton found something related to the bloody sleeping bag? Like a dead guy stashed somewhere in town.

'Someone broke into Addie Simpson's ambulance.'

A lot of rural communities around the United States lacked a fire department, and their counties failed to provide ambulance service. Private and volunteer ambulance companies were often the only service available for those residents.

With the closest medical clinic to Collier down in Cle Elum and the closest hospital in Ellensburg, an additional twenty-five minutes away, serious emergencies were often flown out to Seattle by helicopter, but less serious illnesses or injuries could be picked up and transported to E'burg by a recent addition to Collier's little community, Addie and her bus.

'When did this happen?'

A paramedic by training, Addie drove the ambulance, which she used to transport people on a volunteer basis. Back in October, the community pitched in with donations to help her get it up and running. She earned some money through insurance companies, but she would never refuse a person without insurance, assuring her community of help in a crisis.

'It could have been any time in the last three days. Addie was down in E'burg working her usual twenty-four-hour shift. She got stuck out of town when the tree came down but wanted to come back to Collier to help Donna at the community center in case of a medical emergency. She got a ride to the spot where the power company is clearing the road and hiked through. I picked her up and brought her home. We're at her house now.'

There could be a lot of narcotics in an ambulance. The 'while you were out' note from Jamie Garcia about an increase in drug use in the area floated through her mind. Drugs had never been a problem in her valley, but that didn't mean that problem might not start to take hold.

'I assume something was stolen?'

'She doesn't keep a lot of drugs on board, but she put together a list of what was taken. There are a couple of items on the list, like morphine, that someone could use to get high or sell. The other stuff doesn't have much street value.'

'Any damage done to her rig?'

'Just a broken lock on the back door.'

'You did a walk-through of her house?'

'All clear. No evidence of any other break-in. Just the bus.'

There was even less of a chance they would solve the break-in of the ambulance than they would the break-in at the rental house.

'OK. Write up the report, take fingerprints, and talk to the neighbors, but I don't think it's something we're going to solve.'

'Yeah. I just wanted you to know since it's not a typical crime around here, and it means she's not as fully stocked as she'd like to be in case of an emergency.'

'I appreciate that.'

Bet thought about the break-in at the rental house again. Could the two be connected? They rarely had burglaries of any kind in Collier, including vehicle break-ins. Two in the same time period felt like too much of a coincidence. But what did the different crimes have to do with each other? It wasn't like there were enough drugs stolen from the ambulance to be worth killing over, though someone drug-seeking could act out violently. Maybe the victim at the rental house got between a person and their fix. But Addie lived miles away in a different part of the valley. Geographically the two crime scenes didn't fit together. After processing, however, they could determine if there were finger-prints common to both scenes.

'Keep me posted,' Bet said.

Hanging up with Clayton, Bet got back on the phone to Alma, spelling out what they needed on the warrant to search the rental house. Bet described everything, including why she'd done the walk-through in advance of the warrant, and what belonged in the request so that a judge would authorize a full crime scene investigation for the house and the garage. Hopefully the house would give up enough clues to point her toward the victim . . . and if it were a homicide, lead her to a killer.

EIGHT

Bet walked up to the front door of the Marsden house to find lights on downstairs and in one upstairs window. Even though it was still early afternoon, the sky was dark from the storm. She knew Doug wouldn't be there, but someone had answered the phone – Doug's older son Bodhi, a likely candidate. He should have more information about where Doug was and if Grant had been out with someone else on the snowmobile. Could Bodhi have been out with his brother yesterday? Caused the accident, then left his brother to die?

Talking to people face-to-face usually prompted more information, so she decided to drive over in person. Until the judge issued the warrant, the investigation at the rental house was on pause.

At the Marsdens', a number of vehicles sat parked out front. A few pickup trucks, older hatchbacks, and one minivan were quickly turning into mounds of snow. The Marsdens must have a working generator, as along with the lights, music played loud enough to be heard over the storm.

Could Bodhi – or whoever was home – have enough people over that they never noticed Grant didn't come home last night?

A drumbeat vibrated the frosted glass windows on either side of the door as she knocked and rang the bell.

No response.

She knocked and rang the bell again, holding her finger down, the buzz insistent against sounds of the storm. The music dropped in volume, and a moment later, a figure appeared on the other side of the glass.

Bodhi opened the door, a beer in his hand and a brace on his leg. 'Hey, Sheriff.' She knew he had recently turned twenty-one as he'd started hanging out in the local bars. 'Everything all right?' His voice was the one she'd heard on the phone.

'Hi, Bodhi. What happened to your leg?' Was the injury from a snowmobile accident yesterday? Had Bodhi caused his brother's accident?

'Stupid snowboard accident a couple days ago. Ski patrol had to haul me down on a toboggan.'

'The Summit?' Bet referenced the closest popular ski resort because she could confirm the accident and rule him out for snowmobiling with Grant yesterday if he was already injured.

'Yep.'

'Bummer. How long do you have to wear the brace?'

'Couple weeks.'

'Is your dad home?' It would be interesting to see if he gave the same answer to her as he had to her voice on the phone. He didn't appear to recognize her from the earlier call. The noise in the background had probably made that impossible.

He shook his head. 'He was down in E'burg, so now he's stuck until the road is cleared.'

Doug's absence, leaving Bodhi the only adult in the house, might explain why no one contacted Bet about Grant's disappearance. Bodhi probably didn't pay attention to the location of his younger teenage brother, and Doug hadn't been home when his son went out on the sled.

A young woman wandered into view. Bet recognized Rebecca Sanchez. Not yet twenty-one, the girl took one look at Bet and scurried out of sight. Bet raised an eyebrow. Bodhi shrugged as if to say, *what can you do?*

'Just a few friends over to wait out the storm,' he said. 'We have a generator.'

'Underage drinking is still a crime, regardless of the weather.'

'I didn't see a beer in her hand.'

He waited, an unspoken dare for Bet to pursue it further. He was right, Rebecca didn't have a drink in her hand, so Bet only had her instincts that the girl was drinking without her parents' consent. But it wasn't a battle that Bet had time to fight.

'Let's keep it that way. No one leaves the house under the influence, OK? Driving in these conditions is bad enough sober.'

Bodhi gestured toward a bowl of keys on a table near the door. 'No one is going anywhere.'

'That includes you.'

Bodhi dipped his head in a mock bow. 'Trust me, I'm not leaving. I'm playing host. Is there something else I can do for you?' Bodhi narrowed his eyes. 'I can't believe anyone complained about our music in this weather. What brought you over here?'

Grant was a minor, so Bet needed to tell Doug about his son's death first, before she gave any information to Bodhi. But she also didn't want him to go out looking for Grant if he expected him home anytime soon.

'Is your brother home?' she asked. Where did Bodhi think Grant had been all night?

'He's riding the storm out at a friend's house. He's been there all weekend.'

Bet could have abandoned Grant's friend out on the ridge in the storm. A possible victim of the same accident that claimed Grant's life.

'Whose house would that be?'

Something new flashed across Bodhi's eyes. The last thing Bet wanted to do was pique his curiosity enough to ask questions she couldn't answer.

'Checking up on us Marsdens? You must have better things to do in the midst of all this.' Bodhi gestured out at the tempest as it roared around the house, fresh snow sliding down the collar of Bet's heavy coat.

'Now that I know your dad isn't home, I just need to know he's OK. Grant is still a minor.' Bet fought the urge to cross her fingers behind her back.

Bodhi relaxed. 'He's with Aimee Johnson,' he said. 'Her parents are out in Seattle and she didn't want to stay home alone. He's fine.'

The Johnsons were longtime residents and lived past the cemetery on the other side of the valley from where the Marsdens lived.

'OK. Thank you. Can you tell me where your father is staying and give me his cell number?'

Bodhi hesitated, probably worried she would out him to his dad about having at least one underage girl drinking at the house while Doug was down in E'burg. 'You still haven't explained why you're here.'

'I just need to talk to your father about a construction question. Don't worry, no one's in trouble.'

Bodhi rattled off Doug's number, which she put into her cell. She recognized the name of the motel he gave her in E'burg. Bet paused a moment when he was done to see if he would say anything further or ask if she planned to track down his brother. He merely rubbed his arms and complained it was too cold to stand in the open doorway.

'I'm glad to know Grant is OK,' she said. Guilt shot through her at the deception over his brother's death, but she didn't want Bodhi trying to call Aimee before she visited the girl. It was important that Bodhi believed she wouldn't follow up.

'See you, Sheriff.' Bodhi pulled the door shut and Bet watched his form disappear through the frosted glass as he limped away. The music grew louder again. At least she didn't have to worry about Bodhi's concern for his brother sending him out in the storm.

Getting back into her SUV, she considered calling Doug right away, but with the road still blocked, there was nothing he could do from a distance, and at least she knew he couldn't be out looking for Grant and wasn't involved in the accident. Doug wouldn't be able to see his son to identify him, so he might not believe it was Grant until he did.

Would she want to know immediately if it were her child?

She pictured the moment when officials notified her of her father's death. She thought he would recover from his illness, so she wasn't expecting to face his death so soon. Two park rangers Bet knew well arrived at her doorstep. The second she opened the door she knew something terrible had happened by the neutral look on their faces.

Her father had been undergoing cancer treatment, the reason she'd come home as interim sheriff. But he'd died from a fall off a trail on National Forest land, so the initial inquiry fell to the rangers. As next of kin, she wasn't allowed to participate anyway, so the sheriff station in Cle Elum assisted with the investigation, determining the fall an accident, though Bet wasn't so sure.

But the manner of death didn't matter. The loss was the same. Life would be irreparably changed for Doug Marsden *and*

Bodhi. Maybe it was a mercy to give them a few more hours before she tore their world apart.

As she backed up, she glanced at the windows upstairs. A figure stood in the shadows. Bet could only see the movement of a hand on the blinds. Were they curious about the sheriff's vehicle parked in the driveway? Or hiding out until Bet left?

NINE

B et pulled up in front of Aimee Johnson's house. All the windows were dark. Sitting a moment in her SUV, Bet sent Alma a text to have her confirm Bodhi's accident at the Summit ski resort. Then she put a call in to the hotel in E'burg where Bodhi told Bet that Doug was staying. She wanted to confirm he was there so that if she needed to, she could have the E'burg police go over to give him the news about his son. She explained who she was to the clerk and asked about Doug's whereabouts. He assured her no one by that name was staying at the hotel and hadn't in the past few days.

Annoyed at having to add 'tracking down Doug Marsden' to her list of things to do, she got out of the car. Without knowing his location, she didn't have the option of the E'burg police making the notification and couldn't confirm he wasn't involved with the accident.

She decided to locate Aimee first, then call Grant's father on his cell. If she couldn't find Aimee, she could use that as an excuse for contacting Doug, explaining she was looking for the girl. She would never tell a parent their child was dead over the phone, but maybe she could find out where he was staying during the course of the call and have the locals perform the death notification. There were protocols for a notifier to follow: do it in person, have a second person on hand in case the receiver needs assistance, don't leave them alone until assessing their well-being or a support person arrives.

It might be better to wait until Doug was back home in Collier, but making the notification as soon as possible was also important – she had a tight lid on Grant's death, but a leak could get out on social media. If Doug learned of his son's death through unofficial channels, it would be a disaster.

There was no sound of a generator running, but Bet knocked anyway. Aimee could be home despite the power outage. No one answered after her repeated knocks and doorbell rings. Bet walked over to the garage to see if the Johnsons owned snowmobiles. Aimee could have been in the accident too, her sled leaving the trail farther down. She could have been missed with everyone's attention on the wreck. Or she could have been a passenger, thrown far enough off the machine to have landed out of sight. If her parents were out of town, no one would know she was missing.

Bet shoved aside a mental image of the girl buried in the snow.

Peeking through the window of the garage, she saw the space was empty and only large enough for two cars. Aimee was probably somewhere with one car and her parents were out in Seattle with the other. If they did own snowmobiles, they must park them elsewhere. Bet walked around behind the garage to find an outbuilding in the backyard. The doors were locked, and there were no windows for her to look through.

If they owned a snowmobile, Aimee could be stuck or injured in the middle of the worst storm they'd had in years, or be dead just like Grant.

Someone shot an arrow at Grant. Could Aimee have been the one who fired the crossbow?

Or Bodhi had it wrong and Aimee was holed up with her parents or another friend somewhere else. Or, Grant lied to his brother about who he was with. Bodhi could know that his brother went out on a snowmobile, but thought he'd gone to Aimee's on it.

Lots of reasons to worry about where Aimee might be.

Bet got back in her SUV and called Alma.

'Bodhi was in a snowboard accident on Wednesday,' Alma said in greeting. 'He was hauled off the mountain on a toboggan and fixed up at the hospital in E'burg.'

'Great, thank you. Now I need you to check on whether any snowmobiles are registered to Craig and Marta Johnson.' Snowmobiles didn't carry titles, but owners were required by law to register them.

'This related to what you found this morning?'

'I'll explain when I come back in.'

Bet could hear the keys clicking as Alma accessed the database.

'I don't see any snowmobiles registered in their names.'

'Damn it,' Bet said. That didn't mean they didn't own any. People didn't always register their machines. Failure to do so carried a maximum fine of one hundred and fourteen dollars, and registration cost fifty, so some people just played the odds and let it go.

Alma's voice cut through Bet's thoughts. 'What do you want to do?'

'Track down cell phone numbers for the Johnsons. I need to find their daughter.'

Alma promised to get on it.

It was time to check in on the progress the electric utility had made on clearing the road and getting the power back on. With one dead kid and another potentially missing, a crime scene up on the ridge underneath several feet of snow, and the crime scene at the Collier summer rental, she wanted to open up the road to emergency services and the crime scene tech she brought in from Ellensburg for anything more complicated than fingerprinting. Plus, she'd like to get the coroner's van up to send Grant's body down to Ellensburg for a complete autopsy. If Grant was high or drunk, that might have played a role in events, and maybe Carolyn could still get a more accurate time of death.

Bet tried not to think about the fact that Aimee might have bled out on a sleeping bag in the rental house. And if it wasn't Aimee, Bet still had the possibility of another victim from that house and Aimee stuck on the ridge and alone in the storm.

She'd wanted to prove to her community that she could handle the job. Evidently, she was going to get the chance.

TEN

Bet pulled up in front of the station and shut the engine off. Just as the Bluetooth disconnected, her cell began to vibrate. By the time she dug through layers of clothes to get to it, the call had gone to voicemail. She glanced at the screen and read Rob Collier's name. The prodigal son of the town's founding family, Rob arrived back in town and got under Bet's skin. Now he was out of the country dealing with a variety of issues that concerned his father, an ex-pat living in Vietnam. Bet understood why Rob felt he needed to see his father in person, but the fourteen-hour time change made it hard for them to connect on the phone.

Probably just as well. Having an ocean between them gave her breathing room. They had only met a few months ago, during her first homicide investigation, and she wasn't sure what she wanted from the man. It was easier to put off dealing with the intimacy of their dynamic.

Even if that distance was only temporary.

At some point, she'd have to decide how she felt about him and face up to telling him whatever those feelings were.

Though if she waited long enough, maybe he would tell her first.

The ding from the voicemail notification sounded, but she tucked her phone back into her pocket. She'd listen later. Rob would understand she had other priorities.

After getting out of the SUV, she unloaded Schweitzer, and they walked up to the front door – both hunched against the strong wind and blowing snow. She struggled to get the door closed behind her and let out a sigh of relief to find the station house warm and brightly lit.

'Glad to know our generator is holding up.' Bet unzipped her coat, planning to go to her office. The ancient generator was on its last legs, but in the face of budget cuts, it wasn't at the top of her list of priorities for their fiscal year.

'When are we going to replace that damn thing?' Alma didn't look up from greeting Schweitzer as she ruffled his ears and scratched his chest. The dog was often the focus of her and Bet's attention when they didn't want to look at each other but had something important to discuss.

Alma had leaned hard on Bet last summer to get a new generator before this year's winter weather started up, but Bet hadn't given in. Alma always thought she knew best where the sheriff's station budget was concerned. Even though Bet was getting better at not second-guessing herself when their agendas didn't match, she still prayed the generator held out through the storm so Alma wouldn't turn out to be right.

Bet would never hear the end of it.

'Any luck finding the phone numbers I asked for?'

Alma tore a sheet of paper off her memo pad and held it out to Bet, her eyes still on the dog. 'Top one is the landline, the bottom three are cell numbers.'

There were no names next to the cell numbers. Chris and Marta Johnson probably each had one, with Aimee using the third. With all of them on the same plan, there was no way to know which number belonged to whom.

'Thank you, Alma.'

Alma looked up then, tearing her eyes from the dog. 'You doing OK?' The concern in her voice was genuine. No matter how much Alma might disagree with Bet's choices, her support was unflinching. Alma was the perfect example of unconditional love. Tough love, but unconditional.

Alma had been the public face of the office since Bet's grand-father was the sheriff, then Earle, and now Bet. Collier was her town, and her job was to protect the citizens any way she could, even if that meant disagreeing with the sheriff. New worry lines around her mouth showed Bet how much Alma feared the impact of the storm. It didn't help that Bet hadn't told her who she'd found dead this morning. But the more people who knew it was Grant, the more possibility it could leak and Doug would learn of his son's death before Bet could inform him properly.

'What's the radar look like?' Bet asked.

Alma glanced back down at her computer. She twisted the monitor around so Bet could see the giant storm. It spun coun-terclockwise, because the winds pushed in from the south, but the entire storm came down from the Arctic, bringing cold air, snow, and high winds.

The dark-blue expanse filled the computer screen, as if the tiny town of Collier and its adjacent lake disappeared into an abyss. The swirling bands of the storm meant the bad weather would come in waves, with a few hours of heavy snowfall and wind, followed by a few hours of calm, then another round of snow and wind, as each weather event slammed across their valley.

Based on the enormity of the total disturbance, they had a very long way to go before it came to an end. And if it stalled on top of them or another storm materialized behind this one, it could last a lot longer than a few days.

'Any word from the power company?'

Alma shook her head. 'I figured you might want to lean on them a little bit.'

Bet would, though she knew they were working as fast as they could in the treacherous conditions.

'Grant Marsden,' Bet said, though Alma hadn't asked. 'I haven't contacted his father, so that information isn't public yet.' Even though Alma maintained the website and the social media accounts for the station, Bet knew she'd keep the information private. Alma might be a pain sometimes, but she was a loyal pain.

'Crap,' she said. 'He's just a kid.'

Bet nodded. There wasn't anything to say to that.

'What happened?'

'I'm not sure.' She went on to explain about the arrow trapped underneath the snowmobile. 'But I can't speculate about it without going back up and getting the evidence and investigating what Grant was up to, and with whom, before he went out on that ride. It's even possible Grant had the arrow with him and landed on it in the accident. I need to get a better look. Who knows what evidence is spread around in the snow.'

Bet hoped it wouldn't take next spring's thaws to figure out what had happened to Grant.

'Let me know what I can do.'

With a nod, Bet headed into her office, Schweitzer on her heels, to make a few phone calls before she went back out.

The dog plopped down on his bed with a loud sigh and began working on one of his squeaky toys. Schweitzer loved Alma, but Bet was his person, and he was most content when they were together. It had taken months after her father's death for them to bond, but now that they had, Bet couldn't imagine life without him.

Bet set the pink note with the Johnsons' cell numbers on her desk as she put in a call to the power company. She eyed the note from Jamie Garcia taped to her monitor. What kind of drugs was the reporter referencing? Sitting on hold, she pulled open her email and sent the woman a note: *Details?*

After several minutes of getting passed around and sitting on hold, she learned the crew had already pulled the trees off the power line, but the road wasn't cleared yet. At least they were making progress. She was impressed they had finished that much while contending with high winds, freezing temperatures, and the relentless snowfall.

Ending that call, she went back to the phone numbers for the Johnsons. The home number went to voicemail, so she hung up and dialed the first cell number on the list. It also went to voicemail, but a male voice identified himself as Craig and said to leave a message. Bet hung up without speaking and called the second number. It also went to voicemail, where a female voice identified herself as Marta.

Third time's a charm. Bet dialed the last number.

'Hello?' came a tentative voice.

'Aimee?'

'Yes?' the girl's voice went up on the end as if she was asking a question, but Bet took it for an affirmative.

'This is Sheriff Bet Rivers. I'd like to ask you a few questions if that's all right.'

Aimee paused long enough that Bet thought she might have lost her. 'This is about Grant, isn't it?'

Bet felt a jolt. Maybe Aimee did have some useful information.

'What makes you say that?'

'I told him he was going to get in trouble. But why are you calling me and not his dad?'

What was Grant up to that would get him into trouble? Why wasn't Aimee more surprised to have the sheriff calling her?

'I'd like to hear your side of the story.'

'Shit! I mean . . . damn. I told him to leave me out of this. I told him it was stupid.'

'You're not in any trouble,' Bet reassured her, even though it might not be true. 'Just tell me what you know.' Silence met her again. 'It might help Grant.'

Bet feared the girl had hung up.

'Bodhi said your parents are out in Seattle.'

If only Aimee would fill in the blanks about where she was now. Bet would rather talk to her in person, but nothing in the background indicated her location.

'Yeah. They're stuck there . . . what did Bodhi say?'

The tone of Aimee's voice changed from anxiety to suspicion. Bet wondered if she'd made a tactical error mentioning her conversation with Bodhi. Silence often prompted people to say more.

'Was he . . . is he ticked off?'

Now Bet was confused. What would Bodhi have to be angry about?

'Let's talk about Grant.'

A murmur of voices came through the phone. Clearly Aimee wasn't alone. Bet heard her explain to someone she was on the phone with the sheriff.

'Aimee, where are you?' Bet tried to win her attention back.

'I'm—'

Before the girl could answer, something – or someone – cut her off. Bet heard a struggle before the call ended. Either Amy hung up, or someone hung up for her.

Bet dialed again, but it went straight to voicemail. An automated recording spoke – no personalized greeting. Bet waited to leave a message. She asked that Aimee return her call.

Bet hung up again. 'Crap.' Her tone made Schweitzer lift his head to gaze in her direction. 'The good news is, at least I know Aimee isn't dead.'

But Aimee thought Bodhi would be angry and someone didn't want Aimee speaking to the sheriff.

What kind of trouble was Aimee in?

ELEVEN

Bet wished she could track Aimee on her cell phone, but a recent Supreme Court ruling put an end to that use of technology. Officers needed a warrant to obtain a person's cell phone location, otherwise it became a Fourth Amendment violation. Concerned as she was about Aimee's situation, she didn't have a legitimate reason to track the girl, so a warrant was out of the question.

She could, however, call Aimee's parents and ask them to

locate her phone. As the registered owners they could legally trace its location if they wanted to. But she needed a logical reason to ask them to locate their daughter's phone. Something that wouldn't raise their suspicions that Aimee was in trouble, which could make them unwilling to help.

Why had Aimee thought Bodhi would be angry? And why did she think Grant was in trouble with Bet?

Bodhi or Grant could be into something illegal.

'Our legal system says innocent until proven guilty,' Maggie told her once. 'But that's in a court of law. We have to keep an open mind when we interview suspects, but assume everyone *could* be guilty of something. That way nothing takes you by surprise.'

Bet woke up her computer and started looking into Bodhi's background. He hadn't been in any trouble in her jurisdiction, but he'd been gone from town for a few years just as she had been. Collier was a small town, so even though she'd been in Los Angeles until recently, she knew a lot of the people in the valley. Still, she wasn't intimate with everyone, and the whereabouts of people who left town certainly weren't something she tracked.

Bodhi didn't have much of an online presence. She searched through social media and ran his name through a few search engines, but little showed up. He went to college in Seattle, placing him there until June, after which he apparently returned to Collier.

He didn't have a police record, but that could just mean he'd never gotten caught.

Wet snow slammed against the window, rattling the glass in the frame, reminding her that she had better things to do than research Bodhi Marsden. She shut her computer down.

Deciding on a course of action with the Johnsons, she called the first cell number back again.

Voicemail once again announced it belonged to Craig.

'Hi, Mr Johnson, this is Sheriff Bet Rivers up in Collier. Don't worry, this is not an emergency.' Bet knew hearing from law enforcement could strike fear into a person's heart. 'I'm trying to locate a friend of your daughter's, and I'm hoping you or Aimee can help. Could you please call me back at your earliest convenience?'

She left the same message with Marta Johnson and decided

that was all she could do for the time being. Without clear evidence a crime took place on the ridge – the arrow wasn't proof of anything yet – and no idea what Aimee had alluded to, she had bigger worries on her plate. Like a bloody crime scene at a vacant house and an entire community buried in snow. At least she knew Aimee hadn't fallen off the back of a snowmobile or died on the sleeping bag.

Though with that much blood, someone could have.

She called Clayton to find out his whereabouts. He'd finished fingerprinting the ambulance and was back out patrolling the community. But Bet knew he hadn't stopped for lunch, so she sent him on break for an hour. It wouldn't do for either of them to get run down. Schweitzer looked up as she stood. With Clayton on break, she'd patrol the streets to check for stuck motorists and other storm-related emergencies before she dealt with the other situations.

'OK, Schweitz, let's go see how things are going.' If the road wasn't going to open soon, she would have to tackle processing the scene at the rental house. She'd prefer to bring one of the crime scene techs in from E'burg because the experts would do a better job. But with the dangerous weather, that might not be possible.

She'd wait until the warrant came through and make a decision then.

Schweitzer popped up to his impressive height, stretched out with a giant yawn, then the two headed out into the storm.

At least she didn't have to face it alone.

TWELVE

Bet made a circuit around town, eating the bag of almonds that Alma had pressed into her hand as she left the station. It was dark now, even though it was not yet five o'clock. Most Lakers stayed home, and the few vehicles that were out had studded tires or chains or were heavy four-wheel drives. One thing she could be confident about was that Lakers knew how to drive in the snow. As with most small mountain towns, folks in the valley were fearless and confident in winter driving conditions. Collier probably wasn't the best year-round choice for people who weren't.

Driving toward Pearson's Ranch at the Train Yard, Bet's intention was to make the full loop around the valley. If anyone had a car break down, hypothermia could set in quickly, and phones didn't always work. Even Lakers needed a hand sometimes, and Bet wasn't about to let someone freeze to death on her watch.

On the way to Jeb's place, she brought Rob's voicemail up over her car speakers.

'Hey, it's me.' The sound of his words filled the car, and her heart rate spiked. 'It's two in the morning here. I was just on the computer and saw the storm warnings out there. I thought I'd check in and see how you're doing.' His laugh came through low and quiet, a rumble in his chest. Bet knew exactly what it felt like when she rested her head there. 'Not that I can do anything about it from here.' Fatigue suffused his tone.

The sounds of honking and traffic filtered through the silence. He liked to sit in the window of his hotel, looking down on the busy street scene below him. He sent her photos from his bird's eye view at various times during the day. Crowded streets in the morning rush hour, car lights stretching out below late at night. With a population of over seven million, Hanoi never slept. She imagined heat and humidity, the smell of exhaust. The cadence of another language rising from the bustling street.

'OK. I'm going to try to get some shut-eye. Just know . . .' He paused. So many things he could say but wouldn't. 'If I were there, I'd clear the snow off your front walk.'

It was about as close as he'd come to saying 'I love you' since they'd met.

They hadn't known each other long. Not long enough to make declarations. And their 'dating' had never been formalized with deep conversations about monogamy or 'where they were heading'. But the situation in which they met, with Rob mixed up in the middle of her first homicide case, had an intensity to it that sped up her feelings for the man.

Did that make her feelings any less real?

Bet saved the message and turned her full attention back to the storm.

She hadn't gotten very far when the station's number showed up on the screen and Alma's no-nonsense voice came over the speakers.

'The warrant came through for the rental house.'

'That was fast.'

'Caught my favorite judge at just the right time.' Alma chuckled at her ability to move the right mountains.

Bet was relieved to have Alma on her side. If the woman ever turned to a life of crime, she'd get away with everything.

'Good work, Alma.' The two fell silent as Bet considered next steps.

The warrant coming through and the blocked road prompted Bet's decision. Time to see what information the crime scene could provide her team.

THIRTEEN

Bet tucked into Jeb Pearson's driveway, ready to turn around and head back to the station. In the dark and the snow, she could barely see the outline of the buildings closest to the road. Nothing stirred. Bet pictured all the animals in their spots in the barn, warm and waiting out the storm. Cyd, one of Jeb's mares, was due soon. Jeb hadn't planned to breed her again, but a stallion jumped a fence at another farm nearby and Jeb didn't find out about it until after the horse had gotten in with Cyd and the two consummated their brief – but successful – love affair.

Hopefully, both Cyd and Clayton's wife Kathy could hold off having their babies until after the storm ended.

Bet could just make out smoke rising into the air like ashy geysers from the chimneys in the main building and the cabin the Crewses had rented.

'I'll call Clayton,' Bet said in response to Alma's news about the warrant. 'Since the road's not clear, the two of us will have to process the scene. Someone could be hurt out there waiting for us to track them down. The sooner we figure out what happened there, the better.'

She didn't say 'if we *can* figure it out', though Alma probably thought so too. 'Anything else going on I should know about?'

'If there was, I'd tell you.' Alma took the sting from her words with another chuckle. 'I liked to irk your father that way too.' Alma had outlived two sheriffs and made the transition to Bet in charge with minimal fuss. Bet was grateful for the woman who sat behind the desk, day in and day out, as much a part of the station as anyone who carried a badge. But like all family, sometimes they got on each other's nerves.

'I miss him too,' Bet said before she hung up the phone. Another thing she and Alma had in common – a constant, underlying grief over the loss of Earle Rivers. The bedrock on which so much of their lives had been grounded had eroded under their feet with his death. Bet wondered if she had the constitution to get them back on solid ground.

Clayton didn't have many opportunities to work on investigating a crime scene, so despite the complications created by the blackout and the weather, she wanted to use the rental house as a teaching moment. It struck her that she had to play the mentor role to Clayton just as her father and Maggie had played the role for her. How well could she do that without their years of experience?

Clayton picked up after the first ring.

'Talk me through your process,' she said after establishing Clayton wasn't in the middle of a crisis and could meet her there.

'First, I do a walk-around of the building, looking for anywhere someone might have broken in. Then I move indoors.'

'Are you forgetting anything before you go inside?'

Bet could hear Clayton's windshield wipers pushing snow off the glass and the click of his turn signal.

'Secure the premises and mark the boundaries with crime scene tape.'

'Good. Just because you know I've already been there doesn't mean I've done that or done it well. It's good to have that in your mental checklist, even if it's just to confirm what I did, and it's OK to point out if I miss something.'

Clayton continued to describe the basics of crime scene investigation. He would gather his overall impressions of the scene. Look for blood evidence in other rooms, or footprints, which could be found in dirt or blood. Then he would photograph the interior, paying close attention to the dining room with its bloody sleeping bag, and places where intruders had clearly left evidence, such as the impressions on the furniture in the living room.

If someone left hairs behind it could give them a clue to the person who left it, since forensics could determine not just hair color, but also age, gender, and racial origin through a single hair. If they could get DNA along with fingerprints, that could narrow down a suspect list of who had been in the house. With George as thorough as he was with cleaning, it would most likely have been left after the final renters of the season had gone home.

Throughout his investigation, Clayton would need to write copious notes.

'It can take months or even years before anyone goes to trial on a homicide,' Bet reminded him. 'You're going to have to remember what you saw and what you inferred and why you inferred it no matter how much time has passed.'

'You sound confident this is a homicide.'

'At best this was some kind of accident, but no one contacted us, so until we learn something that tells us otherwise, we have to believe the blood could have been left through the course of a serious crime.'

Bet turned into the driveway as she said these words, pulling up next to Clayton. She'd told him it was OK to park there. Snow had covered all the tire tracks, and both she and George had parked there already.

Bet trailed behind Clayton as he made his way around the building, checking windows for broken locks and searching for evidence outside, despite the heavy snow. He reached the back door and snapped a few photos of Bet's repair job over the broken glass with his digital camera. If there ever was a trial, he might be called to verify what she had done. They both used digital cameras for anything that might be used in court so their cell phones wouldn't be subpoenaed. Bet mixed her experience from Los Angeles with her father's life as Collier's sheriff. She hoped, for Clayton's sake, that would be enough.

Clayton completed his circuit of the building, with Bet walking behind. Once back at the cars, they gathered what they needed from their vehicles for the interior evidence sweep and stopped at the front door. They both put on booties and gloves to wear inside the building. Bet pulled a knife out of her pocket to slice the crime scene tape where she'd sealed the front door and they stepped into the entranceway.

Bet set a notebook and pen on a small table near the door to track anyone visiting the house. She and Clayton signed in and noted the date and time. It might only be them at the crime scene, but Bet followed protocol regardless. Her father would expect her to. Bet wouldn't forgive herself if someone got away with murder from a technicality. She documented everything they did.

Clayton carried the evidence vacuum in with them, which he'd picked up at the station on his way over, and they both had evidence bags. The vacuum was only used at crime scenes, to gather microparticle evidence such as hair and fibers. They would use it here at the scene and secure the bags to send to the crime lab if and when their investigation warranted it. She'd rather collect material she never needed than lose out on the chance to secure something that might break an investigation wide open. The tiniest of clues – little things criminals never expected would trip them up – could solve a crime and put the right person in jail.

After Clayton finished vacuuming around the sleeping bag and the floor under the table, Bet moved in to do the immunochromatographic procedure to test if the blood on the sleeping bag was human.

It didn't take long for the pink line to appear.

'Definitely human.' Bet gestured with the test strip in her hand before dropping it into an evidence bag and sealing it with the date across the tape.

'There's a lot of blood on that sleeping bag.'

'But we don't know yet if it all came from one person.'

'What about . . . someone having a baby?' Clayton said the words casually but with a catch in his voice. Impending fatherhood must impact his feelings about the idea of a woman in trouble giving birth. It was also probably why it was on his mind.

'I hadn't thought of that. The lab can tell us if there are signs of other biologics, like amniotic fluids, mixed in. Good thinking, Clayton.'

Clayton nodded and went back to work.

'How's Kathy doing?' It must be hard for him to be stuck in Collier with his wife so near her due date.

'So far so good.' Clayton smiled, but there was tension in his body language. 'Why do you think the sleeping bag was put here on the table to begin with?'

He clearly wanted to change the subject, and it was a good question. 'I'd like to know that myself.' His idea about a woman in labor made sense. And if that was the case, had someone been helping her? Why use the table? Or hide the birth? Could it be someone underage?

Clayton continued with the vacuum. Once he'd collected all of the material throughout the house, he would seal it into an evidence bag along with the filter. They would use a fresh filter at the next crime scene to keep from cross-contaminating evidence.

Even in a tiny town like Collier, there was always another crime scene.

Whenever he moved into a new location to vacuum, Clayton methodically inspected the carpet, furniture, walls – even the ceiling – using a high-intensity flashlight to look for blood evidence that someone might have tried to clean up or was tricky to see because of location or size. Spatter could travel a long way or consist of tiny droplets, which were difficult to identify.

Bet took extensive photos of the sleeping bag in place on the table before carefully moving it into a clean cardboard box. She'd already lined the bottom with paper. If anything fell out of the sleeping bag, a fingernail, a hair, she would fold it inside the paper and send it into the crime lab along with the sleeping bag.

Because the blood was still wet, she needed to remove it from the box, air-dry it, and then reseal it in cardboard or a paper bag as soon as possible. More than two hours sealed up and wet and it could potentially grow microorganisms that would degrade the evidence. The cold temp inside the rental house had slowed the process, but she didn't want to risk losing anything.

Without access to the crime lab in Ellensburg, the evidence would have to be dried at the station. She sealed and photographed the box with her signature across the tape to preserve the chain of custody, proof she'd had control of the evidence at all times.

Bet followed the sound of the vacuum cleaner back into the

bathroom, the one with the missing shower curtain. She waited until Clayton caught sight of her in the mirror over the sink and shut off the machine.

'I'm going to run the sleeping bag back to the station to dry. Do you feel confident about working the scene alone?'

Clayton ticked off the rest of his list: fingerprinting, collecting the dust covers from the furniture in the living room, and checking the garage, which Bet had only taken a cursory look at through a window. She had already confirmed that separate space was on the search warrant the judge had signed.

'I also want to take out the trap under this sink and check for hair or anything that might be useful. With all that blood, maybe someone washed up in here. We know someone came in to steal the shower curtain.'

'Smart thinking.' Bet thought about all the work in front of Clayton. 'You aren't going to finish this tonight. Where are you planning to sleep?' With the road blocked, Clayton couldn't go home, no matter how much he might want to. 'You know you're welcome to stay in my guest room.'

'I thought I'd sleep on the cot in the break room.'

Bet understood him wanting to stay at the station in case an emergency came up. They would both be on duty throughout the night, with one of them awake at the station at all times while Alma kept them company.

'Call me if you need anything.' Bet heard the vacuum turn back on as she made her way to the front door.

She secured the cardboard box in the back of the SUV and headed into town, wondering what hints the bloody sleeping bag would give up. The idea someone might have given birth weighed on her. If they did, what happened to the baby? And where was the mother?

Someone used the missing shower curtain for something, like wrapping up a body – or two – to dispose of elsewhere. As unlikely as it sounded, teenagers sometimes hid pregnancy from their parents, including giving birth. Could a teenager have killed a baby, then panicked?

Whatever happened at the rental house, the evidence she and Clayton collected would give them a path forward to discover the truth.

Bet just hoped it wouldn't be too late for whoever spilled so much blood at the scene.

FOURTEEN

Bet arrived back at the station hungry and cold. It was past dinner time and the bag of almonds she'd gotten from Alma was long gone. But there wasn't time to eat now; she had to deal with the sleeping bag as fast as possible.

'The Stenleys called,' Alma said as Bet came through the door. 'It's going to be a real bear to plow the snow from the road all the way to the highway. The electric company has finally cleared the downed trees, but more snow has fallen than anyone anticipated. They aren't going to be able to do that and keep up with the loop, let alone the side roads. The county said they'd get to us, but they have a long list of places under their purview to dig out.'

Bet wished for a few more snowplows at her disposal. 'Let's check with our local volunteers and get a call in to the governor's office.' Bet didn't want to be an alarmist, but she also didn't want to wait too long to ask for outside help. 'We may need to enlist the help of the National Guard to dig us out, and I want Collier's name high on the list.'

Alma said she'd call about the National Guard first and then follow up with the community members with snowplows on their trucks and tractors.

'Just make sure no one gets hurt trying to help. Remind them no drinking and plowing.' Bet wasn't kidding. Blizzard parties were no doubt in full force around the valley, and Bet didn't want anyone to think clearing a road felt like a good idea after a few cocktails.

Alma got to work on the phone as Bet took the cardboard box with the sleeping bag through the locking door into one of the holding cells in the back of the station.

The best way to dry the sleeping bag was to hang it up. She got out a stepladder and tied a couple spring clips to a pipe that ran across the ceiling of the cell. She laid a clean tarp on the floor underneath and laid more paper down. Then she clipped the sleeping bag up to dry and locked it in the cell. Before she left, she taped over the cell door with evidence tape and signed it with a black sharpie. Bet wasn't taking any chances that a defense attorney could argue someone went into the cell and tampered with the evidence while it hung up in the station.

She'd just finished locking the cell door and snapping a photo with her digital camera, when her phone rang. Bet recognized the incoming number.

'Hello, Sheriff.' Aimee's mother sounded stressed. 'This is Marta Johnson returning your call.'

Bet reassured her there wasn't any emergency. 'I need to locate a friend of your daughter's, and I believe they may be together.'

'Would you like me to call her and find out where she is and who she's with?'

Bet didn't want to tell Marta she believed her daughter would lie to her. Or that Bet had already spoken to Aimee. She paused for a moment, considering the best tack to take. Marta stayed quiet on the other end.

'Do you believe your daughter is at home?' Bet asked instead.

'That's where she's supposed to be.' A hitch in Marta's voice showed Bet an uptick in the woman's anxiety. 'She's not there?'

Bet realized she'd ramped up the woman's fears rather than keeping her calm.

'I just spoke to her a few hours ago,' Marta said. 'She was fine—'

'And I'm sure she is fine,' Bet said. 'And I don't mean to alarm you. I spoke to your daughter as well, but we were cut off. The storm is creating some issues with cell reception here in Collier.'

'Why don't I call her and find out where she is?'

'I have a better idea,' Bet said. 'Are you near a computer connected to the internet?'

Marta explained she was in a hotel in Ellensburg with power and internet access. The storm had reached her location, but they weren't getting the severe snowfall or high winds that currently battered Collier.

Bet asked Marta to locate her daughter's cell by GPS and then give Bet the coordinates.

Marta followed her instructions but balked at giving Bet her daughter's location. 'Are you sure Aimee's not in some kind of trouble?' Suspicion competed with the concern in Marta's voice. 'I don't want her talking to you without me or my husband there.'

Bet found it interesting that the woman would casually leave her teenager at home alone with the storm of the century bearing down, but didn't want her to talk to Bet by herself.

'No trouble that I'm aware of. I just need to ask her a few questions to help me find one of her friends.' Bet hoped that by keeping Marta's attention focused on the friend and away from her daughter, she wouldn't worry so much about involving her daughter with the police.

'Who is this friend?'

Bet considered withholding the information, but she wasn't giving anything away by stating his name. She wasn't going to tell Marta that he was dead.

'Grant Marsden.'

Marta made a sound as if it wasn't a surprise that he was the person the authorities were looking for, then she paused, and Bet feared she had hung up just like her daughter. Or that she planned to tell Bet to drive over to the Johnsons' house first, when Bet already knew the girl wasn't there. She didn't want to waste the time.

'This is what I'm going to do.' Marta's voice filled with the confidence born of taking control of a situation. 'I'm going to call Aimee and ask where she is and what she's doing. I'll know if she's lying about her location because I'll look at the GPS. If she lies to me, I'll call you back. If she doesn't lie, you can call and ask your questions over the phone.'

It was the best Bet could hope for. If Aimee at least knew her mother was aware of the situation, she might be more likely to finish a conversation with Bet.

And Bet had a strong intuition the girl was going to lie.

Marta ended the call. Five minutes went by while Bet watched the weather radar, answered emails, and texted with Clayton to check in on the processing of the rental house, all while eating a granola bar that she pulled from a box she kept in her desk drawer.

Jamie Garcia had sent a quick email back. *Collecting some interesting statistics on meth use in our region. Opioid stats pale in comparison. Much higher overdose numbers. Most of the retailers and users are white, poor, and uneducated. Mexican cartels flooding the market across the border. Would love to discuss with you further after the storm subsides. Buy you coffee?*

Bet had just shot off a quick 'we'll chat' to Jamie when her phone rang. Marta had an answer for her.

'OK, Sheriff, you win. Aimee told me she was at home, but I can tell by this GPS thing she lied to me. Please go see what she's up to and call me back. She wasn't supposed to leave the house.'

Bet promised to do so. 'Where is she?'

Marta gave her the location.

'Well,' Bet said to Schweitzer as she hung up the cell, 'isn't that interesting.'

FIFTEEN

The question was whether Aimee had been at the Marsdens' house the whole time, or if she went over to visit after Bet's call to her. Had Bodhi been the person who cut off the earlier call? Regardless, the girl who was supposed to be with Grant was now at the house where his brother was throwing a party, and Bet knew for a fact Grant wasn't there, so where did Bodhi think his brother had been all this time?

What was Bodhi's relationship with Aimee?

Was anyone in Collier where they were supposed to be?

Bet pulled back into the Marsden driveway to find the same number of cars parked out front. If Aimee had driven over, either her car had already been there when Bet visited earlier, or she'd arrived with someone else. Or she'd arrived not long after Bet and then left again right after the call with her mother to head home so that Bet never saw the vehicle. Bet hadn't passed anyone on the road, however, so she thought one of the other scenarios more likely and that Aimee was still there.

The last thing Bet wanted to do right now was track a lone teenager all over the valley in the storm. But she really needed to know if Grant had been out with someone else on that ridge, and as it stood now, Aimee was her only lead.

Bet took the time to clear snow off all the license plates and write down the numbers of all the vehicles parked out front. If she needed to run them, Alma could do it later to find out whose cars had been there.

Darkness combined with the white blanket of snow and turned the world gray. The party was quieter than it had been a few hours ago; the sound of the storm and the generator now topped any noise from inside. Bet knocked and rang the bell again. She wanted to indicate urgency in her arrival.

Bodhi reappeared through the glass, and the outdoor light flicked on, sending Bet's black shadow across the white snow behind her, the world in monochrome. He opened the door without a beer in his hand this time.

'Sheriff.' The relaxed smile from this morning was gone.

'Bodhi.'

'What can I do for you?'

'I'd like to speak to Aimee Johnson.'

Bodhi started to deny her presence, but Bet raised a finger. She remembered her father had done the same when he wanted her attention. She wondered how long she'd been making the identical gesture without realizing it.

'Don't. Do *not* pretend she's not here.' Bet hoped Aimee hadn't just left and that her tough woman act would be for nothing – or, worse, make her look foolish.

'I'll get her.'

Apparently tough woman worked. 'Are you really going to leave me out here in the middle of a dark and stormy night?' She gave him a smile to balance out her earlier show of confidence and prove she was the good guy and not a threat.

Bodhi looked like a kid to her now. He didn't know what to do. He didn't want to invite the sheriff into his house, but leaving her on the doorstep in the worst storm of his life probably didn't feel like a good idea either. Bet gave him one last nudge.

'Invite me in, Bodhi.' She kept her voice quiet and calm. In her time as sheriff, she was learning she could play good cop and bad cop simultaneously when necessary. 'I'm just here to talk to Aimee.'

He stepped back to let her enter, then led Bet to the opposite end of the house from the rooms filled with Bodhi's friends. The sound of people talking and laughing faded along with the babble of a television as she and Bodhi reached a home office.

'I'll go get her.' Bodhi turned stiffly on his leg brace and disappeared down the hall.

An old desk with an even older computer sat in front of Bet. A single window behind that looked out on to a large expanse of white. Two dented metal file cabinets and a couple mismatched chairs filled out the furniture.

Bet walked over to see what might be in plain sight on the desk. She found a stack of bills, many stamped THIRD NOTICE, with threats to send to collections. It appeared that the Marsdens were having financial troubles. The recession had hit a lot of people in the valley, and they weren't recovering as fast as the high-tech communities out near Seattle.

She heard voices in the hall and walked back around to the front of the desk before Bodhi caught her snooping.

'What's going on, Bodhi?' a young woman's voice said. 'I want to see who gets the rose.'

Aimee stopped short when she saw Bet waiting for her. The beads on her long cornrows clicked together as she whipped her head around to glare at Bodhi. 'What's this? Why is she here?'

Bet didn't expect a warm welcome, but the antagonism in Aimee's voice was a surprise. Bodhi started to leave. 'Stay, Bodhi, this concerns you too.'

Bodhi stepped into the room. Identical fear showed on both their faces. Bodhi might be over twenty-one, but anxiety turned his expression back into that of a teenager.

'I'm having trouble locating your father, Bodhi. He's not at the hotel where you said he was staying.'

The surprise on his face appeared genuine. 'That's where he always stays in E'burg. Maybe he couldn't get a room and went somewhere else.'

Bet directed her next question at Aimee. 'When did you last see Grant?'

Aimee looked at Bodhi.

'Don't look at him.' Bet used her bad cop voice. 'Look at me. It's a simple question.'

Aimee gave an exasperated sigh, rolling her eyes and telegraphing disgust as only a teenage girl could do. 'Yesterday morning.'

'Where?'

'He came by my house.'

Bet realized she wasn't going to get any information from Aimee unless she specifically asked for it.

'Why didn't he stay at your house like he was supposed to?'

'He was going out on that stupid machine with his dumb friend.'

'You mean a snowmobile?'

'Yeah. Isn't that what you told Bodhi when you were here before?'

So that's why Aimee thought Bodhi was angry. Bet watched Bodhi's expression shift from neutral to confused at Aimee's words. 'That surprises you?' she asked Bodhi.

Bodhi looked caught, and Bet didn't think he could invent a lie quick enough to cover his shock.

'His snowmobile is broken.' He turned to Aimee. 'Whose sled was he going to ride?' Now Bet heard anger.

Aimee shrugged.

Bodhi's expression turned menacing. 'Why didn't you tell me that?'

'Why would I?' Aimee's voice turned frustrated. 'Plus, I thought you knew after you talked to the sheriff. Why did you hang up on her when she called my cell?'

Bodhi shot a glance at Bet, but him not wanting Aimee on the phone with law enforcement was the least of her concerns right now. 'What dumb friend?' Bet asked instead.

'I don't know. Some White kid I don't know.'

Bet's mind went to Jeremy Crews. Could the two have been together? Aimee would know all of Grant's friends from the valley, but Jeremy would be a stranger.

Bet turned to Bodhi. 'You own more than one snowmobile.' The registration she pulled from the wrecked snowmobile had Doug Marsden's name on it. The sled could belong to anyone in the family.

'We've got three, but Grant's not allowed on mine or Dad's.' Bodhi took a beat as his anger escalated, and his voice turned harsh. 'That little shit.'

He wheeled around and started out of the room as fast as his leg brace would allow. Bet followed to see what had upset

Bodhi. At this point, he appeared too frustrated to worry about her presence. Aimee trailed after the other two, clearly curious about the unfolding situation, even if she didn't yet grasp the gravity.

Bodhi sped through the kitchen and out the back door with Bet on his heels. A group of young people sat in the living room watching a big-screen TV. They barely looked up as the trio went out into the snow. No one seemed bothered by the local sheriff rushing through the house after their host.

Bodhi crossed over to a large shop in the backyard. He walked to one of the tall roll-up doors, opened a combination lock, and pushed up the door to reveal a clean and orderly workspace. Snow drifted inside the building from where it had piled against the door. A large pickup truck sat parked in front of the other roll-up door, DOUG MARSDEN CONSTRUCTION lettered in white against the blue paint job.

Tools hung on the walls in neat rows. A table saw and a drill press sat on one side, and two snowmobiles were parked on the other. One had been partially dismantled. There was clearly room for a third, but the space was empty.

'Dad's gonna kill that little bastard.'

'I take it Grant took a snowmobile without permission?'

'Dad told him he wasn't allowed to touch his sled. Grant broke his own machine doing something stupid, so he had to earn the money on his own to buy the parts to fix it. He knows better than to take mine.'

The growl in Bodhi's voice and his considerable bulk showed Bet why Grant might leave his brother's untouched. With his father out of town, he must have thought he could get the machine back before anyone noticed it was gone.

'How would he have gotten the snowmobile out of here yesterday without you hearing him?'

'He probably did it when I went to the store for supplies. He wasn't home when I got back, but it never occurred to me to look out here. Grant would know I wouldn't be out here until the storm was over at least. It's not like I'm going riding anytime soon.' He tapped the brace on his leg.

Aimee had reached them by this point. Barefoot in the house, she had stopped to pull on a pair of snow boots before coming outside. She squinted into the shop, the fluorescent lights bright against the dark of the storm.

'You knew about this.' Bodhi swung around to face Aimee, focusing his annoyance on her.

She looked down, scuffing her feet in the snow.

'You told me he was seeing another girl.' Her voice carried hurt, her emotions close to the surface. 'Why else wouldn't he have come home last night?'

'I said,' Bodhi spoke slowly and clearly as if to a child, 'that he *could* be with someone else. I didn't say he *was*. You should have told me he went out on a sled.'

Snow swirled around the three of them, drifting in through the open shop door. The sound of the trees whipping back and forth competed with the sound of the generator, louder now that they were outside. For a moment – despite the power of the storm – Bet felt as if they had stepped inside a bubble and everything stood still. Both pairs of eyes locked on her.

And Bodhi knew.

'What happened to Grant?' Bodhi asked. 'That's why you're here. You aren't trying to track Dad down because you're worried or need to ask him some construction question. You're tracking him down because something happened, and you want to tell him first.'

Aimee looked back and forth between Bet and Bodhi. The confusion on her face told Bet she hadn't put two and two together as fast as he had.

'Tell him what?' Aimee's voice sounded panicked. 'Tell him first, what?'

Bet took a deep breath. Bodhi was over eighteen and Grant's father was missing. He was the next of kin if something had happened to Doug, and she knew Bodhi hadn't caused Grant's accident. Alma had confirmed Bodhi's injury occurred on Wednesday.

But this wasn't how she wanted to tell him. She would have preferred to have Clayton or another care worker with her – even Alma would do in a pinch. It often worked to Bet's advantage that the woman knew everyone in the valley.

'Aimee, go back in the house,' Bet said. 'I'll be in to ask you a few more questions in a minute.'

'I want to know—'

'Go in the house, Aimee.' Bodhi's voice held an authority Bet hadn't heard before. The unsure young man had been replaced with someone a little more in control.

Aimee made a noise of frustration, but did as Bodhi requested and stomped across the yard, slamming the door behind her.

'I'm sorry to have to tell you this, Bodhi, but your brother was in a fatal accident on Iron Horse Ridge yesterday.'

'An accident?'

'On the snowmobile.'

Bodhi regarded her for a long moment, and his face took on a stillness she hadn't seen before. 'He's dead?'

It was best to say the words. It made death real. 'Yes, Bodhi. Your brother is dead. I'm sorry for your loss.'

As the words left Bet's mouth, the generator shut off. The world became still in the pause of the storm, as if Bodhi's grief controlled the events. Bet waited for something to fill the silence.

'The power's back on,' Bodhi said. The generator was no doubt wired to shut off automatically when power was restored. The two stood for another moment. Bet wanted to see how Bodhi would react to the news. She believed he was unaware of his brother's activities, but what she didn't understand was Aimee's role, or why Bodhi had lied about his brother being with the girl if she'd been there the whole time, though it could be as simple as not wanting Bet to investigate further into how many of his guests were underage and drinking.

'What now?' Bodhi asked.

'Now, I need to find your dad. I would also prefer that you don't share this information with your friends. I appreciate that you might need someone to talk to, but I don't want this going out over social media until your father has been told.' She also wanted more time to investigate the situation, but she didn't need Bodhi thinking his brother's death was anything more than a tragic accident.

'Don't worry. There's no one here I want to talk to about this, and social media isn't my thing.'

His lack of a social media presence backed up his comment.

'Does that include Aimee?'

Bodhi nodded. 'She doesn't need to hear this from me. Better that her parents are back before she finds out.'

Bet considered the danger of people driving in the storm if Bodhi sent them all home. She didn't want to leave him with a group of revelers, but asking them to leave created an even larger safety concern. 'What are you going to do about the party?'

'It's fine. They're hardly paying attention to me anyway. I can go up to my room if I need to be alone. I won't send anyone out into the cold.'

He didn't appear as shocked as Bet thought he might. Whatever emotions he felt about his brother's death, he wasn't going to show them to her. 'Any guesses about where your dad might be? I take it he has another car?'

'Yeah, he's got a Honda Accord. He only uses the truck for work. He's not answering his cell for me either.' Bet could hear that troubled him, even if he didn't want to admit it to her.

'He's never done that before?'

Bodhi shook his head. 'He always picks up or calls back right away if it's me.'

'Do you have access to his cell phone account information?'

Bodhi nodded.

'If you look up his location via GPS, I can find him.'

Maybe technology would work for her twice.

Bodhi started to walk back to his house when he stopped abruptly and grabbed Bet's arm. 'Shit.' This time his emotion came through loud and clear.

What could be worse than hearing his brother was dead?

'If Dad's missing, so is Ruby.'

SIXTEEN

There was another Marsden child, a younger sister. Bet's desire to find Doug ratcheted up a notch at the reminder of the girl. Bet and Bodhi walked back through the house. The people watching the screen in the living room barely looked up as they did, unaware that a real tragedy unfolded in their midst, far more important than a bachelor finding love in an artificial world.

Bet noticed Aimee wasn't in the living room, and hoped the girl hadn't done something foolish, like drive away in the storm. But when they arrived in the office, Aimee sat curled up in a chair.

'I'm not a baby – you can tell me what happened.' Her teenage sulkiness had returned. She wasn't a baby, but she wasn't an adult yet either.

'I really can't, Aimee. Not because of your age, but because I have rules I have to follow,' Bet said. 'I will talk to you again, but Bodhi and I have to do something first. Can you please wait in another room for us?'

'You can go back upstairs to Grant's room if you want.' Bodhi's voice was soft, surprising Bet with his thoughtfulness. The maturity she had seen in his face outside in the storm remained.

Aimee looked at the two of them for a moment, as if weighing how much fight she had in her, but acquiesced and left the room.

'What did she tell you when she showed up?' Bet asked as Bodhi started up his father's computer. 'About why she wasn't with Grant?'

'She said he ditched her for someone else. I assumed she meant another girl and told her that he was probably cheating on her.' His demeanor shifted again. He looked chastened. 'To be honest, I wasn't paying that much attention. Mostly I was just messing with Grant. I had no idea what he was up to. I'm sorry I lied about knowing where Aimee was – I never thought you were looking for her. I had no idea this was so . . .' His voice trailed off as he faced the impossibility of his brother's death.

'You weren't worried he wasn't where he was supposed to be?'

Bodhi gave Bet a look that made her feel old. 'My brother wants to sleep with another girl, who am I to stop him? Whatever he's got going with Aimee is between the two of them. I sure wasn't going to out him to you. You said you weren't going to follow up on my brother. You weren't honest with me from the beginning, either.'

He wasn't wrong.

'I said I wasn't going to call your father about your party.'

Bodhi sighed but said nothing more. She hadn't been forthcoming, but the situation had a lot of moving parts and she was doing the best she could to feel her way forward.

'But you let Aimee crash here?' Bet prodded him to keep talking.

'Aimee's a good kid. I've known her for her whole life, basically. She's a little defiant.' He laughed at this. 'It keeps my brother on his toes.'

As the words left his mouth, a new emotion crossed his features. The reality of his brother's death would take a while to sink in, but it had started to grab hold.

'It did,' he said. 'It *did* keep him on his toes. I wouldn't have lied to you if I'd known.' He let the truth of his brother's death sit between them as he went back to his task. She could read in his tone he meant it was her own fault that he'd been less than honest.

The computer made a few sounds as Bodhi tapped the keyboard. 'OK, here's where to log in to his cell phone account.'

'Do you know the password?'

'I have some guesses.' Bodhi made a few attempts, but nothing worked. 'It's nothing obvious. But I know how I can track his phone on the internet.'

Bet needed a warrant to track a cell phone, but a family member didn't. Bodhi could share that information with her without violating the law or her own ethical standards. The fact Doug didn't respond to Bodhi's calls worried her a lot more than the fact he hadn't called her back. A lot of bad things could happen to people in rural areas with weather like this.

Bet hoped his disappearance was nothing more than an inconvenient flat tire and poor cell coverage.

'I'm going to go and ask Aimee a few questions. I'll be back in a few minutes.'

Bodhi turned his attention back to the computer to work whatever digital magic he could to find his father, his silence giving her permission to wander through the house.

The bedrooms were probably upstairs, so she headed there first. If she didn't find Aimee upstairs – she could have gone into the living room – it would give Bet a chance to look over Grant's room undisturbed. Maybe she could find some evidence about who he'd been hanging out with lately. There could be another 'White guy', as Aimee described him. It didn't have to be Jeremy Crews.

The doors were all closed in the upstairs hallway. She opened the first, guessing it to be Doug's room. It had a king-sized bed and the feel of an adult's space. Though the bed was unmade, the rest of the room was relatively neat. The door to an en-suite bathroom indicated this was the primary bedroom. Doug's room might have evidence of his location as well, but she wanted to talk to Aimee first. If Bodhi's tracking worked, she wouldn't need anything else to find his dad's location.

She opened the next door but found it empty. It was clearly Ruby's bedroom, with a Disney bedspread, stuffed animals scattered across the pillow, and Breyer horses on the shelves. Bet closed the door and went across the hall. The first room was also empty and felt like a guest room, with minimal personal knickknacks or mementos. A suitcase in the corner overflowed with clothes. This must be Bodhi's room, and his stay was meant to be temporary.

'Fourth time's a charm,' Bet muttered under her breath as she opened the last door.

Aimee lay on the bed in a ball. Bet saw the tears before the girl could hide them.

'Knock much?' Aimee sat upright, a scowl returning to her features.

Bet wasn't going to admit she'd chosen not to knock to see what she might catch Aimee doing.

'Sorry, I thought this was the bathroom.'

Aimee gave her a look to show she knew Bet was lying, but let it go. The girl's outward demeanor hid something other than anger or defiance, and Bet wanted to understand what emotion lay underneath the surly expression. Bet sat down in a chair next to the wall and let the silence grow between them.

'What's going on, Aimee?' Bet finally asked, once the girl made no indication that she was going to fill the silence on her own.

'You tell me, Sheriff. You're the one with all the answers.'

'If I had all the answers, I wouldn't be here with you, would I?'

Aimee looked surprised at that. An adult – the sheriff no less – admitting she didn't know everything. Then fear crossed her features.

'Where's Grant? Why can't you just tell me?'

'I'll tell you about Grant's situation as soon as I can, all right? But first I need to ask you a few questions. It's to help your friend.'

The girl's face showed a complex set of emotions, with anger the dominant expression. Bet considered everything that might make Aimee angry. She'd been left alone by her parents during the worst storm in years. Her boyfriend abandoned her to go snowmobiling with another person, and Bodhi told her Grant was probably seeing someone else. Now the authorities were questioning her without telling her anything she wanted to know. There were a lot of reasons Aimee could be angry. Would anything she knew help Bet understand what happened to Grant?

'Fine.'

'Tell me about the last time you saw Grant.'

'What about it?'

'Everything that you can remember. When, where, what he said . . .'

Aimee thought for a moment, drawing her legs up underneath her, so she sat cross-legged on the bed. She looked younger than she had a moment before.

'He showed up at my house about nine yesterday morning.' Aimee looked to Bet as if confirming this was the right way to start. Bet gave her an encouraging nod.

'He was supposed to stay at my house for the weekend. Through the storm. I don't mind staying alone, but . . . we knew the storm was coming, and I didn't want to be by myself in the dark if the power went out.'

She paused, as if embarrassed to admit this personal failing.

'I don't like to be left alone in the dark either,' Bet said. 'That's why I have a big dog.'

Aimee laughed at that, and for a moment she looked like an innocent girl too young to be left alone. Bet wondered why her parents felt OK about leaving her by herself or letting Grant stay at her house in their place. Grant didn't appear to be the most dependable of teenagers. Why not encourage Aimee to stay at a friend's house where the parents were home instead? Or take her with them?

'He showed up in his truck, but he had his dad's snowmobile in the back.'

Bet waited. This time her silence worked, and Aimee continued.

'He said he was going to show this guy a cool trail. The one up on the ridge. I guess the kid was tired of hanging with his parents for his whole vacation and wanted to go out on his own. He was up here in the valley because it's mid-winter break, but he's from somewhere out in Seattle. His parents gave him permission to go out with Grant, because he's a local and knows the terrain.'

If the 'guy' was Jeremy and Grant had told Aimee the truth, that meant Julia and Mark Crews knew who Grant was before they 'found' him on the ridge. They also lied about going snowmobiling together as a family yesterday.

'Did you see the guy?'

'No. He was going to meet Grant out at the cemetery. They thought that was a cool place to meet – Grant wanted to show it to him anyway. Then they were going to ride all the way around the valley and up on the ridge. It would take all day. No way was I going to sit on the back of a stupid snowmobile and get bounced half to death in the cold. I told Grant I didn't want to go.'

'They were going to use forest service roads?'

The one Grant and Jeremy started out on probably hooked up with the road near Jeb's place that went up on the ridge and to the spot where Grant died.

'I knew they were going to get into trouble for riding out there. I told him to stop riding on the roads marked closed. How much trouble is Grant in? Is he sitting in your jail cell right now because you can't find his dad?'

Aimee still thought Grant was in trouble for doing something illegal. It hadn't crossed her mind he could be hurt or dead.

Bet started to ask Aimee how she knew Jeremy was White if she'd never met him, when a knock on the door stopped their conversation.

Bodhi stuck his head through the door. 'I found him.'

SEVENTEEN

Bodhi took some convincing to stay home while Bet went to look for his father, but she managed to talk him out of following her before it had to become an order.

'You've got a house full of people here, some of whom are underage, and a wicked storm outside. Your responsibility is for the people here.' Bodhi looked at Aimee, who had pulled the comforter up around her ears and lay on the bed with her back to them. 'Not to mention I can't have you out in these conditions with your leg like that.' She pointed to his brace.

'OK, Sheriff,' he said. 'But I want an update from you as soon as possible.'

Bet found it interesting that Bodhi wanted an update from her, not that he requested she have his father call him. Did Bodhi think his father would be incapacitated or under arrest?

They left Aimee in Grant's room and started to walk downstairs.

'Whatever is going on with Dad, my little sister is with him. Please look out for her.'

Bet studied Bodhi's face. Something was there she couldn't read. 'Is there anything about your father that I should know before I go look for him?'

Bodhi glanced in the direction of the living room, where a shriek followed by a gale of laughter showed the visitors were still engaged in whatever reality show they were watching on TV. His expression softened, as if amused by the 'kids' in the other room. He started to say something when the phone in his hand buzzed. He looked down. His features hardened and he sent the caller to voicemail.

'No. Just . . . don't let anything happen to my sister too, OK?'

Bet promised to do what she could. Another burst of laughter and the smell of pizza came through from the living room. Bet hoped Bodhi couldn't hear her stomach growl. She had to eat soon or she'd pass out and Alma would have to come rescue her in the snow.

With a last glance in the direction of the crew in the living room, Bodhi gestured toward the door. 'I'll walk you to your car.'

As they made their way to her SUV, Bodhi held out the map he'd printed off the computer, complete with the blue symbol showing exactly where his dad's phone was currently located. She opened her door and set the paper inside to keep it from getting destroyed by the falling snow.

'I hope I'm not going to regret giving you that.' He looked younger again as he studied her, snow sticking in his hair. The responsibility for a dead brother and a missing father and sister was too heavy even for his broad shoulders.

'You have my word. I will do everything I can for your sister.'

Bodhi looked down at his hands as if he couldn't quite bring himself to go back into the house.

'Bodhi.'

He looked at her with trepidation, as if she might say or ask something he didn't want to think about.

She kept her voice calm, quiet. It was something she needed to ask but knew how hard it might be for him to hear. 'Has your father ever expressed any thoughts about hurting himself?'

The surprise on Bodhi's face looked genuine. 'No. Never. You can't think—'

'I don't think anything yet.' She spoke quickly so he wouldn't change his mind about following her on her search for his dad and Ruby. 'But I have to consider all the possibilities. Does your father own a handgun?'

Bodhi was already shaking his head. 'He would never do something like that. Especially not with Ruby there.' Bet wondered if he heard the contradiction in his words. If he *really* wouldn't do it with Ruby there, then deep down, Bodhi thought he might if he didn't have Ruby with him – otherwise the answer would just be 'never'.

'Let's assume you're right,' she said. 'You know him better than I do. But I still have to ask. He could be in some other kind of trouble where he might want to be armed. Does he own a handgun?'

'No.'

Reading Bodhi's body language, Bet guessed he was lying about the gun, but she didn't think it was worth the time to argue with him right now. Doug hadn't done anything illegal that she knew about yet. Better to check the location of Doug's phone and have more information to go on. She pictured the rental house with its bloody sleeping bag and missing shower curtain. If this was a murder/suicide, did Doug take his daughter to the rental house to do it? Why kill her in a sleeping bag in a strange house? Just so Grant and Bodhi wouldn't be the ones to find her? And if he did, where did he off himself?

Or had someone else killed Doug, and Ruby was just collateral damage, with a third person disposing of both their bodies? She didn't think Bodhi was such a good actor that he could pretend he didn't know anything about their whereabouts. Or so cruel that he could do that to his father and sister.

But he was hiding something.

'OK.' Bet got into the front seat and buckled up. He nodded and stepped back, giving the window a double tap on the glass as if to wish her luck.

He walked back toward the house, his gait awkward on the slippery drive. The heavy snow obscured the front door from her view.

Bet dug another granola bar out of her glove box and tore open the wrapper. It would have to hold her over until she could get an actual meal. She pushed the thought about how good the pizza smelled out of her mind.

Putting the SUV into drive, Bet tried to remember a storm as bad as this one in her valley's history. The valley got snow every winter, but for it to fall so relentlessly was nothing she'd ever seen. Normally, she enjoyed the snow; fall and winter were her favorite times of the year. She loved how dry snow squeaked under her feet. The pure smell of ice in the air. The way the flakes drifted down, light as feathers, to pile up on the hushed earth.

This was more ominous.

The wind had picked back up again, the break in the storm forgotten, the sky once more blotted out. The heavy flakes splatted against her windshield like a wet rag. The valley wasn't being swaddled in winter white. The valley was being buried alive.

Bet called in to Alma over the radio to tell her where she'd be. She explained she was following up on a report that someone might be stuck there. Then she asked that Alma do a search on Doug Marsden owning a handgun.

Alma paused for a long beat. She knew Bet wasn't giving her the whole story about what she was up to and why.

'Ten-four,' Alma said reluctantly. 'I'll be standing by.'

Alma would wait on high alert until Bet checked back in. If she didn't check in within the hour, Alma would no doubt send Clayton out her way. That kind of thinking would have annoyed Bet in the past, but now she found it comforting. It wasn't a bad thing to have other people looking out for her.

Bet signed off and turned her full attention to driving. The streets were quiet, with most folks hunkered down indoors. Despite the storm warnings they'd heard all week on the news, no one could have imagined the amount of snowfall they saw today. Hard to believe that a week ago there had been only a few inches on the ground. Now it felt as if the snow would always be there. Winterfell brought to life in Washington State.

The roads were still passable. Jack and Sally had kept the town road cleared, and local volunteers were doing a good job with the loop, but a lot of people wouldn't be able to get out of the side roads or even their own driveways. At least she hadn't heard about any medical emergencies in the midst of all this.

Addie had reported to Clayton that she'd gotten chains on her rig, so she could handle the conditions if they had to get someone out of the valley. The ambulance was ready to go – minus the supplies stolen during the break-in.

Bet hoped the coroner could get out to pick up Grant soon, but it wouldn't be safe until the storm cleared completely. She wouldn't ask him to drive out to their little hamlet until the weather changed.

Passing through town, Bet saw the lights on at the community center. Then she passed the station, where Alma waited for the storm to subside and her town to dig back out again. Alma raised a hand, her eagle eyes finding Bet's as the SUV drove by.

Bet continued out toward Aimee Johnson's house, and Robert Collier's rental property – where someone might have come to a grisly end – and the service road behind the cemetery, where Doug Marsden's phone appeared as a blue dot on the computer printout.

She turned on to the road leading into the cemetery, glad of her four-wheel drive and studded tires. This road hadn't been cleared recently, and the snow drifted deep in front of her.

Doug Marsden could have lost his phone out here before he went down to E'burg. It would explain why he wasn't answering his calls. But it didn't explain why he would go so long without checking in with his sons. Or why he wasn't staying at the hotel Bodhi expected. He could have called Bodhi to update him from whatever hotel he landed in.

And what would he be doing on the service road behind the cemetery in the first place?

Bet just hoped he and Ruby were safe, with a simple explanation for all of this.

The SUV's forward momentum remained steady up to the second turnoff.

The cemetery, which had been there since the founding of the town, spread out across the hillside along this stretch of the valley. Each ethnic and fraternal group had its own section, separated by various fences – some wood, some wrought iron, some stone – and one low hedge of boxwood that had grown for more than a hundred years.

It wasn't long before the SUV started to labor in the deep snow.

The vehicle was still moving forward, however, when she arrived at a downed tree across the road.

Bet parked next to the Italian section of the graveyard and got out. As far as she could tell, the tree hadn't been on the ground long. There was snow underneath it, and not much piled on top, indicating it had fallen recently. Glad to be wearing her snow boots, Bet left her hat in the SUV and pulled the hood of her coat up to keep snow from slipping down her collar. With a quick look around, she climbed over the fallen pine. Then she headed up the hill, past the memorial for the dead miners put in by the townspeople twenty-five years after the accident that claimed one hundred and twelve lives in 1910, one of the largest mining accidents in Washington State history.

Bet continued to trudge up the road, the going slow as snow came up past her knees. More snow whirled around her, covering the shorter headstones until the graveyard looked like a series of small rolling waves broken up by the taller stone monuments to the dead, rising out of a vast white sea.

Fatigue had already set in by the time she reached the turnoff for the service road and plunged into the woods that surrounded the graveyard. But with Ruby's safety weighing on her, she had no choice but to continue forward.

She unsnapped the holster on her gun, though she didn't think she would really need to pull her weapon out. Her movements were already slowed down by the layers of clothing she wore and the bone-chilling cold. She was grateful for her Mechanix gloves. Tough enough to protect her hands from the cold but still sleek enough to allow her to use her Glock if she needed it.

There weren't any fresh tracks in the snow. Had Doug driven out here and then gotten stuck when the tree fell? If so, why would he stay in the car instead of walking back down to safety? Or take his phone if he did? If Doug had been parked out here long enough for the snow to cover his tracks, Bet feared she wasn't going to find him – or Ruby – alive. He was far enough out of sight from the cemetery that his car wouldn't be visible even in the best of conditions. And if he had walked in, it appeared he never walked out.

Bodhi could be wrong, and the man *was* suicidal. She'd seen the piles of bills on his desk. Perhaps he'd become distraught over his financial situation. But if that were true, where was Ruby? Domestic violence was the most common cause of a child's unnatural death. The likelihood of a murder/suicide sent a cold spike of fear down her back. Though she'd been serious when she asked Bodhi about it, it hadn't been at the top of her list. Now she wasn't so sure. With little serious crime in the valley, domestic abuse and violence toward children was, sadly, something that happened even in her small, quiet town.

The evergreens around her looked alien under the blanketing of white. Big chunks slid off trees, the unburdened limbs snapping up when released from the weight. The sound of the ice slamming on to the ground competed with the rush of the wind. The uproar and vibrations kept Bet uneasy, as if something stalked her through the storm, hidden by the snow and the trees. Something that lurked around in the graveyard and tracked her progress up the service road.

Something that had already fed on Doug and Ruby and was looking for its next meal.

Reining in her imagination, Bet shook off the eerie feeling of being watched and paused for a moment to catch her breath. After her heart rate slowed and her breathing evened out, she started up again.

Rounding a curve in the road, her flashlight picked up a car parked ahead. There were no lights on and no signs of life. With the engine shut off, anyone inside would be very cold on a night like tonight.

No other vehicles were in sight. Bet checked her radio, but both that and her phone were out of range. Nothing to do now but move forward. She needed to get this done and report back to Alma before the woman came out here herself to make sure Bet was OK. Bet could imagine her plowing through the snow, Schweitzer leading the way.

Bet scraped the snow off the windows to look inside. Part of her expected to find Doug's body in the front seat, his head blown off by a self-inflicted gunshot wound and the disturbing sight of his daughter in the seat next to him.

Her own reflection in the glass startled her before she realized what it was. Her gasp came out in a cloud, like the wispy smoke of dragon's breath. Until she saw the vapor, she hadn't even realized she'd been holding it in. Gripping her flashlight tighter, she leaned forward for a better look inside, not at all sure what she hoped to find.

EIGHTEEN

The car was empty.

The doors were locked.

First, she felt relief. Then she looked at the trunk.

It was large enough to hold a body, maybe even two. There was also the possibility one or both of them were injured, but still alive. If so, they wouldn't be for much longer. She had a duty to intervene if they were, and she had to be quick. It wouldn't be easy to get an injured person, let alone two, back out to civilization from here.

The Bust a Cap she kept on her Maglite had been designed by Todd Summers, a longtime sheriff who saw a need for that kind of tool. It was now widely used by law enforcement, and Bet had recently put one on hers, never expecting she'd need it so soon. A pointed metal tip replaced the factory cap on the end of her flashlight, turning it into a glass breaker. She just hoped it worked.

The window broke immediately, a sizable hole appearing in the 'shatterproof' glass. Bet reached through to flip the lock, then dug enough snow away to open the door and search around for the trunk latch.

If Doug and Ruby were in the trunk, it wouldn't matter to Bodhi that she'd broken the car window. And if it led to information that aided in their safe recovery, it wouldn't matter to her.

She heard the clunk as the catch of the trunk let go, but the lid barely moved under the weight of all the snow.

Plunging through the deep drifts around to the back of the car, Bet managed to catch the edge of the trunk lid with her fingers and stop it from closing again. She held it up while shoving several inches of snow on to the ground with her other hand. With a heave, she pushed open the trunk and shined her flashlight inside.

She hadn't held her breath this time, but relief washed over her as soon as she could see that neither Doug nor Ruby was stuffed into the trunk. While finding his empty car abandoned on this lonely road was bad, it still meant there was a chance Doug and Ruby were fine and just unable – or unwilling – to contact Bodhi.

Bet began a methodical search of the car. The trunk didn't hold anything useful. A tub filled with several reusable grocery bags. An old, dirty T-shirt. A box of spark plugs.

The weather made it challenging as she dug snow out from under the passenger's side and back doors. She pushed the hood off her head while she worked, and more snow fell down the back of her neck. The cold turned her hands into ice, as she'd peeled off her Mechanix gloves in favor of latex while she searched the interior. The car was a potential crime scene, depending on what had happened to Doug and Ruby, and she didn't want to contaminate evidence.

Doug's phone sat on the passenger side front seat. It perched in the middle, as if he had deliberately set it down there rather than accidentally leaving it behind. It struck her as strange because if he set it on the seat while driving, it would have slid around. Why would he deliberately leave his phone behind after he parked the car?

Unless he didn't want to be found through GPS.

Or someone else didn't want him tracked.

After Bet searched through the back seat and the floorboards, she checked the snow around the immediate area. There were no signs of anyone else nearby. It was deep enough that if another vehicle had parked here, the tracks were long gone. There were no receipts or notes left from Doug indicating where he'd been or where he might go. She picked up his phone, but the screen was locked.

She stood in the cold, dark woods, near the old graveyard with the wind howling, and thought about the little girl. There must be something else she could learn from the vehicle.

Half frozen, she decided to go back to her SUV, make sure nothing urgent had come in while she'd been out of cell phone range, and warm up. Trudging back down, she sat a moment, heater running full blast to thaw out her face and hands, thinking about Doug's car.

GPS.

The car was new enough to have that on board.

Exhaustion rolled over Bet in waves. She had been working for more than fourteen hours straight with very little food or breaks. What she wanted was a hot shower, a hot meal, and a comfortable bed. Instead, she toiled back to Doug's car to check for GPS and found a blank screen in the dashboard indicating the car could have information stored from any recent addresses Doug had input into the map program. It wouldn't be as comprehensive as a fancy onboard computer with all of Doug's travels listed, but it didn't require anything more sophisticated than starting the engine to access.

Bet made yet another trip down to her SUV to get into cell range to call Bodhi to ask about an extra key for the car. She didn't want to have to drive back to his house, but if she could get a hint about where Doug had been, she might be able to locate where he and Ruby were now, making it worthwhile.

The phone only rang once before Bodhi picked up, as if he had his phone in his hand waiting for her. His anxiety came through loud and clear. Bet explained what she'd found and why she wanted to start the car.

'There's a key bolted up underneath.'

Bodhi went on to explain how his father bolted a spare key to a hole on the frame, using a wing nut so it wouldn't require tools to remove it in an emergency. Bet would have to dig the car out and hope for the best getting the frozen key off.

'Want me to drive over to help?' She could hear the eagerness in his voice. Waiting was always harder than actively doing something.

'You'd never make it to the car in this snow,' she said, reminding him about his injured knee. She'd kept the information minimal, not telling him about the fallen tree, and reminding him he had a house full of people.

She promised to keep him posted.

Back at the car, Bet dug it out enough to crawl underneath it. A Sisyphean task. No sooner did she get snow out, when more fell to refill the hole. It took several minutes before she managed to clear enough space to lie down on the ground next to the passenger side of the car and reach underneath. Feeling around, fingers stiff and frozen once more in nothing but latex gloves, she found the spare key. Sending a silent prayer of thanks to whatever gods looked out for stranded motorists and lone sheriffs, she worked at the wing nut. Darts of pain shot through her fingers from the cold, but at least they still *had* feeling.

By the time she finished, she lay on the ground panting with the effort and a key in her hand.

Brushing the snow off, she got into the driver's side to start up the car. The engine cranked over a few times, but the lights dimmed.

She was going to have to jumpstart it.

'Damn it!' Bet pounded out her frustrations on the steering wheel. 'I just want one thing to go right!'

To jump Doug's car meant getting her SUV past the downed tree and through the cemetery. Bet felt tears threaten. Every time she got one step forward on this, she slid another step back. She took a deep breath to calm her thoughts and an image popped into her mind. The portable battery pack. She had limited storage space in the SUV, but she'd stuck it into the back in preparation for the storm.

She hiked back down to the SUV once more to get it. Slogging back up the hill in the snow with the added weight of the device had her gasping for breath, sweat running down her back, but she didn't see a route to drive around the fallen tree. She could have tried to find another way around the cemetery, but with the worsening conditions, she'd just as likely get stuck, and she didn't want to spend the time searching for another route.

After a struggle against the weight of the snow, she got the hood of Doug's car up and clamped her penlight between her teeth to hook the unit up to the battery before hopping back in the front seat.

'Come on, baby,' she muttered under her breath as she turned the key. The car hiccupped but started. Heaters blew full blast and windshield wipers tried to push the snow off the glass. Bet struggled to turn everything off, managing to turn on the blinkers and the headlights before finding the right knobs in the strange car.

It took her a few tries to navigate the unfamiliar GPS system, but she soon found recent destinations.

Home appeared, with the Marsdens' address. She also found a hotel in Cle Elum. Why would Doug need a hotel so close to home? If he had been in E'burg and drove all the way to Cle Elum, he'd be almost back in their valley. It didn't make sense. Unless he was meeting someone that he didn't want Bodhi or Grant to know about. A woman? Someone he didn't want to be seen with in town? Maybe she was married? But why take Ruby with him? She could understand if he didn't feel like leaving her with her older brothers, however; Grant wasn't responsible enough and even Bodhi was questionable.

There was also an address out in Federal Way, a neighborhood south of Seattle. Once she was back in cell range, she would find out if it was a residence or a business.

Bet decided she'd learned all she could. She stuffed the dirty T-shirt from the trunk into the hole in the window to block the snow. Time to get back down to her SUV and see if the hotel in Cle Elum would lead her to Doug and Ruby's whereabouts or dance her down another frozen dead end.

NINETEEN

Bet tried to look up the hotel from Doug's GPS on her phone, only to find her bars nonexistent. While snow didn't impact cell reception as much as heavy rain, with snow this thick and the air heavy with water, the weather must be interfering.

The radio went through to Alma, however, at least that system still worked. Using as cryptic language as possible, Bet explained the situation and requested that Alma get online and check for the hotel phone number, then call and ask if Doug Marsden had rented a room and if so, ask if he was there with his daughter. She didn't use his name over the radio, just 'the guy we're looking for.'

Alma took a beat before she replied. 'We've got a problem.'

Bet sighed. She was getting tired of hearing that statement.

'The landline went out.'

'Turn on the Hughes.'

The sheriff's station used a backup communication system in case the landline went out. They had a satellite dish on top of their building, which kept them connected to the internet even if their usual lines went down. Bet liked the redundancy and had decided it was worth the cost, having it installed last summer.

'The Hughes is on, but it's not working. I think it's blocked by snow. Clayton is going to go up on the roof and try to clear it as soon as he gets back to the station.'

The idea of Clayton up on the roof in the storm by himself made Bet uneasy, but she also didn't like being isolated from the outside world.

'OK. I'm coming back to the station. Don't let Clayton go up on the roof until I get there.' Bet knew if she didn't stop her, Alma would be out in the storm holding the ladder for Clayton, no matter that the wind was strong enough to blow her across the parking lot.

'Ten-four,' Alma said. 'Over and out.'

Bet placed Doug's extra key into an evidence bag, which she sealed, signed and dated, and stuck in her glove box. She was going to hang on to that key until she located Doug. She considered driving over to give Bodhi an update – he might even know why his father would be at a hotel in Cle Elum – but she had too many other priorities. She sent him a text to let him know she hadn't found his father or Ruby yet, but she would update him with additional information when she had something. She wanted to find Doug before Bodhi did.

He buzzed back almost immediately with *I'll be waiting*. Bet doubted he would sleep at all tonight if she didn't come up with Doug and Ruby's whereabouts.

Clayton's SUV sat parked in its usual spot at the station. The exterior lights barely illuminated anything through the blinding snow, but she could just make out a bright orange aluminum ladder disappearing around the back of the building.

Bet followed the large footsteps her deputy left behind and found him extending the ladder against the back wall. They had to shout to be heard over the storm.

'This is the most protected side of the building,' he said. 'But I'm sure glad you're here to hold the ladder.'

Bet thought about going up in his place – she was the boss after all – but her falling and getting injured wouldn't help the town any. Plus, Clayton was an experienced and accomplished rock and mountain climber, so he was a better choice to do the dangerous task. He'd be steadier up on the roof than she would be, and less likely to get blown off with his heavier mass.

'Do you want to wear a harness?'

He shook his head. 'The good news is, even if I do fall off the roof, this snow is so deep I'll have a soft landing. Let's just get this over with.'

She gestured for him to go up. The ladder bent under his weight. The force of the wind tried to rip him off the side of the building. For one terrifying moment she felt the ladder slip sideways as he shifted his weight from the rungs to the roof, but he stuck to the tiles like Spiderman.

Clayton disappeared from her view, and Bet imagined him tumbling off the other side and falling to the ground outside her line of sight. Her heart hammered in her ears as she waited, unable to look up for long or her eyes filled with snow. The wind roared around her and yanked her hood off. The cold slunk down the back of her neck, but she didn't want to let go of the ladder long enough to pull it back up again.

Her body ached to let go of the ladder and get out of the storm.

Just when she thought she couldn't stand another moment in the cold, she felt a shudder through the ladder and looked up to see Clayton climb on to the top rung. He came down with dizzying speed and helped her bring the ladder down.

'Leave it here,' Bet shouted in his ear. 'We might have to clear the dish again before the storm passes.'

Clayton nodded and they stuffed the ladder against the side

of the building, then he followed her into the station. As they came around the front of the property, the intensity of the storm had lessened from when they first put the ladder up. Hopefully it meant a break in the weather, even for a couple of hours.

'Good work,' Alma said as they came in through the front door. 'We have internet again.'

Schweitzer popped up from under Alma's desk. Nothing cheered Bet more than the look on Schweitzer's face when he was happy. She'd never known a dog could smile until she met him.

His grin went from ear to fuzzy ear as she tussled with him, no longer embarrassed by the amount of 'Who's a good dog? Who's a good dog?' baby talk she used in front of Alma and Clayton. He gave her a sense that all could be right in the world. And a little humility was good in a leader. It was healthy to show her human side. It was something that Earle had never done, at least not when Bet was around; maybe Alma had seen a different side of him.

Maggie had never shown a softer side either, except on the rare occasion Bet saw her working with kids.

It could be a mistake to let Alma and Clayton see her like this, but it was a chance she was willing to take.

Alma handed Bet a phone number after the wrestling match ended and Schweitzer went over to greet Clayton. 'Here's that information you wanted.'

Bet pulled her phone out and dialed the number to the hotel. It rang several times. It was after ten at night, so she wasn't surprised no one answered, but it was strange there wasn't voicemail.

'No answer,' Bet explained as she hung up the phone. 'I could have Cle Elum police check for us, but let's try email first. Does their website have that on their contact info?'

Alma got back on her computer. 'They do. What do you want me to write?'

Bet dictated an email for the hotel, stating this was official business, following up on a missing person, and asking if they had any record of a Doug Marsden. Bet had Alma add that he might be traveling with a little girl and included a description of them both.

'End with reminding them again this is official business, and that if Doug is registered, not to check if he is in his room or talk about the request to anyone, just to contact us as soon as possible.'

Bet, Clayton, and Alma reviewed the unfolding situations: the bloody sleeping bag and potential crime scene, the missing Marsdens, and the information about Grant borrowing his father's snowmobile. Bet went on to explain that Aimee's description of Grant going out with some kid who was visiting with his parents made her suspect the Crews had lied about them riding together.

'What now?' Alma asked.

'First, please run this address for me.' Bet gave Alma the Federal Way address saved in the GPS in Doug's car. Alma's fingers clicked away on her keyboard.

'It's a Polaris Dealership,' Alma said, looking up from her computer. 'How does that help us?'

Doug owned snowmobiles. He could have ordered some parts.

'Lots of reasons he might go there,' Clayton said. 'Why do you look so pensive?'

'If he needed a part, why not have it shipped? That's an almost two-hour drive each way. Four hours of driving time for something he could have delivered?'

'You said he was in financial trouble,' Alma said. 'Maybe he's looking to sell his sleds?'

Doug might have planned to fix Grant's sled so he could sell it but didn't want his son to know what he was up to. But selling through a dealer didn't quite make sense. 'He'd get more money selling the sleds himself to a private buyer.'

The other two looked at Bet like she might have insight into why a middle-aged, White guy in financial distress would visit a Polaris dealer. She didn't like to admit all the answers didn't come with the badge. Or if they did, it was the badge they buried with Earle Rivers.

'We don't know that address has anything to do with the current situation.' Even if Doug did visit it a few days before he disappeared, Bet couldn't see how the information helped them in this moment. 'Let's table that for now and go with what we do know.'

Dread sidled up to Bet again. What if she was going about things all wrong and she should be spending her time looking into the Polaris dealership? Maybe Doug was close with someone there – someone who knew where he and Ruby were. Bet pushed her anxiety aside. She couldn't let her fear of making a mistake keep her from doing anything at all.

'Whatever you do, don't get stuck,' Earle would say.

'Make a choice, but be prepared to shift as the situation changes,' would be Maggie's advice.

Echoes of the same idea. Unfortunately, neither one of them ever explained how to make the *right* choice. She'd need to have a little faith in herself for that.

'I think Jeremy rode out with Grant and was there when he crashed yesterday, but for whatever reason, no one reported it until this morning. We don't know where the arrow came from. Jeremy could have left the scene fearing for his own life and now the Crews don't want to be involved in an investigation.'

'And we have no way to know when, or what, Jeremy told his parents,' Clayton said.

'Right,' Bet said. 'We can't assume they knew anything until they informed Jeb this morning after "finding" Grant on the ridge.'

'So, here's what we have to do.' Alma ticked the items off on her fingers. 'Find Doug and Ruby. Figure out who shot the arrow at Grant and whether it was an accident or not. Sort out what the Crews knew and when.' Alma held up one more finger. 'And finish processing the crime scene at the rental. What do you want to do first?'

Clayton looked to Bet for the answer, but she was curious about his thought process. 'What do you think, Clayton?'

'Ruby should be our number one priority.'

Bet nodded. She could understand his concerns for the young girl.

'Think about what we know.' She watched his face to see if he would arrive at the same answer she had.

Clayton thought a moment before his shoulders sagged. 'We don't know if she's a missing person or if any crime has even been committed that involves her.'

'Right.' Bet knew how hard it could be when something looked obvious but didn't rise to the level of a formal investigation.

'I know you want to find her,' Bet said. 'I do too. But currently we only have an adult male we can't locate. Legally, that's not the same thing as a missing person. And, unless we have strong reasons to suspect foul play, we can't assume it's anything more.

Adults can go missing, with their children, and unless there are custodial issues, it's not illegal. Ruby's mother is dead, and Doug has full custody. Bodhi might know more than he's telling us. He could have his own agenda that we aren't aware of.'

Bet looked to Alma for confirmation on custody of Ruby. 'I can check,' Alma said, 'but as far as I know, Doug has sole custody. I remember when his wife died a few years ago. Cancer.' Alma clucked about the loss. 'Such a young woman too, and poor Doug left to raise those three kids on his own.'

Bet turned her attention back to Clayton. He'd revised his thinking. 'We do have reason to suspect a crime took place at the rental house, so that's our priority.'

'There *was* a crime,' Bet corrected him. 'We know there was a break-in. What we don't know is if there was also an assault, an accident, or a homicide. That's what we need to sort out.'

Concern had etched itself on Clayton's face. 'It seems like a big coincidence that Mr Marsden and his daughter are missing, you found his car not far from the rental, and there's so much blood at that house.'

The cemetery was only a few miles from the crime scene, though it would be a very long walk.

'It is. But never make the mistake of jumping to conclusions. It gives you tunnel vision at the start of an investigation. Evidence is as much for ruling things out as it is for ruling things in.'

It was clear he understood her point, but the missing child weighed on him. Clayton would do whatever Bet asked, but she wanted him to fully understand the situation. Following orders was important, but understanding the reasoning behind orders mattered too. This must be how Maggie became a mentor; she'd been good at wanting Bet to understand not just what, but why. Bet hoped she could do as good a job with Clayton.

'We have no reason to think Doug was ever there. If Doug's prints are in the system somewhere, we can compare them to any we find at the scene. We can also do a DNA match to Bodhi to see if the blood on the sleeping bag could belong to Doug or Ruby, but that can take weeks or even longer, which isn't going to help us today.'

Bet thought about the neighbor, Wanda Dupree. Maybe she would recognize a photo of Doug or Ruby. It would be strange that Wanda hadn't mentioned noticing a young girl at the rental house recently, but Bet couldn't make assumptions any more than Clayton could. She needed a photo of the two to take over to show her. Maybe Wanda had seen them in the neighborhood.

Bet looked at Alma, who sat behind her desk, ready for her next task.

'If we confirm Doug Marsden has a room at the hotel in Cle Elum, the Cle Elum police station can do a welfare check on him and Ruby,' Bet said. 'If he's there with Ruby, problem solved. They can also handle the death notification.'

It would be a simple solution. Perhaps Doug and Bodhi had a fight before Doug left. That could explain whatever Bodhi wasn't being honest about in his conversation with Bet. He could just feel bad about his last interaction with his dad. If Doug left his car voluntarily, forgot his phone, and had his own reasons not to be at home with his boys during the storm, he and Ruby could be holed up somewhere perfectly fine.

Clayton continued outlining his thoughts. 'So, if Ruby isn't our priority, then I guess Grant's death is the most serious investigation. Then second is finishing up at the rental house.' Bet nodded her agreement with Clayton's assessment. 'What do you want to do first?' Clayton asked.

'Let's do this. I'm going to call Bodhi and get photos of Doug and Ruby and find out if he knows anything about his father staying at that hotel in Cle Elum.' Bet looked at Alma, knowing the next thing she said wouldn't make the woman happy. 'Then, since there's a break in the storm, I'm going to drive back up to that ridge and see if I missed anything important at the scene of the wreck. I might be able to get that arrow out from underneath and confirm no one else was thrown from the vehicle.'

Alma started to argue about the late hour and the dark, but Bet shut her down. 'I will be fine. Then I'll come back here and grab a few hours of sleep. I promise.'

'What about me?' Clayton asked.

'Your priority will be to finish processing the crime scene at the rental house and, once I have the photos of Doug and Ruby, visiting Wanda Dupree to see if she recognizes them. It's too late to visit her now. That can wait until tomorrow morning.'

Alma reminded Clayton and Bet they needed to eat. She'd had

food sent over from the Tavern and had it waiting in the little kitchenette in their break room in the back.

Alma was right. Wearing themselves too thin wasn't going to help anyone. 'Why don't you heat up the food for us,' she said to Clayton, 'while I have a quick chat with Bodhi.' If Doug and Ruby's vanishing act turned out to be nothing more than a family squabble, she would be relieved. Annoyed, but relieved.

Instincts, however, told her it was something else.

TWENTY

B odhi had texted a few times to let her know he was still awake and waiting for an update. She appreciated that he hadn't called repeatedly – the wait couldn't have been easy. When she got him on the phone, she explained she hadn't found anything concrete yet and asked him to email photos of his father and Ruby. Then she asked him about the hotel address down in Cle Elum as a possibility for their whereabouts. She hoped he might know why Doug would visit a hotel there.

'I can't imagine why he'd plan to stay so close to home.' Bodhi's words echoed Bet's confusion. Bet asked about the possibility he was seeing someone, a woman he didn't want his kids to know about. Bodhi's voice sounded confident again. 'He wouldn't take Ruby along if he was hooking up.'

Silence on the other end of the line while Bodhi considered Bet's update.

'Maybe he thought the storm would catch them on the road and he stopped—' Bodhi cut himself off when he realized that didn't make sense with his father's car abandoned in Collier. He tried another angle. 'Maybe Dad's car was stolen.'

When a situation didn't make sense, the human mind worked overtime to fill in a logical explanation. Bodhi wanted to create a narrative that made sense. A stolen car wasn't outside the realm of possibility, but Bet already had Alma run a check on Doug's vehicle; if it had been stolen, Doug never reported it. Plus, if it had been stolen, what kept Doug from calling his sons to let them know his phone was gone too, or reporting the theft to law enforcement?

Bet reassured him the best she could. 'We're doing everything we can to find them, Bodhi.' He told her he appreciated that, but she knew he was thinking about what he could do to look for his family. 'I need you to stay home in case your father contacts you on the landline.'

'He would never call me at the house. He'd call my cell.'

'Cell phones aren't working very well with the storm. Your father might use the landline if he can't get through. I also don't want you out running around and becoming another accident victim. You can't get down the road to the highway anyway. Stay with your friends at the house.'

'That's my father and little sister.' Bet heard anger in Bodhi's voice, but it wasn't directed at her as much as a situation where he had no control. 'You can't stop me from trying to reach them.' Bodhi's voice grew louder, and Bet hoped no one was around to hear him. Especially not Aimee, who was suspicious enough.

'A police officer's first job is to keep the peace,' Maggie's voice whispered in Bet's ear. 'Talk him down by staying calm.'

Bet took a deep breath.

The last thing Bet wanted was Bodhi leaving the house. 'Bodhi, I know you're upset, but if you get in the middle of things, it will slow me down and potentially put your father and Ruby in greater danger. Not to mention, I can arrest you for impeding an investigation. I know that's not what you want.'

His breathing came hard and fast on the other end of the line. Fear could look a lot like anger. She softened her voice, de-escalation training kicking in. 'I'm very good at my job, Bodhi. Let me help you and your family.'

She hoped she was telling him the truth, but sometimes sounding confident was just as important as feeling confident.

He agreed to stay put and email the photos over.

'One last question,' Bet said before ending the call. 'Did your father drive out to a Polaris dealership in Federal Way recently?'

There was nothing but empty space on the other end of the phone.

'Bodhi?'

'Not that I know about.'

Something in Bodhi's tone gave Bet pause. Why would the mention of a Polaris dealership trouble Bodhi?

'Are you sure?'

'If he did, I don't know anything about it.'

That line of questioning wasn't getting her anywhere, so she let it go but made a mental note to have Alma dig into the dealership a little more.

Alma printed out the photos Bodhi emailed, giving a set to both Clayton and Bet as they ate a quick meal in the break room.

'Thank you for this, Alma,' Bet said as she gestured with a triangle of her favorite club sandwich. 'Did Schweitzer get his dinner?'

Alma harrumphed at the suggestion that she hadn't fed her favorite dog.

'See?' Bet looked down at her buddy where he sat expectantly at her feet. 'I knew you were exaggerating when you said you were starving.'

Schweitzer lay down at her feet with a big sigh.

'Don't worry, Schweitz, you can keep working Alma for treats,' Bet said. 'I'm not taking you on the snowmobile with me.'

Schweitzer flopped over on his side, resigned to the situation, but he eyed Alma as if considering the likelihood that he'd get something yummy out of her soon.

Clayton said he would put another hour in at the crime scene before he caught a nap on the cot in the station. He left for the rental house and Bet started to follow, but Alma stopped her before she could get out the door.

'There's something you should know.'

Bet wasn't sure how much more bad news she could handle.

'It's about Clayton. Kathy went into labor.'

'Oh shit.'

Alma laughed. 'You do have a way with words.'

'Why is he still here?'

Alma cocked an eyebrow.

'Right.' Clayton couldn't safely get down to Cle Elum with the road blocked, but she anticipated he wanted to try.

'What should we do?' Bet hoped Alma had some words of wisdom. Having a baby wasn't something Bet knew anything about on a personal level. Not that Alma had any children either, unless you counted every citizen of Collier.

'She's at the hospital in Ellensburg and it could take hours. She's not very far along, so I think Clayton is hoping the road opens up first thing in the morning and he can get down there before the baby arrives. But he's going to need you to tell him to go. He won't leave if you don't give him an order.'

They both knew how loyal Clayton was; he wouldn't leave Bet solo in the midst of the storm. But he'd be torn by his loyalty to his wife and soon-to-be-born child. He'd feel tremendous guilt no matter what he did. Bet had to take the responsibility for making the decision off his shoulders.

'OK. Thank you for telling me.'

Alma nodded. 'I overheard him taking the call or he wouldn't have told me – you know how stoic he can be.'

Bet did know. And she wasn't sure what to do to help him. She didn't want to be the lone law enforcement officer in the midst of multiple investigations. She had been trying to fill the part-time deputy spot, but it wasn't easy in her isolated community. Her previous full-time deputy had made some bad choices in the fall, which moved Clayton into the full-time spot, so now she needed to plug the vacancy left by his move up. There wasn't much chance she'd find a part-time deputy in the midst of this storm.

With the road blocked, there was nothing they could do for the moment. Kathy was in good hands. Bet would just have to help Clayton make the best choice he could as the situation developed.

She headed back out, hoping they weren't all just chasing their tails in the snow.

Bet considered having another conversation with Jeremy and his parents at Jeb's place before heading up to the ridge, but she didn't want to lose any time during the break in the storm. Besides, she wanted to have the arrow and any other evidence she might find before she talked to Jeremy again. She double- and triple-checked the weather report before she left Jeb's on the snowmobile, confirming she had time for a trip up and back before conditions worsened again.

'I should go with you,' Jeb said for the third time.

'I've checked the Doppler radar,' Bet assured him. 'I've got time. You know the exact route I'll be taking.'

Jeb didn't look convinced.

'You're too important for search and rescue. If I go missing, who's going to go after me?' She didn't have to remind him that if she got caught in an avalanche and he was riding with her, they'd both be buried.

'Do you have a PLB on you?'

When Bet said she didn't have a personal locator beacon, Jeb ran back into the main building to grab one of his.

'You know this only works if you send out a distress signal, right?' he said as he handed her the device.

It meant she had to be conscious to activate it.

'You taught me exactly how they work.'

He tapped on the top of her helmet. 'Godspeed, Bet.'

She sped out of Jeb's driveway and a bone-jarring, freezing hour later, Bet arrived back at the scene of the wreck on Iron Horse Ridge. She stepped off the sled and stood listening to the quiet now that the storm had paused. It was only a temporary reprieve before another arm of the storm slammed into Collier, but Bet would take what she could get.

The forest lay hushed under its blanket of snow. With nothing but stars out, everything went dark once she turned the headlight off on Jeb's machine.

Bet was glad to be still after the vibration of the snowmobile. There were no sounds around her, except the occasional soft thunk of ice chunks sliding off the trees. But the air still held the taste of ice, the storm dormant, not dead.

Determining herself to be alone, Bet clicked on the headlamp strapped to her helmet. The snow was deep, but up here on the ridge, it was a drier snow, and it compacted under her feet as she pushed through to reach Doug Marsden's sled and the place where his son had died.

The sled wasn't as deeply buried as she expected. It looked as if someone had dug it out since the storm started. She searched the area around the tree where the sled lay smashed, but with all the recent snowfall, she couldn't tell if there were new tracks since she and Jeb had escorted Julia and Grant back down into the valley. She searched as far as she felt a passenger might have been thrown.

Back at the wrecked sled, she fully dug the machine out. Bet pulled her phone out to look at the original photographs of the wreck. Flipping through them, something nagged at her. She pulled up an earlier shot of the snowmobile and held it up to compare to the scene in front of her.

The extra gas can was missing.

Doug's sled was outfitted with an aftermarket rack that carried a two-gallon plastic gas can.

Why would someone come all the way up here just to retrieve a gas can? And who would know it was here? Someone riding with Grant when he wrecked? It felt unlikely that someone happened by, realized the can could be useful and grabbed it. The idea that someone could have been watching from the woods while they loaded Grant's body in the Snowbulance gave Bet a chill.

Perhaps the Crews came back; they knew about the wreck. But why? The gas can wasn't worth enough to risk their safety on this ridge in the storm. They could buy one for less than fifty dollars.

Bet took photos of the machine with the missing can before turning her attention to the arrow stuck farther underneath the machine and the snow. She dug all the way down to the ground without success.

The arrow was also gone.

Someone had cleaned up the scene of the crime.

TWENTY-ONE

Back at Jeb's place, Bet parked the snowmobile and returned the PLB. She assured him she wasn't going back up on the ridge anytime soon. Then she hopped into her SUV to drive to the station, putting in a call there as she drove. Clayton answered the phone, explaining he'd made Alma take a nap on the cot. Alma was convinced she was bulletproof, and sometimes Bet wondered if that might be true, but she was relieved the septuagenarian agreed to take a break.

Things had been quiet since Bet left, and the main road down to the highway was almost clear, though traffic was still not yet allowed in or out of the valley.

Relief flooded her that there had been no emergencies while she was up on the ridge, but she still had to figure out what to do about Clayton's impending fatherhood.

'I haven't finished at the crime scene,' he continued. 'I'll do that first thing in the morning. But I did find something that might be useful at the rental house. I brought it back to the station with me.'

'I'll be there soon.'

Bet arrived to find Clayton and Schweitzer waiting for her. 'Alma wanted me to wake her up when you got back,' he said. 'But I'll leave that to you. Meanwhile, here's this.' He held out an evidence bag. 'I found it when I took apart the P trap in the sink.'

Bet held the bag up to inspect the contents. It held part of a human tooth.

'This is great, Clayton.' She sat for a moment, trying to decide what to do with it. 'So, here's what we know. Someone was seriously injured at the rental house, and now we have a tooth from the bathroom where the shower curtain disappeared. This tooth could belong to our injured person.'

'And Doug Marsden is missing.'

'Right.' Bet thought about how long it took to get DNA.

'The tooth looks too big to be a child's.' Clayton's comment telegraphed his concerns.

'I agree. So, the question is, does this tooth belong to Doug?'

Clayton shrugged. 'How do we find out?'

Bet considered her options with no access to experts outside the valley. 'I know just the woman to see, but it will have to wait until the morning.' Bet updated him on her discovery up on the ridge. Neither one had any ideas about what else they could do tonight.

'I guess we should all get some sleep.' He was right, and from Clayton's calm exterior, Bet wouldn't know anything more serious was going on in his life than the job. 'I can sleep with the phone ringer next to me in case any emergencies come in.' Or his wife called.

'What have you heard from Kathy?'

Clayton grimaced, as if Bet had exposed a weakness.

Bet laughed. 'You knew Alma had to tell me.'

Clayton smiled – they both knew Alma would never have kept that secret from Bet. 'I know.' His face showed genuine vulnerability – it wasn't a look Bet saw very often. 'I just didn't want to add to the problems around here.' He regained his usual expression of quiet competence. 'Currently she's fine. She's at the hospital with very little progression, so it could be a while. I don't want to leave you here all by yourself.'

Bet laughed. 'Careful there.'

'I don't want to leave you here with no one but Alma.'

'Better not let Alma ever hear you say otherwise.' Bet considered what constituted an emergency versus what Clayton would remember as one of the most important events in his life. 'OK, Clayton. Let's do this. You can't leave until the road is clear anyway. We'll reassess the situation when that changes. For now—'

The phone on Alma's desk rang. Clayton still sat in the chair, so he picked up.

'Sheriff's station.' He listened for a long moment before he said, 'Sit tight. I'll get right back to you.' He hung up the phone and turned to Bet. 'We've got a problem.'

Of course we do.

'That was Addie. Charles Weare may be having a heart attack. She arrived at his house and has him stabilized, but wants to get him to the hospital in Ellensburg. Want me to check the latest news on clearing the road?'

Bet waited as Clayton put in the call. Charles Weare was the owner of one of the two service stations in town. She couldn't remember ever seeing him without a cigarette in his mouth. He was her father's age and not the picture of health.

Bet sat in the chair across from the desk and leaned her head back. She craved sleep so badly she could feel herself drifting off, no matter how hard and uncomfortable the chair felt. Schweitzer put his chin on her knee, his presence bringing her a sense of peace.

She'd almost dozed off when Clayton's voice brought her back. 'Road is passable but not advisable.'

Bet took a deep breath. This was one of those moments she might regret for the rest of her life.

'Clayton, I want you to go with Addie. She shouldn't make the trip alone, and that way you get a ride to the hospital.'

'But then you'll be on your own.' He paused as his smile returned. 'You and Alma will be here alone.'

'True,' Bet said. 'But Kathy won't be.'

They waited together in silence until Addie arrived in the ambulance. Bet watched through the window until Clayton climbed into the driver's seat, allowing Addie to get in back with her patient.

Hanoi was fifteen hours ahead, so it was sometime in the afternoon. Too tired to do the math, she called Rob. Four rings and his voicemail picked up, asking her to leave a message.

'Hey.' All the things she could say but wouldn't. 'I got your message. I could sure use someone to shovel my house out, it's buried . . .' And then keep her warm while she slept . . . 'Spending the night in a jail cell.' She laughed at the image of herself under lock and key. 'Alma is asleep on the break room sofa, so that's all I've got.' The bedroom at Rob's house had a king-sized bed and a fireplace. For a moment she imagined Schweitzer and her tucked in under the down comforter, pine logs popping on the hearth. She stopped short of imagining Rob there with her. 'There are too many hours between us.'

She ended the call and made her way to the cells alone.

TWENTY-TWO

Bet didn't wake Alma, and she even managed to get a few hours of sleep after dragging the phone extension in with her in case a call came through to the station with another emergency.

It was after six when Bet walked out into the front room to find Alma seated at her desk and Sandy – the owner of Bet's favorite espresso stand – in one of the visitor chairs with Schweitzer at her feet.

'Did you see Clayton's text that Kathy is still in labor?' Alma asked as Bet set the extra handset back on its charge.

'I did. I'm glad he got to the hospital before the baby came.' She turned to Sandy, happy to see her friend.

'Thought all of you could use a pick-me-up.' Sandy pointed to the two other coffees on the desk in a cardboard carrier. 'It's hard to wake up when it's still dark outside.'

Alma sat sipping her chai tea latte and eating a fresh poppy-seed muffin. Sandy baked wonderful treats that everyone knew had to arrive alongside Alma's chai.

'You're a peach.' Bet took a sip of her latte before unwrapping another muffin, still warm from Sandy's early morning baking. 'You're all caught up on Clayton's situation?' She gestured toward the third coffee Sandy had brought over for him.

'Hell of a time for the poor woman to give birth, but I'm glad he got down to E'burg before the baby arrived.' Sandy stood up, handing Schweitzer one last treat – she viewed him as part of the team as well. 'OK. I'll be over at the coffee stand if you guys need anything. With this break in the weather, I'm sure a few Lakers will be out and about needing their early morning caffeine fix before the weather turns bad again.'

Bet thanked her and said she'd be by later for another round to keep her and Alma going. After Sandy left, Bet explained to Alma about the tooth and put a call in on the direct line to her local expert at seven.

'The doctor is in.' Her dentist sounded awfully perky for so early in the morning. 'I'll meet you at my office.'

Bet arrived at Dr Kerry's office to find the lights already on – the office had a generator. Bet had told her she could pick her up if she didn't want to drive in the snow, but the dentist just laughed and said she'd see Bet in twenty minutes, then hung up the phone.

Bet walked in to find Dr Kerry behind the front desk where her office manager Laura usually sat.

'I've pulled up Doug Marsden's records. Let's see the tooth.' Dr Kerry had always been no-nonsense, which Bet appreciated in a dentist. Born and raised in the valley, Dr Kerry only left long enough to get her degree. She'd returned and set up shop as the only dentist in Collier. That had been more than thirty years ago, but she showed no signs of slowing down or retiring

anytime soon. If she did, Lakers would all have to troop down
to Cle Elum to get their teeth cleaned.

Bet handed the tooth over in the evidence bag, which Dr Kerry
slit open with a knife. She already wore latex gloves and held
the tooth up to the X-rays that Bet could see mounted on the lit
screen.

'Can't rule it out with a visual exam. Give me a few minutes
while I get this under a microscope and do a few X-rays.'

Bet sat impatiently in the waiting room. Usually the room was
bright from the overhead lighting and a TV would be turned to
the local access station, close captioning on and the sound muted,
while music played over a few discreet speakers. But with the
office closed, most of the lights were off and the rooms were
quiet. Bet could hear Dr Kerry humming to herself through the
open door of her small onsite lab.

Dr Kerry stepped into the hall to hit the button and take an
X-ray before slipping back inside. Bet tried to place the tune the
woman hummed but failed. It sounded a little like she might be
making it up.

Ten minutes later, Dr Kerry returned to the front office, shaking
her head and holding out the tooth, which she'd placed back
inside the evidence bag for Bet to reseal and date.

'I can assure you, that is not Doug Marsden's tooth.'

'But it does belong to an adult.'

'Absolutely.'

'Can you tell me anything about whose tooth it might be?'

Dr Kerry shook her head. 'Sorry, Sheriff. Other than "adult",
there's nothing I can tell you for sure. The break looks like a
fracture, probably done with some force as opposed to the tooth
having a structural problem. The person brushes a lot – I can see
microscopic lines where they brush their teeth hard.' She made
a side-to-side motion with her hand. 'The person brushes hori-
zontally, not in a circular pattern, though I'm not sure how that's
of any use to you.'

She nodded toward the bag now in Bet's hand. 'If you find
the rest of the tooth, or the person whose mouth it belongs in, I
can tell you if it matches the break.'

Bet thanked her and promised to come in for her overdue
cleaning. She had been a patient of Dr Kerry's since she was a

child, but hadn't been in since she moved home. She wasn't going to admit how long it had been since she saw a dentist in Los Angeles.

The two women went back out into the weather together, and Bet watched the dentist hop into her old Subaru Outback and zoom out of the snow-covered parking lot.

At least Bet knew the tooth didn't belong to Doug. That did not, however, mean he wasn't the one who bled on to the sleeping bag. She wondered how long the tooth might have been in the P trap in the bathroom. Time to have another chat with George. Despite the early morning hour, she knew the man would already be awake. Hopefully, he could give her a sense of when the tooth ended up in the sink at her crime scene. Instincts and Dr Kerry's observations told her it had been knocked out in a fight.

TWENTY-THREE

The road to George's house was neatly plowed. He had probably cleared the road all the way to the Colliers' house that morning, even though Rob was out of the country. George was a very conscientious caretaker and would be checking on the empty house regularly. She hoped he was home, as the break in the weather could have him out surveying the storm damage on the properties he managed.

Rolling up in front of the cabin, Bet pulled over and shut off the SUV. Smoke rose from George's chimney, and the lights were on. The wind had picked up again and the smoke blew sideways like a translucent flag into the trees, rather than escaping straight up into the sky.

Despite the deep forest around George's house, there was still heavy snowfall on the ground, but the walkway up to the porch had been shoveled. Bet tromped up the steps and knocked on the door. She wanted to make a little extra noise to announce her presence as George had a tendency to answer the door 'locked and loaded' if he was surprised. She didn't want to do anything to set him on edge.

'Hello, Younger,' George said as he opened the door. He looked around to see if she was alone, then held his door open. 'Best come in and warm up.'

She had been inside George's place a few times in the past, but she was always surprised at how much bigger it felt inside than it looked from the road. The log walls were chinked with plaster that created a thick barrier against the outside world, and the sound of the wind disappeared as soon as George closed the solid wood door.

He gestured for her to follow him into the kitchen. 'Got news for me?'

'No, but I'm hoping you might be able to answer a question for me.'

She said yes to a cup of coffee, freshly made in George's coffee press. As he poured one for each of them, she explained what they'd found and why she'd come looking to him for advice. 'How long could that tooth have been in the P trap?'

'That's a good question, Younger,' he said as he blew across the top of the hot drink. 'It would depend mostly on the water pressure and how much the tenants used the sink. If I recall, a family of four rented the property last. They had it the entire month of September. Seems the kids were homeschooled, so they didn't need to be back in Seattle after Labor Day.'

Bet didn't doubt George's memory.

'It would be useful for me to have the information on all the renters in the last six months,' Bet said. 'I doubt any of them were involved in any way, but I may want to run a background check on people who have stayed in that house. Or at least call and ask if any of the adults broke a tooth. Can you provide that information to me?'

'I surely can.' George walked over to his computer and printer – the only modern technology in the house that Bet knew about. 'I am the legal representative for Mr Collier the Elder where the rental properties are concerned, and our contracts with renters state we will provide information to police in the case of any investigations.' George gave her a grin. 'Makes people less likely to steal things from the properties.'

It relieved Bet that she didn't have to wait for a warrant.

George brought up a spreadsheet and it didn't take him long

to print out what she needed. There were no familiar names, though that didn't surprise her. It had been a long shot that she would have interacted with any of the renters in an official capacity.

'The family that stayed at the place in September. How old were the kids?'

George closed his eyes a moment. In the silence, Bet heard a sound in another part of the cabin. She looked at George, startled to discover he had company, but he gave no explanation about a guest.

'I remember seeing them when I met the family at the house to give them the keys and do the walk-through. They had a boy and a girl maybe ten or twelve years old, very polite.'

Dr Kerry had been confident the tooth didn't belong to a child, so it couldn't be as simple as a lost baby tooth.

'And the parents? What can you tell me about them?'

'A man and woman. White. I'd say upper middle class. They drove a nice minivan, an older model, but well cared for. The parents were probably in their late thirties or early forties. I know the man was in IT. He wanted a high-speed internet connection. We have one in that house, which is part of why they chose that specific rental. He brought a laptop with him to work while he was on vacation. Had all his teeth, far as I know.' George said this last bit with a smile.

'I don't suppose you had reason to do any plumbing repairs at that house.'

George took another sip of his coffee. 'Sorry, Younger. I wish I could be of more help.'

'So . . . a tooth could be stuck in that trap a long time? The water pressure wouldn't wash it down?'

'There is one thing that might help. I pour bleach down the drain after every rental. It keeps from having problems with hair clogging the plumbing for the next renter. If that tooth had been down there, it might show signs of that.'

Bet made a note to call Dr Kerry and ask if there had been any signs of exposure to bleach. 'But no one should have used the sink after you put bleach down it the last time?'

'That's right. I would have done it after the last renters were out of the house. Anyone using that sink would have come in after the house was closed up.'

'Thanks, George,' Bet couldn't think of any other questions. 'I'll let you know when we finish processing the scene. It shouldn't be too much longer.'

'I appreciate that. I'd like to get that broken glass fixed and replace the shower curtain. Don't worry about putting the trap back together. I'd rather do it myself.' He didn't have to say he had to clean up the blood on the dining room table; they both knew that was foremost on his mind. Bet anticipated George would burn the wooden table and put something new in its place. 'No other signs of break-ins at any of the Collier buildings. I've checked on all of them.'

He would have called right away if he had found anything, but it was nice to have it confirmed. George paused a moment and looked at her with an intensity that piqued her curiosity. It was clear the man had something else on his mind. 'Since I've got you here. There is one other thing I'd like to talk to you about.'

Bet waited. George looked slightly uncomfortable – an awkwardness she'd never seen before.

'What's up?' she finally asked when it became clear he didn't know where to start.

'It's my nephew. Great-nephew, actually. He's staying with me for a little while.'

George paused again. That explained whoever moved around in his guest room.

'Oh?'

'Here's the thing, Younger. Kane got out of the military a while ago and he's having some trouble readjusting to being back stateside.'

She now had a sense of where the conversation would lead.

'He was military police. Army. Over in the Middle East.'

'And you know I need another part-time deputy.' Her instinct was correct.

'The thought had crossed my mind.'

Bet considered Clayton, a long way out of their mountain valley with his baby on the way. She definitely needed help, but the wrong help was worse than no help.

'What do you mean by having some trouble readjusting?'

George looked her in the eye. 'Nothing that would interfere

with his ability to serve you and this community. But he was trained as a warrior, and now there's no war for him to fight.'

Earle Rivers rose in Bet's memory. Her father was also a warrior who returned home with few outlets for his wartime experiences. To be a warrior during peacetime could be a tricky way to live.

'Send him over to see me.' Bet didn't want to meet this Kane for the first time at his uncle's house. She wanted to meet him on her own territory.

'Thank you, Younger.' Something in George's voice cracked. A hint at emotion Bet knew he hadn't intended for her to see. She touched his arm. 'Happy to talk to him. What's his last name?'

'It's also Stand. You won't find a blemish.' He gave her Kane's date of birth. 'I know you have to check his background.'

'I hope it works out. Anyone you recommend would be high on my list.'

Walking outside, Bet considered driving up the road to Rob's place. She'd come to love the house. It made her feel safe and peaceful, though that likely came from Rob himself, not his property. Although there was something special about it that went beyond its grandeur. There wasn't any legitimate reason to drive up there, however, with him so far away. She didn't like to admit that she missed him and wanted to remember what it was like to travel that private drive to see him. Turning around, she headed toward the station instead. She'd meant it when she complimented George's recommendation, but she also knew the blinders people wore about the folks they loved.

Arriving at the station, Bet could see Alma through the glass door. She sat at her desk, a pair of reading glasses on as she studied the computer screen in front of her, a look of intense concentration on her face. Schweitzer sat next to her peering at the screen too, as if his opinion might be needed with whatever Alma studied.

They both looked up as Bet walked in, smiles on their faces. 'What have we got?' Bet asked, her spirit bumped up by seeing her team.

Alma's face grew serious again as she sat back and slipped off her glasses. They hung on a beaded strap that sparkled in the overhead light. Schweitzer dodged around the desk to greet Bet, toenails clicking on the hardwood floor.

'Looks like at least another twenty-four hours of repeated cycles of snow and strong winds. And another storm is building up behind it.'

Bet rubbed her dog's face and reminded him that he had to sit nice for a cookie.

Alma eyed her with an expression Bet knew well. 'You're wondering if you did the right thing letting Clayton go down to E'burg?' Alma always read her mind with remarkable accuracy, and right now she knew the conflict in Bet's heart.

Bet made a noncommittal noise, keeping her focus on Schweitzer.

'You did the right thing. He only gets one shot to be at the birth of his first child. You would have regretted asking him to miss that, even for a possible murder investigation and a couple of missing persons. Cases get solved or don't, but a child's birth is once in a lifetime.'

Maybe Bet should let Alma's voice overtake her father's and Maggie's.

Bet pictured Grant, lying cold in Jeb's walk-in freezer, and Ruby, out there somewhere in the storm with her missing father. Other people's children she felt responsible for. Clayton might have put other people's children first before, but could he now? Fatherhood had to impact him on some level. Her own father hadn't always put Bet's welfare first. At least, that was her perception. But maybe he had and she'd just never realized it. Or at least he did the best he could. She was starting to understand what it meant to put an entire population's welfare over her own.

'You,' Bet said, 'are my right-hand woman no matter what, so let's get the information we have up on the whiteboard and figure out a strategy for moving forward.'

The two of them walked back to her office and Bet pulled out the board that they used to track major crimes. They hadn't needed it since that first homicide investigation back in September. She started to list the information they knew, putting Grant Marsden at the top.

'Are we considering this a homicide?' Alma asked.

'We're keeping that a very real possibility.'

Alma stared at the white space as if it could fill her in on the missing details. 'Someone cleaned up the crime scene,' she said, 'but we don't know intent.'

'We could also be looking at manslaughter,' Bet reminded her. 'Or reckless endangerment. Plus, a snowmobile is a motor vehicle, and a driver could be charged with vehicular homicide if that person caused Grant to wreck.'

'That's a class A felony.'

If Jeremy was involved with Grant's accident, he could be in a lot of trouble.

First, they had to determine who else was on the ridge and who cleaned up the scene. The actual charges would come later from the district attorney.

Bet looked at the information they had on the board. 'I do think it's a strange coincidence that Doug and Ruby are missing, Doug's car is abandoned at the cemetery, and his son's sled was hit by an arrow on the ridge. I'm not drawing conclusions, but somehow this web could connect.'

Alma cracked her knuckles as if readying herself for a fight. 'What's next?'

Bet looked over the whiteboard as well, but she and Alma could only do so much.

She had no access to a crime scene investigator, the crime scene where Grant died was still buried under snow, and the arrow was gone. With another round of storms coming in, she still couldn't ask anyone to drive in from E'burg. She couldn't get Grant to the morgue for a full examination, and she had no body from the rental house, no tracks to follow, no obvious witnesses, and a potentially missing ten-year-old girl.

'Time to go talk to the person who knows the most about the comings and goings in Collier.'

'Isn't that me?'

Bet laughed at the expression on Alma's face. 'You're right. The second most. Come on Schweitz, we're heading to the Tavern.'

TWENTY-FOUR

Rope and his partner Tomás had run the Lake Collier Tavern for years. Rope was quite the character, heavily tattooed with bits and pieces of embedded metal sticking out from his skin. Contrary to his tough exterior, however, he was a sweet man who wouldn't hurt a fly.

The building that housed the Tavern fronted the lake, the deck reaching out over the water without access to the surface. Lake Collier was deep, dark and cold. It was also devoid of life, a situation currently under investigation. It was also dangerous, with a long history of drownings and strange disappearances. The locals went elsewhere for boating, fishing and water recreation.

But it was beautiful to look at from a distance.

The sheer banks and warning signs kept most visitors at bay, but the water still drew people like a magnet. Something about the danger pulled them in. Bet understood the allure, even if she was able to resist it herself.

Parking in the lot outside the Tavern, Bet wasn't surprised to find a good crowd at the bar. It was midmorning already, and a number of snowmobiles and four-wheel-drive vehicles shared the lot, exhibiting the spirit of the Lakers, a resilient group who weren't going to let the storm of the century keep them from a cheeseburger and all-day happy hour drink specials. Schweitzer let out a quick bark of delight when he recognized where they were going.

'Bet!' Rope called out as she walked in with Schweitzer on her heels. 'How's my favorite customer?'

'Schweitz would love a burger patty made just the way he likes it.'

They both knew that meant rare and delivered to him on a paper plate.

Rope tossed a cocktail napkin down on the bar. 'And for my second favorite customer? Water? Or Coffee? Tea? I should get you something hot to drink. You look half frozen.'

'Coffee would be great.'

Other than the dinner Alma had brought over for her and Clayton last night, she hadn't eaten anything more than the muffin from Sandy at six o'clock that morning. Just keeping warm right now burned energy, and she was running on little sleep and a lot of physical activity out in the cold. The smells coming from the kitchen made her stomach growl.

'Eat when you can,' Maggie always said. 'You never know when all hell is going to break loose.'

Bet ordered a cheeseburger and fries, plus another to go that she planned to take back to Alma. Calories and cholesterol weren't something she was going to worry about until the storm and the investigations were over.

After she got her order in, Bet pulled out the photos Alma had printed off.

'Do you know the Marsdens?'

Rope picked up the photos. 'Oh sure, that's Doug and his son Grant. He's got a couple other kids. Bodhi and Ruby.'

'Have you seen any of them recently?'

'Bodhi comes in a lot now that he's twenty-one. He likes to hang out in the bar section here. I haven't seen him since the storm started. Grant was in here, let's see, three or four days ago. He was shooting darts with a kid I didn't recognize.'

Bet thought about Jeremy. Collier didn't have many places to eat, so it would have been easy for them to meet at the Tavern. Kids under twenty-one could be in the restaurant, which included the gaming area – a pool table, a pinball machine, and two dart boards – until ten at night. Teens often gathered in the gaming area, leaving their parents behind at the tables in another part of the restaurant.

'Was Doug around, or was Grant on his own?'

Rope thought a minute. 'I don't remember. Let me check with Tomás.'

Bet noticed a group of teens over at the pool table. She considered talking to them while she waited for Rope, but decided they weren't going anywhere soon.

Rope and Tomás hunched over the photo, engaged in animated discussion. A moment later, Rope returned to where she sat.

'Tomás doesn't remember seeing Doug. We both think it was

just Grant. And Tomás is sure it was three days ago.' Which was the day before Grant went out on the snowmobile.

'Can you describe the kid you saw him with? The one you didn't recognize?'

Rope's description was generic, a teenage White kid with dark hair and an average build. It could certainly be Jeremy, but nothing distinct enough to confirm.

While Rope went off to check on some other patrons, Bet sauntered over to chat with the teens. She wanted them to respond to her, not shut down in the face of authority, so she kept her body language relaxed and kept the serious cop expression off her face.

'Hey,' Bet said to the five young people. Two stood with pool cues in their hands, while the other three perched on stools at the round high-top tables against the wall.

'Hey, Sheriff,' said one of the girls. Bet guessed she was the leader of the group. She looked familiar, but Bet couldn't place her name. 'What can we do for you?'

'I'm trying to find someone that might be a friend of yours.' Bet set the photo of Grant down on the edge of the pool table. She noticed a line of quarters tucked in under one of the bumpers, the order of players laid out on the felt. Some things never changed. She could remember placing her own quarters there years ago when the Tavern was owned by someone else. She came here with her closest friends, Eric and Dylan. Her mind shied away from those childhood memories and focused on the task at hand.

'Oh, sure, that's Grant.' The boy who spoke was shorter than the others, his sandy blond hair and round glasses making him look thoughtful and a little bit like a miniature John Denver. She had no doubt he would hate to hear that – if he even knew who John Denver was.

The taller boy standing next to him poked him in the shoulder with an elbow. 'What?' the short boy said, with a sharp glance at his friend.

'Don't tell her anything.'

Bet had to stop herself from laughing. She'd never thought of herself as 'the man' before, but these kids apparently did. Of course, she was wearing a gun, a uniform and a badge.

'Grant's not in any trouble.' Not anymore and never again.

'But I'm wondering if you can tell me if he was in here three days ago? Maybe talking to a kid from out of town?'

Turning toward each other, the teens used a couple words, eye signals, and various expressions as they carried on a complicated, unspoken conversation only they could understand.

The leader of the group finally spoke out loud, stopping their private dialogue, a level of exasperation in her voice. 'Come on, you guys, Sheriff Rivers isn't out to get anyone. No one here has done anything wrong. Stop pretending to be savage.'

Bet managed to keep a straight face. She felt about a hundred years old.

The leader continued. 'He was in here three days ago with all of us.'

'With a kid named Jeremy, right?'

'Did *he* do something?' The short kid's voice held a note of anticipation. Something exciting to spice up an otherwise boring snowstorm.

'Why would you think that?' Bet asked.

'He was kind of rude.'

Maybe it was more about the rude kid getting into trouble that piqued their interest than something to make the day more interesting.

'What's your name?'

Expressions got wary as Bet pulled out her notebook. They had already started talking to her, so now she could focus on useful information. Bet took down all their names, not because she thought she would ever need to call any of them in for more formal questioning, but to sober the atmosphere and maybe invest them with the seriousness of her inquiry. They could be witnesses to Jeremy having a relationship with Grant prior to the accident on the ridge.

'So,' Bet said after she had all their information. 'You met a boy named Jeremy.'

'We did,' said Roger, the John Denver look-alike. 'He was in here with his parents, but he played pool and darts with us for a while.'

'Did he plan to go out snowmobiling with Grant the next day?'

The teens weren't sure.

'He might have,' Roger said.

'How did you all get here today?'

Gina, the leader, pointed to a table some distance away, where several adults were eating together and laughing, unaware the sheriff was talking to their kids. 'You aren't going to talk to them, are you?' For the first time, Bet could see a crack in the girl's confident façade.

These teens were unlikely to be involved in anything nefarious, but keeping them a little anxious would likely keep them talking. 'Did any of you go snowmobiling with Grant?' She watched them closely. If someone had witnessed Grant's crash, she found it hard to believe they would be so casual now.

'None of us are into snowmobiling,' said a girl named Hillary. She had wild hair and a scattering of freckles that she'd unsuccessfully tried to hide behind foundation. Bet hoped she'd give that up someday and embrace the characteristic that made her unique. 'Grant might have gone with Aimee, though. You should talk to her. Aimee Johnson.'

The rest of them looked at Bet with expressions of curiosity. No one looked guilty or acted like they hid anything. Teens could be capable of great deception, but not an entire group all at once; there was always a weak link. Bet found it interesting that Aimee had been hanging out at Bodhi's house rather than with this group. Why wasn't she here with them now? Maybe they were more Grant's friends than Aimee's. Or was this a racial thing? These kids were all White. Or was it just because Aimee's parents weren't here like the rest of them?

Bet could also be reading too much into the situation, but it was her job to observe, and it was hard not to draw conclusions.

'If you think it could be a racial thing,' Maggie would say, 'it probably is.'

'Are you guys close to Aimee?'

The teens gave each other those looks again. Bet wished she could interpret 'teenspeak', though whatever dynamic was at play, it probably had nothing to do with Grant's death.

'Close enough,' Gina finally said. 'But she usually only hangs out with us when Grant's here.'

Bet decided she was going too far afield from what she needed to investigate and thanked them for their help. She returned to

the bar, where Schweitzer had held down her spot by tucking in
under her bar stool. No one was going to ask a dog that big to
move. Rope brought over her burger when he saw her sit back
down. She knew Schweitzer had already enjoyed his, since he
rested quietly, though he did keep one eye open in case she
decided to share her fries. She relented and tossed him a few
before she doused them with vinegar and started on her meal.

'Find out what you needed from the kids?' Rope slid the wooden
condiment holder over to her, and she grabbed the mustard.

'I think so,' Bet said. 'Very interesting.'

Her next visit would be back out to Pearson's Ranch to visit
Jeremy and see if she could throw him off guard with what she'd
discovered and find out what really happened on that ridge.

TWENTY-FIVE

A text from Alma came in just as Bet finished her meal.
Bet had given Kane Stand's name to Alma for a background check. She picked up her phone expecting to find
the message to be about that, but instead she discovered Kane
was waiting for her at the station.

'No time like the present,' Bet said to Schweitzer, who stood
up as she did. She sent Alma a response that she'd be right there.
Dropping some cash on the bar next to her empty plate, she
picked up the carryout for Alma and headed for the door.

Bet tipped her hat to Roger, who watched her from the pool
table as she exited the Tavern. The kid gave her a small wave,
his back to his friends so the gesture went unseen by the others.

It heartened her. She liked to believe that most kids were basically good and that even the ones who did bad things were worth
saving.

George's old Willys sat parked in front of the station. Kane either
didn't own a car or it wasn't suitable for the weather. He could
have something parked behind George's house that he wouldn't
get out again until the storm cleared.

A man sat in the same chair as George had been in the day before. He turned to look up at her as she walked through the door. She knew from his birth date that Kane was one year older than she was, but he had an ageless quality about him that he shared with his uncle.

Kane resembled George physically as well – the same angular features, full mouth, and eyes so black the pupils disappeared. But the similarities ended there. Where George barely topped five and a half feet, Kane stood an inch or two taller than Bet, putting him over six. Though not as broad-shouldered as Rob Collier, he carried himself with a bearing clearly honed in the military. A soldier in civilian clothes.

Bet introduced herself and led Kane back into her office.

'Your uncle tells me you were with the military police.'

'Yes, ma'am.'

His voice carried the cadence of the south. George's people were from Georgia. His great-great-grandfather came out with the first Robert Collier not long after the civil war. George and his sister were born and raised in Collier, but the sister moved back to Atlanta before Bet or Kane were born.

'Bet, please. Ma'am makes me itchy.'

'I'll do my best.' There was an undercurrent of amusement in Kane's voice that warmed Bet to him. She liked a person with a sense of humor, even if she was the cause of their merriment.

Bet asked Kane questions about his service and his intentions for staying in Collier, watching his face and body language as much as listening to his answers. 'Do you see yourself here a year from now?'

Kane pursed his lips, watching Bet with an unblinking gaze. She fought the urge to break the silence, thinking how good he must be at getting suspects to spill their guts with that particular expression. She fought the urge to admit to any infraction she could think of if only he would blink.

'I'd love to tell you yes, but I don't like to lie. I *am* being truthful when I say I'd like to work for you, and I'd like for this to fit. But I can't guarantee I won't pick up and move down the road again.'

'Why is that?'

Kane's eyes drifted to the photo on the wall behind her. There had always been a photo of the current sheriff behind the desk, and Bet didn't buck that tradition. His face showed no change in expression, but he studied her image as he put his thoughts together.

'I'm having a little trouble staying put. This town might be a little . . . tight for me.' His attention dropped back to Bet's face.

Bet had moved to Los Angeles a few years ago. She'd gone, in part, to get out from under her father's shadow, *the* Earle Rivers, Sheriff of Collier. She had only come back to fill in while he was sick, and when he died, she'd seriously considered returning to LA. She loved the anonymity of a big city. After an entire childhood in one house in one tiny town, where her family had lived for generations, she liked not putting down roots. Now she was back in tiny Collier, where she was *the* Bet Rivers, Sheriff of Collier. The yoke might fit well, but that didn't mean it wasn't heavy on her neck.

'Come with me.' Bet stood up from behind her desk. 'I'm going to go talk to someone, and I want you to join me. I'll explain the situation on the way over.'

Bet figured she might as well see if Kane could follow orders. Discover if he could stand in the room while she questioned the Crews without speaking. Plus, she'd learn a lot more about him and how he saw the world by hearing his thoughts afterward. If he had trouble answering to a woman, she might as well know now, not down the road when she needed someone to rely on only to find he wasn't going to back her up so much as run her over.

They arrived at Jeb's with lights on, but no siren, and parked in front of the roundhouse. The red and blue flashers lent an aura of danger to the scene. Jeb met them at the door and agreed to bring the family over to the roundhouse for questions. Bet wanted them uncomfortable, and the roundhouse would make them feel more exposed than their little cabin. Walking past the SUV with the light bar flashing might increase their anxiety and push them to say more than they intended.

The Crews arrived in the big front room where Bet and Kane waited for them. Mark looked angry, Julia looked troubled and Jeremy looked scared. Bet nodded when Jeb asked if he should leave the room.

'What's this about?' Mark asked as they walked over to the table and chairs that Bet pointed to.

'Why don't you sit down, Mr Crews. I have some questions for you.'

Mark looked about to argue when Kane took a step forward. He didn't have to make any other move and Mark abruptly sat down, though the expression on his face didn't change. Bet was impressed. She had told Kane she wanted him there to observe, not to speak, but she hadn't said don't use non-verbal communication. His action served the right purpose. He caught her eye, and she could tell he wanted to know if he'd done the right thing, which she also appreciated. She gave him a quick nod of approval and turned back to the Crews.

Bet didn't introduce Kane, and he now stood with that impassive expression on his face. His neutral cop face was more intimidating than any other expression he could display. Bet let the tableau settle in, her and Kane standing, the Crews sitting. The intimidation tactics felt right. The Crews had proved they would lie to her, so she wanted to rattle them a little and see what they did in response.

'It's come to my attention that the three of you haven't been honest with me about a few things.'

Jeremy looked ready to bolt. Julia's face paled, but Mark's expression turned even more belligerent. In Bet's experience, when alpha males felt their authority questioned, they puffed up and made mistakes.

'We've told you everything we know.' Mark's tone echoed the red flush of anger on his cheeks. Fury leaked from his pores. She wondered if his emotional state came from arrogance or fear, or both.

Bet sat down across from them, so the Crews continued to face Kane standing behind her. She and Kane were a united front threatening Mark's domain.

'Use the idea that men have of women being weaker,' Maggie had said one night over a beer after a long day. 'You don't have to show them you aren't until it's to your advantage.'

Bet brought her voice down, quiet, noncombative, but also confident, unafraid of him for all his bluster. Sometimes angry men were thrown off when the other person didn't match their anger. Bet had learned long ago that another person's anger was an internal situation, and she didn't have to take on someone else's emotional state if she didn't want to. 'We all know that's not true, Mr Crews.'

Mark tore his eyes from Kane and focused on her. Bet sat eye-to-eye with him, not fighting, but not backing down. Mark looked away first. Body language carried a lot more weight than many people realized. In this battle with Mark for psychological control, Bet and Kane were ahead two to nothing.

After another moment of silence while Mark calmed down – Bet never underestimated how much a good shot of adrenaline impacted a person – she continued. 'First of all, we know that Jeremy went out snowmobiling with Grant Marsden without you.'

'He didn't know the dead kid!' Mark jumped in again, giving himself away just as Bet had hoped he would. She had him in the right state of stress, not so much that he went ballistic, but just enough to say things he shouldn't.

'How do you know the victim's name was Grant Marsden? I just said he went snowmobiling with someone. I didn't say it was the boy who died.'

Jeremy blanched at this, looking at his father with open disgust. Bet wondered at the family dynamic playing out in front of her.

'Just shut up, Mark.' Julia's voice was controlled, but her anger was also very clear, and it wasn't directed at Bet. 'You are not as clever as you think you are.'

Mark looked startled. Bet didn't think his wife spoke to him like that very often, if ever. Her inner mama bear had come out to protect her son.

Bet decided to change up her tack. 'I'd like to hear Jeremy's account about what happened on their ride.'

'And you will.' Julia put her arm around her son. 'As soon as we have a lawyer.'

Bet had misjudged Julia's role in the dynamic. But she'd learned a lot during their interactions – and created a rift within the family, which might help down the road.

The Crews couldn't take back the fact that everyone knew they had lied about knowing Grant, and Mark had helped confirm their son was on the ridge when Grant died.

Bet was on the trail to the truth.

TWENTY-SIX

B et continued to study the Crews, their body language, who looked at whom. The power differential between the parents had shifted from the overbearing father to the overprotective mother. Mark got up from his chair and moved away from his wife and son to stand at one of the big windows – originally the doors into the roundhouse for the trains. He looked out at the snow, which alternated red and blue from the flashing lights on top of Bet's black and white.

'That's your right,' Bet said. 'Though I'm not accusing Jeremy of anything, I just need to know what really happened on that ridge. How the accident happened. Grant's family deserves some answers.' Bet held back the information about the arrow. She didn't want to play a card until she knew it was the right time.

Bet hoped her comment about Grant's family might get through to Julia. Her maternal instincts might be triggered to remember that Grant had people who loved him too.

'Do you even have a lawyer in this godforsaken place?' Mark spoke from his spot by the window. Bet recognized he was a man who lashed out in anger rather than look at his own actions too closely. He probably found it painful to admit failures of his own. 'Or do we have to wait for the storm to lift and bring someone in from Seattle?'

Bet was used to people underestimating folks from rural communities. She'd seen it with how people interacted with her father over the years. He never let it get to him, explaining to Bet how underestimation on the part of another person was always to his advantage.

It was something Earle and Maggie would have agreed on, if for different reasons. 'I'm a woman and I'm Latina,' Maggie would say. 'No one knows I'm the smartest person in the room until I prove it, and I only do that when it will get me what I want.'

Kane shifted his stance to match Mark's, where he stood at

the window. Kane still stood impassive, but he also moved his weight forward on to his toes, ready to spring into action.

Mark didn't strike her as a man who got physical with law enforcement officers. Sticking to angry outbursts probably served him well in whatever world he lived in, but she was glad to have Kane there just in case things changed. She could handle Mark in a fight, but she'd rather not have to do it alone.

There was also the additional danger that either Julia or Jeremy would join him and get injured in the fray. Even when there were fissures in a family's dynamic, members would often bond together when facing a common 'enemy'. Or if Mark made a move toward her or Kane, Julia might step in to stop it and end up injured herself.

'We have an attorney you can call.' Bet reached into a coat pocket to pull out a small notebook she carried. She wrote out Sandy's name and phone number. The woman might run the espresso stand at the market, but she was also a criminal defense attorney who had practiced in Seattle up until a year and a half ago when a heart attack sent her back home to Collier to regroup.

Sandy said she never missed the law, but she'd been so quick to help Bet with her election campaign last fall, Bet thought she might be ready for a little more action than making the perfect cappuccino.

Mark made a move as if to go back to his cabin, but Bet held up her hand.

'Feel free to call her now. We can wait.'

Bet didn't have a legal leg to stand on. The Crews could leave the room and call Sandy or not call Sandy – she couldn't force them to talk to her – but she hoped they wouldn't think about it too much. Best for her if they brought Sandy out to Jeb's. A lot of people thought they had to talk to police if the authorities wanted to question them, and Bet had no reason to tell them otherwise.

Bet started to ask a question, but Julia cut her off. 'We have nothing to say until the attorney gets here.'

While they waited, Bet got on her phone to check the progress of the storm. The break in the weather looked to be holding for the time being. But she'd keep a close eye on the next wave threatening to slam into the valley.

It wasn't long before Sandy's Kia Telluride pulled in next to

Bet's SUV. She glanced at Kane standing unmoving against the wall, a look of curiosity on her face. Then she put her hand on her hip and looked at Bet with a cross expression and a spark in her eye.

'Have Miranda rights been read?'

'I'm just asking questions.'

Sandy watched Bet for a moment, a knowing look in her eyes. Police could arrest a person after they said something incriminating, and as long as that person wasn't in custody when they said it, Miranda rights didn't apply.

'My clients and I would like to chat in private, so either you and whoever the new muscle is you've got standing over there by the wall can give us the room, or we are going back to their cabin. The choice is yours.'

Bet looked at Kane. The glimmer of amusement that she'd seen earlier at her office flashed across his eyes. Other than that, his expression never changed.

Bet and Kane went back to Jeb's office, promising Sandy that they would close the door and for her to knock when she and her clients were ready to talk.

Guessing Jeb was there, Bet knocked.

'Come on in.' Jeb's voice came through the solid wood door.

Bet opened it up and peeked inside. 'Can we wait in here with you?'

The office was much like Jeb himself, small but neat. 'Be my guests,' he said from his chair behind the desk. He watched while Kane and Bet settled into the two other chairs in the room.

'I've got a question for you while we wait.' Bet pulled out her cell phone. 'Either one of you might be able to answer.' Bet brought up the photo of the arrow where it was stuck under the snowmobile. At least the image was fairly clear. 'What can you tell me about this?'

Jeb slid on a pair of reading glasses and inspected the photo before handing the phone over to Kane.

'Looks like an Easton six millimeter,' Jeb said. Kane nodded his agreement and handed the phone back to Bet.

'What would those be used for?'

'Hunting,' Jeb said. 'Those aren't target arrows. Those are the real deal.'

'That's an expensive arrow.' Kane looked over at Bet, the glint of amusement still dancing in his eyes. 'Sorry, is it OK if I speak now?'

Jeb raised an eyebrow at the two of them, but Bet laughed. Kane's humor was one notch below cheeky, which she enjoyed. 'Yes. You did an excellent job of looking intimidating in the other room.'

'Is that what he's here for?' Jeb asked. 'I wondered where Clayton was.'

Bet gave Jeb the quick rundown of Kathy going into labor down in E'burg and nodded toward Kane. 'He may be my next deputy.'

Jeb assessed Kane. 'Afghanistan or Iraq?' Bet wasn't surprised that Jeb didn't need to be told about Kane's service to see it. Kane wore his military history like a suit of armor.

'A little bit of both.'

'Welcome home, brother.' As Jeb said these words, he pulled up the sleeve of his shirt, revealing a military tattoo. 'I did a little bit of time in the sandbox back in the nineties.'

Kane dipped his head in response and his body language relaxed. Someone else in the room knew what he'd endured. Like finding someone who spoke your language while traveling in a foreign land.

Bet shook off thoughts of warriors finding their place in peacetime and considered the number of people in the valley who bow-hunted instead. Lots of people augmented their groceries with game they killed legally. Hunting wasn't allowed on the valley floor, but there were plenty of places nearby where hunters could go. Target shooting was also legal on private property.

'Let me see that again.' Jeb held his hand back out, then looked closer at the photo. 'Is that under Grant's sled?' The image Bet had given him was the close-up of the arrow, but the edge of the snowmobile was visible.

'Yep.' Bet said nothing else, and Jeb let it go. 'Don't suppose you know who would use them.'

Jeb shook his head. 'Sorry, Rivers, lots of people do. Myself included.'

'Wait . . . you use these?'

'When I go hunting, sure. But not for target practice.'

'Don't suppose any of yours have gone missing.'

A look of surprise crossed Jeb's face, immediately followed by a look of concern. He got up from his desk and walked out with Bet on his heels. Skipping the front room where the Crews were still holed up with Sandy, he went down the hallway out to a side door with Bet and Kane close behind.

They crunched across the fresh snow, their feet sinking only a few inches. Jeb had cleared a path to the door recently, but more snow had fallen. Bet looked behind them to see their footprints were the only marks in the otherwise pristine surface. Jeb arrived at one of his outbuildings and pulled out a set of keys. Bright colored rubber rings were on each one and his fingers quickly found the one in blue. He tried to slide the key into the lock but failed.

'What the . . .' He leaned over to eye the lock. 'Sheriff, I think I need to report a break-in.'

Bet gestured for Jeb to stand aside and took a closer look. Something was broken off inside the lock. Bet unsnapped the keeper on her sidearm and gestured for Jeb to stay outside. Kane started to follow, but Bet raised a hand.

'You're still a civilian, Mr Stand. There's no footprints in the snow and it's unlikely anyone is holed up in there, but I need to clear the room first.'

She gently pushed on the door, but it didn't give way, so she shoved a little harder.

The door popped open, but Bet had braced herself, so she was ready when it fell away from her. She stepped into the room, drawing her weapon as she called out. She didn't think anyone was inside, but the cost could be high if she guessed wrong.

'Bet Rivers, Collier Sheriff's department. If anyone is in here, please step forward and put your hands up where I can see them. This is Sheriff Rivers, I'm coming in.'

She reached around on the wall near the door and found the light switch with one hand. With a click, the room burst into light from the LED track lighting that crisscrossed the ceiling. Instinct told her no one was in the building, but she stated her name a third time as she did a quick survey of the room. She could see lockers and worktables and various cabinets, but nothing stirred. She opened the only closet but found shelves and no room for anyone to hide. There was also a small half-bathroom, but it too was empty.

She re-holstered her weapon and called for Jeb and Kane to join her. 'I'm thinking someone bumped your lock.'

Jeb looked perplexed. 'What does that mean?'

Bet explained the process of using a regular key, the identical make as the lock, but filed down in a special way. After inserting the filed key partway into the lock, the perpetrator used a hammer to tap it all the way inside, forcing the pins to jump and the lock to open.

'Hit it too hard and the key can jam.' Kane kept his eyes on Bet. 'That could explain why a key is broken off inside.' She nodded her agreement.

'That's an expensive lock,' Jeb said. 'Shouldn't it have held up better?'

'Expensive locks actually make bumping easier,' Bet said. 'The parts inside a good lock are harder, which makes them stronger, but easier to bump.'

Burglars who used the technique carried a 'set' of keys for all the major brands of locks. Expensive locks were used on the most expensive houses with more valuables to steal, so those were the most likely filed keys to carry. The broken key could indicate the person who used it wasn't an expert at the technique, as someone with more experience would know not to tap so hard.

Jeb kept a variety of bows, along with fishing and other sporting equipment in the room. His guns and rifles were all locked in a safe in the roundhouse, but there were still plenty of valuable objects in the room. Jeb pulled out a container with arrows just like the one Bet saw on the ridge.

He began to count.

'Any missing?' Bet asked.

'A set of six.'

'What about a bow?'

It took a few minutes for Jeb to go through all the equipment. Some of the crossbows were in hard cases, which he opened to confirm each crossbow was still inside.

'No bows are missing.'

'That doesn't mean a crossbow wasn't used and returned,' Kane said from his spot by the door.

'Do the Crews know what's in here?' Bet asked.

'I did a demonstration for them when they first arrived. It's something teen visitors usually enjoy and I always offer to families. One of them could be the cause of the break-in.'

Should she have told Jeb about the arrow at the scene of the crime? That would have pointed her in this direction sooner. She'd kept it to herself because Jeb wasn't a member of the force.

No use second-guessing herself now. The damage was done. She could only move forward, but how?

TWENTY-SEVEN

Jeb's outbuilding was now a crime scene. Bet hated the thought of asking Clayton to return from E'burg, but she could only do so much alone. She had yet to receive a text that the baby had been born, worrying her about complications. Bet knew little about childbirth, but she didn't think it should take this long.

She turned to Jeb and Kane to discuss the best course of action. The Crews had lied about knowing Jeremy, but that didn't mean they'd committed another crime. Grant's death could still be an accident, which Jeremy didn't tell his parents about until the following day. Someone had stolen arrows similar to the one under the sled. And someone had removed the arrow after she and Jeb got Grant down off the mountain.

'You said you gave the Crews a demonstration with the bow. Was Jeremy overly interested?'

'The kid didn't show a lot of interest in anything, but that doesn't mean he wasn't more curious than I gave him credit for.'

She started to ask Jeb if the Crews had left their cabin again at any time after they'd retrieved Grant's body when her phone rang.

She clicked on the call from Alma, 'I hope you have good news for once.'

'There was a fight at the Tavern. Rope called in for help.'

'Crap. On our way.'

The immediate altercation took precedence over a break-in.

Bet stuffed her phone back in her pocket. 'Here's what's going to happen now. Tell Sandy that we will be back to talk to her clients as soon as we can. If it's going to be more than an hour, I will call her and let her know. No one is to come near this door. I'm going to seal the door with crime scene tape, so I'll know if anyone tries.'

Bet turned and looked at Kane. He stared back at her with those impossibly dark eyes. She couldn't read anything about his state of mind. 'I need to deal with a couple drunk and disorderlies at the Tavern. It would be nice to have backup. Are you serious about the job?'

'I am.'

'Good. Raise your right hand.'

Kane did, and Bet swore him in. She'd have to trust her instincts and George's recommendation that Kane was the right man for the job. Bet handed him the crime scene tape and watched him seal the door while she sent a text to Alma to get the paperwork started on Kane's hire.

He signed and dated the tape – showing Bet he understood how the process worked – and turned to look at her. She took the tape from him with a nod. 'Let's go.'

Reaching the SUV, Bet eyed Kane. 'Do you feel confident driving in the snow?'

'Yes, ma'am.'

'Back to that, are we?'

'You're my boss now.'

Bet chuckled. 'How about "Sheriff" then? You know how much I love ma'am.' She handed him the keys. 'Guess I'd better assess your driving skills.'

Kane took the keys. He got into the vehicle and moved the seat back. He adjusted the mirrors and took a moment to acquaint himself with the unfamiliar vehicle.

'Lights and sound?' he asked. She nodded and he turned on the siren. With an efficient three-point turn, Kane maneuvered around the banked snow and Sandy's vehicle before heading back out on the loop road into town.

The studded tires roared, and Kane's eyes moved between the road in front of him, the area around him, and the mirrors to see the road behind. His hands were relaxed on the wheel, but Bet could feel his concentration. Snow had started to fall again, and the road conditions had worsened since Bet drove them out to Jeb's, but he showed nothing but confidence. Bet relaxed. It wouldn't do to underestimate the importance of a law enforcement officer being able to handle the weather conditions in their isolated valley. It could be the difference between a successful career as a deputy and driving one of their few patrol vehicles into a tree and dying on the job.

As Maggie had liked to remind her, more police officers were injured annually in driving accidents than gun-related incidents. She always said, 'Driving skills and physical conditioning are two of the most important things for a patrol officer. If you have those covered, you'll be fine.'

A crowd of people jammed together at the front door of the Tavern. Kane parked the SUV behind two vehicles in front, leaving the lights on as he hopped out from the driver's seat. The sound of shouts from inside explained the tenseness of the observers. Bet pulled off her winter gloves and stuffed them into her pocket as they reached the door. The last thing she wanted was to pull a weapon in a crowded restaurant, but no matter what happened, she didn't want to be hampered by her heavy winter clothing.

Bet pushed everyone aside while announcing her presence to the room as Kane followed her in.

She recognized the two men faced off in front of her, circled by the other patrons clearly enjoying the day's entertainment. Other than Rope, no one had tried to stop the fight. Once she had a better look, she could understand the hesitation of the others to get too close.

One of the men, a guy she knew of as 'Skeet', held a broken beer bottle. The other man, whose name she couldn't remember, held his hand on his neck. Both the fighters were large men and looked like the type who never backed down from a fight. Rope had gotten between the two, while everyone else looked poised for flight if the battle came their way.

Bet's voice carried over the din. 'Stop!' She knew how to project when she needed to. 'Skeet. Put the bottle down.' The room fell silent, though the two men never took their eyes off each other. Adrenaline had taken over and the fight, flight or freeze impulse was overriding the common sense of listening to law enforcement. She felt Rope turn his attention to her, but Bet never took her eyes off Skeet. He telegraphed his intention even before he started to move.

Bet lunged for Skeet as he struck at the other man. She caught him under his raised right arm. Hooking his elbow behind his back, she pushed the broken bottle up and away from her. While he wasn't much taller than she was, he had her by more than fifty pounds, and the two of them continued forward, his momentum taking Bet with him. She felt something burn down the side of her thumb.

Kane, moving faster than she anticipated, slipped in next to her. He gave Skeet's hand a twist, causing him to scream and drop the bottle. Rope sidestepped out of the way just before the other three crashed to the floor. Bet regained her footing and got a better hold of Skeet, putting the cuffs on him as Kane rolled away, springing to his feet again. Kane put himself between the other combatant and Bet, assuring her safety while simultaneously eyeing the crowd.

'You stay put,' she told Skeet, who sat on the floor, handcuffed and angry. She walked over next to Kane and looked at Skeet's opponent, who stood holding his neck, a stunned look on his face. Blood began to seep through his fingers.

'I need to have a look at your wound,' Bet said. At the same time, the guy took his hand away from his throat.

'Is it bad?' he asked. A wave of blood drenched his shirt front and sprayed toward Bet and Kane.

Without a word, they moved forward and carefully helped the injured man down to the floor.

'Put your hand back on your neck,' Bet said to the man. She knew how fast a person could bleed out from a sliced artery.

'Bar rags, clean,' Bet said to Rope as she pulled a pair of gloves out of her vest. Tomás tossed several clean towels at Rope from behind the bar, which Rope handed to Bet.

'How are your first aid skills?' she asked Kane as she reached out to help the man hold pressure on the wound.

'Fair.'

She appreciated he didn't brag. It also meant they were probably even.

Bet asked Rope to get a first aid kit, then she turned back to Kane. 'Get Skeet locked up in the back of the SUV and pull the first aid kit out of the far back. Get yourself gloved up.'

Without a word, Kane hoisted Skeet to his feet. His actions were so swift and sure, Skeet didn't appear to know what hit him before Kane had him on his way. The curious onlookers parted like the Red Sea as Kane walked Skeet out the door at a fast clip.

'Let's get a call into Donna,' Bet said as Rope set the first aid kit next to her. 'She's at the community center. Have her come over here immediately. Explain we've got a severe laceration to the neck, which is currently controlled with pressure.'

Kane returned and dropped down next to her with the kit from the SUV as well. He popped open both kits and pulled on gloves then set out gauze, tape and scissors.

She carefully peeled back the bar towel to check out the wound. 'It's not as bad as it looks. It's bleeding a lot, but it's not his carotid or he'd be pumping out a lot more. I don't think Skeet nicked an artery.'

A woman walked toward them from her place at the doorway. Anger radiated from her body language, but her voice shook with fear and the slight slur of someone who'd had a few drinks. Excitement and booze made for a potent mix. 'Is he going to die?'

Kane stopped her forward momentum by getting between the woman and Bet and held his hands up. 'I'm going to have to ask you to stop right there.'

The woman did as she was told. Bet recognized her as a local real estate agent. Tammy something. She'd aggressively tried to get Bet to put her own house on the market after Bet's father died.

'He's going to be fine,' Bet said. 'Is this your partner?'

'Boyfriend.'

'What's his name?'

'Larry. Larry Summers.'

'Tammy, right?'

Tammy nodded, her eyes never leaving Larry.

'OK, Tammy. I'm going to ask you to sit back down over there and wait for Deputy Kane to ask you a few questions.'

'Fine. But tell that son-of-a-bitch he can sleep on the couch.'

Larry's eyes went wild as he tried to speak.

'Stay calm, Larry.' Bet did not want his heart rate to rise. 'You can sort out your personal life after we get your neck stitched up.'

Bet worked to tape a pressure bandage in place while waiting for Donna.

'Take statements,' Bet said to Kane. 'Start with Tammy . . .' The image of a real estate poster popped up in Bet's mind. 'I think her last name is Bishop, but check everyone's ID.'

Kane got up and pulled a notebook out of his coat pocket. Bet wondered if he always carried one, a remnant of his previous life, or if he'd had one just in case he needed to take notes during their interview. Regardless, she liked that he was prepared.

Kane stationed Rope at the front door. She heard him explain that no one could enter or exit except Donna. Few people had left the scene, as the unfolding drama was much more interesting than going home. Kane soon had all the patrons who had been at the table with the two men when the fight broke out isolated in the far dining room – and seated separately so they wouldn't talk to each other. Then he asked everyone else to find seats and wait.

So far so good. Maybe Kane was just the person she needed. Or was he too good to be true, and he had some inner demons that would appear at the worst possible time, jeopardizing someone else's safety, maybe even her own?

A few minutes later, Donna sailed through the front door with a suture kit and a few other supplies. She removed Bet's make-shift pressure bandage.

'This is going to hurt a little,' she said to Larry, 'but it will numb the pain while I stop the bleeding.' Donna shot him up with an anesthetic.

Donna looked at the blood on the floor, then studied Bet. 'You've got blood on your cheek. You should go wash that off now. I don't have to remind you blood is a bio-hazard. All the waste here should be incinerated.'

Rope came over wearing rubber gloves and carrying a plastic garbage bag. He began to clean up the bloody towels. 'I got this, Bet.'

Bet walked over to Kane, who was questioning the people in the back room. 'Did you get any blood on you?' She inspected his face.

'I'm good.'

She trusted the man knew how and when to protect himself and went into the restroom to clean up. She rinsed the blood off her check. As her adrenaline subsided, she felt the burn again that she'd noticed during the fight. She pulled off her gloves.

A long scratch ran along the outside of her thumb. Adrenaline racing, she hadn't noticed it when she'd gloved up.

As she held her hand under the hot water in the sink, she could see it beginning to bleed.

TWENTY-EIGHT

B et knew all about the protocol for her situation. The Los Angeles Police Department discussed ways to deal with possible blood contact during basic training and reinforced it when she was a rookie. But it was her father's words that came back to her now.

Like most of her dad's instructions, they were succinct and to the point. Dad wasn't one to waste words. 'Don't panic. Clean the wound. Wrap it up. Sample the other guy's blood. Get it tested. Get yourself tested. Request a cocktail.'

He wasn't, of course, talking about a Cosmo. The 'cocktail' was an antiviral drug mix designed to prevent an HIV transmission in the case of an accidental exposure. The drugs should be started within seventy-two hours, but the sooner the better.

Bet looked at herself in the mirror. 'Don't panic.'

She let herself go down the list of potential complications from exposure to another person's blood. HIV was only one problem; there was also Hepatitis B and C. She'd had a Hep B vaccine, so that shouldn't be a problem. The likelihood of the broken bottle transferring anything to her were minimal, but the human reactions to potential disasters were often immediate and visceral. Larry had already been cut with the bottle before it sliced her thumb. There was nothing she could do about that now.

Her heart rate bumped up, no matter how small the possibility was that she'd have any issues down the road.

'Just do what you need to do, Bet,' she said to herself in the mirror. 'You are going to be fine.'

She held a paper towel around the wound and walked out to see how Donna fared with the injured man.

Donna had cleaned the cut out and was neatly stitching up the wound. 'Almost done, Larry.'

Bet kneeled next to him. Now that he was out of the woods, she needed to get his contact information and take a statement. She also wanted to determine what started the fight.

Donna tied off the last stitch and began to bandage the wound.

'Does he need to go to the hospital?' Bet asked.

'As long as he doesn't get in any more fights, he should be fine. It would be more dangerous trying to drive out of the valley right now. I'm going to shoot him up with antibiotics and send a prescription for oral antibiotics over to the drug store.'

She taped a large bandage down and got out a syringe.

'You're sure you aren't allergic to antibiotics?' she asked Larry.

'Not that I know of.'

'Let's see if we can sit you up.'

With Bet's help, Donna sat Larry upright and they rolled up the arm of his long-sleeved shirt. Donna cleaned a spot on his arm and injected him.

'Now what?' Larry asked.

'Now we wait a few minutes to see if you stop breathing from anaphylactic shock.'

Bet hoped Donna had a softer bedside manner with the kids.

The nurse must have seen Bet's startled look because she chuckled as she started cleaning up. 'I've got a community center full of people depending on me and I'm over here wasting my time because a couple of yahoos got into a brawl over something ridiculous.'

Bet couldn't fault her thinking.

Donna caught sight of the paper towel Bet had wrapped around her thumb to stop the bleeding. 'What happened?'

After Bet explained she'd been nicked with the bottle that Skeet had cut Larry with, Donna dug back into her supplies. 'Let me check it out.'

She used a topical antibiotic to clean the wound out again and put a bandage on. 'It doesn't look too serious.' Donna didn't say anything more, but Bet could tell she wasn't done.

Bet turned to Larry and helped him get out his wallet to confirm his ID. 'What were the two of you fighting about?' she asked him after recording his contact info. Skeet could get charged with assault with a deadly weapon. Even though the fight had ended without significant injuries, Bet was still going to take the incident seriously. She knew Larry might lie, but she had to start somewhere.

Larry studied Bet, no doubt deciding how to best couch an answer that would get him in the least amount of trouble.

'He owes me money, but he still wanted me to pick up half the tab.'

Donna rolled her eyes and looked at Bet. Bet guessed her own expression mirrored the annoyance in Donna's. It really was a stupid reason to get into a fight and waste valuable resources the community couldn't afford at a time like this.

Bet didn't try to hide her irritation. 'Are you kidding me? We're in the midst of the worst snowstorm this town has ever seen and you two are breaking up Rope's bar over a bill?'

Larry looked sheepish. 'Sorry.'

'Not as sorry as you're going to be. You are both getting written up for disturbing the peace, and I might charge you with assault and battery. Plus, you have to pay Rope restitution.'

'I didn't hurt Skeet.'

Bet held up her hand. 'But one of you did hurt me.'

Larry paled.

'Here's what you're going to do.' Donna pulled another syringe out of her bag of medical supplies. 'You're going to give me your arm and I'm going to draw a little more blood.'

Without a word, Larry held out his arm. After Donna got the blood sample, she pulled Bet aside, leaving Larry seated dejectedly on the floor. 'This will last about two days for testing, even at room temperature,' she handed Bet the vial, 'but you should start a cocktail now. Do you know what that is?'

'I had the same thought myself.'

'Good. You're probably fine, but we should play this safe. I don't have the meds here in Collier. Can we get some in from E'burg?'

Addie had dropped Clayton off at the hospital. Bet wasn't sure if she'd returned to Collier yet. Addie might wait down in E'burg until the weather improved and she would likely stop to restock what was stolen from her ambulance.

'I'll see what I can do.'

Bet had withstood conflicts with armed criminals on the streets of Los Angeles for four years without incident. Was she really going to face a serious complication caused by a minor scratch from a broken beer bottle?

She considered how she could have broken up the fight differently. She couldn't pull her weapon in a crowded bar. She couldn't let Skeet attack Larry with a broken bottle right in front of her. She'd acted quickly and decisively. Sometimes bad things happened.

'What's done is done.' Bet relied on the platitude to stop her rising sense of panic. Nothing she could do about it now. She had a job to do. Worry could wait for later.

TWENTY-NINE

Bet stashed the blood sample in the SUV before rejoining Kane to finish the interviews at the bar. Bet took the statements from Rope and Tomás, the two people she felt were the most likely to have unbiased, and sober, opinions. She took them separately, however, to keep them from influencing each other. Memory was remarkably untrustworthy, and eyewitnesses were easily swayed by other's statements, melding with their own 'memory'.

Skeet and Larry were at the Tavern with their partners, Skeet's wife Paula and Larry's girlfriend Tammy. They sat at a table near the window, farthest from the bar, so Rope didn't hear what started the fight, but Tomás was serving another table nearby.

'Skeet started yelling that Larry was taking advantage of him,' Tomás said. 'Then Skeet threw the first punch.'

Rope had already said he looked up when Skeet started to yell, and while he couldn't make out the words, he also thought Skeet threw the first punch.

Bet allowed Larry's girlfriend to take him home – once Donna felt confident that he wasn't going to have an allergic reaction to the antibiotics. Kane had already interviewed Tammy who, not surprisingly given the trouble Larry was in, backed up the story told by Rope and Tomás. Angry people sometimes made their partners out to be worse than they actually were but, ticked off as Tammy was, she claimed Skeet was the aggressor and that Larry merely defended himself.

Bet had to run Skeet over to the station and lock him up in a cell before he froze to death in the SUV.

'Finish up the interviews,' she said to Kane before she went out into the cold. 'I'll be back to pick you up to go over to Jeb's again.' Bet had already contacted Sandy to let her know it would be at least two hours before they returned to talk to the Crews.

'I'll be home,' Sandy said. 'Be sure to let me know when you're going back over. I want to be in the room.'

Bet heard the energy in her friend's voice.

'Nice to have a client again?' Bet asked.

Sandy laughed. 'It is, but don't tell my cardiologist.' Sandy's doctor wanted her to keep her stress level down even though it had been a full year since her heart attack. Bet thought a person with Sandy's drive would get stressed without anything to stimulate her intellect, and thought this might actually be good for her friend.

Pushing Skeet through the front door at the station, Bet was amused at the raised eyebrow the two of them got from Alma.

'We're booking Skeet on drunk and disorderly and the assault of a police officer.'

'I wasn't trying to assault you.'

'You lunged at me with a broken beer bottle. I'd call that intent.'

That shut the man up.

Alma peered over her reading glasses at the man standing next to Bet. 'Shame on you, Skeeter Douglas. Your mother would be very disappointed.'

Skeet ducked his head. Alma had a knack for making anyone feel repentant.

Bet walked him through the station and passed through the locked door to the cells in the back.

'What the hell is that?' Skeet asked as they reached the first cell with the bloody sleeping bag hanging inside.

'Nothing for you to worry about. Your only job right now is to sober up and think about your sins.'

Skeet went into the cell quietly and sat down on the cot. 'I'm

sorry, Sheriff.' He hung his head in abject misery. Bet almost
believed him.

But she knew it could also be a carefully orchestrated fake.
She had done a breathalyzer on Skeet in the SUV at the Tavern,
and he'd blown a 1.2, so he was legally intoxicated. She thought
about doing a drug test, but decided it wasn't a good use of time
or resources. She anticipated Skeet would get charged with
assault on Larry, which would be fines and a max of one year
in jail, though he'd probably get probation. There weren't death
threats or serious injury, so aggravated assault didn't fit the
crime.

Bet felt her anxiety rise again at the thought of the cut made
with the broken bottle. She'd seen how much blood was on the
glass when she'd bagged it at the scene. Most of it was Larry's,
which meant she had been exposed.

She'd take the cocktail and wait for the results on the blood
test. If Larry was negative for anything she could catch, she was
off the hook. Until then, there was nothing she could do.

Leaving Skeet behind in the cell, Bet arrived in the front office
just as Alma hung up the phone.

'That was the Polaris dealer.'

'Learn anything interesting?' Bet didn't really think Doug's
trip to Federal Way had any bearing on events in the valley. But
it might help build a picture of the man.

'No record of him buying anything with a credit card, but I
said I would send over a photo of him and see if anyone working
the counter recognizes him.'

Bet started to ask for more information when the landline rang
again.

'Yes, she's free.' Alma held out the phone. 'Your new deputy.'

Kane's voice was calm. 'Something I think you should know
right away.'

'Yes?'

'Before the fight started, someone else was at the table with
the two heavyweights. He lit out before we showed up. I think
it's very interesting that he didn't stick around to watch the fight
like everyone else.'

'Did you get a name?'

'Gordon Dupree. Does that name mean anything to you?'

'Gordon, no. But I do know a woman with the same last name. What's the description?'

Bet thought of Wanda Dupree. She lived next door to the crime scene at the rental property and had told Bet she lived alone.

'Twenties, Black, short hair, average height and build.'

Did Wanda have a son? A nephew? Did he live in the valley? Or did he live with Wanda and she lied about living alone?

'Anyone there know where he lives?'

'Negative.'

'OK. I'll get Alma to do a search. On my way back. Good work, Kane.'

'Over and out.'

Bet explained the situation to Alma and asked her to look into Wanda Dupree and this missing Gordon. It felt unlikely two people with an unusual last name could be in tiny Collier without being related, but that didn't mean Gordon was involved with whatever happened at the rental house, even if Wanda lived next door.

'Call me when you have anything,' Bet said. She'd wait to visit Wanda again until she had more information. For now, continuing the interview with the Crews was her next task. 'Any word from Clayton?'

Alma tensed. Her lips tightened as she shook her head. 'Not a word other than the text that he'd arrived at the hospital safely and Kathy was still in labor. Addie is on her way back.'

Bet thought about Grant Marsden as she walked to her office. Protocol dictated the coroner pick up the body to transport to the morgue, but the storm had wreaked havoc on protocol. If Addie took Grant down to the morgue, she could also drop off the blood taken from Larry and the lab could run tests to check for infectious disease. Should she have Addie turn around and pick up a cocktail of drugs before she came back to Collier?

Bet didn't want to alarm Alma, so she hadn't mention the cut she'd received or the exposure to Larry's blood. She had to fill out a report, but she could wait to let Alma see it after she had more information. She'd call Addie herself and see if she could make another run down to E'burg with Grant's corpse.

As she got ready to make the call, the window in her office shook as wind lashed snow against the building.

The storm had returned to Collier.

THIRTY

By the time Bet arrived back at the Tavern, Kane had finished the interviews. On the drive over, Bet had reached Addie on the phone and learned the paramedic carried an emergency supply of the HIV cocktail on her bus.

'It wasn't anything that got stolen during the break-in,' Addie said. 'I'll come wherever you are when I get back to town. It's only two days' worth and you have to take them for twenty-eight, but I can pick up the full prescription when I return to the hospital.'

Addie also agreed to take Grant down to the morgue and the blood test to the hospital lab.

'I know what you're going through,' the young woman said. 'I had a needle stick from a junkie's used hypo my first year on the job. I got your back, Sheriff.'

Bet felt grateful to have so many people in her corner. With both Donna and Addie looking out for her, she didn't feel so alone with her fear.

Rope had finished cleaning up the blood on the Tavern's floor. He would remain open for business and was giving out free appetizers in appreciation of everyone's cooperation with the sheriff. The crowd remained in high spirits, with no one wanting to go home despite the weather.

Kane waited for her near the door.

'Let's get back over to Jeb's to finish questioning the Crews.' Bet noticed Kane checking out the bandage on her hand. 'It's nothing.'

'You got that breaking up the fight?'

His voice gave nothing away. It struck Bet he might think she'd done a poor job of protecting herself, to get cut in a fight with a bloody bottle. She fought the urge to defend herself.

'Are you taking precautions?'

Bet told him about Addie providing her with a cocktail.

'OK.' Kane tucked his notebook into his pocket again. 'Want me to drive?'

Bet parked the SUV in front of the roundhouse. She'd seen enough of Kane's driving to know he was very capable in the snow. Another test he'd passed. He was getting a trial by fire driving in a snowstorm and breaking up a bar fight all on his first day. He was a good man to have her back.

This time, she left the flashers off. The Crews didn't need a reminder that things were serious.

She and Kane got out and trudged their way over to the guest cabin the Crews family rented. She was going to try to ask a few questions before they called Sandy to come back over. Sandy had requested Bet call when she resumed asking questions, but that wasn't the same as the Crews requesting their lawyer. The Crews were not in custody, so Miranda rights didn't apply. If they chose to answer questions, that was their choice. She wasn't legally barred from asking them as long as she clarified they weren't required to answer and were free to leave at any time.

Jeb provided a mix of single-bedroom and double-bedroom cabins, and a bunkhouse that could house up to ten kids at a time. In the summer all of them were in use for the drug and alcohol rehabilitation program he ran. In the winter, he typically closed the bunkhouse and kept only a few of the cabins open. The Crews had rented one of the two-bedroom cabins.

Bet could see lights on, though the drapes were drawn.

'I'll take it from here,' Bet said. Kane stood back as she knocked on the door. A moment later the door cracked open, and Bet found herself looking down into the eyes of Julia Crews.

'Oh,' Julia said, as if surprised to find Bet standing there, even though she knew Bet and Kane would return. Had she expected someone else? 'You're back. What can I do for you?'

'For starters you could let us in out of this storm.' The winds buffeted Bet as she stood in the doorway, and snow blew around her into the cabin.

'Of course, of course, come on in.'

The doors to both bedrooms were closed, and Bet could see a paperback and a pair of reading glasses on the end table by the sofa in front of the hearth. A cheerful fire lent a holiday air to the scene.

'I should call Sandy back if you're going to ask us anything else about . . .' Her voice trailed off, as if she couldn't quite figure out how to talk about Grant now that everyone knew the family had lied about knowing him.

'You can, but I also have some new questions to ask about whether you went into the outbuilding where Jeb stores his bows and arrows.' Julia hadn't actually asked for her attorney yet, so Bet held out.

Julia looked even more startled, a response Bet didn't think she could fake. It definitely wasn't the question Julia expected to hear. The surprise worked in Bet's favor as Julia answered without thinking about calling her attorney.

'We went in with Mr Pearson. He gave our son a few lessons with the bow.'

That jibed with what Jeb told Bet earlier. It would also give a plausible explanation for any fingerprints they found in the room.

'Is there a chance any of you went back later?'

'I'm not sure I understand.'

Bet waited to see if she would add anything. Julia's eyes went back and forth between Kane and Bet as if to find a clue from their expressions.

'Why would we do that?' Julia finally asked. Which didn't answer Bet's question.

'I'd like to talk to your son and Mr Crews as well,' Bet said.

'They're both taking a nap.' She spoke quickly, making Bet wonder if she was lying about their whereabouts. Was it possible Mark had taken their son somewhere? Maybe out of the valley? But if so, why leave Julia behind? To slow things down? Dispose of evidence? Like Grant's cell phone and the arrow from the sled?

'I'm here now, and this won't take long.'

Julia looked at Kane but found no help there. 'I'll go get them.' She turned toward the bedrooms.

'Your son first, if you would,' Bet said. There was nothing to stop Julia from waking her husband as well, but Bet was curious to see what she would do. She'd seen fractures in the marriage. Maybe Julia's concerns about her husband's poor choices in the situation would keep her from bringing him in right away.

'All right.' She crossed over to one of the closed doors and rapped lightly with her knuckles, before slipping in and closing it behind her.

Bet and Kane listened. The sound of voices murmured through the door, but not clearly enough to follow the conversation. A few moments later, Jeremy came out, rubbing his eyes.

Mrs Crews stood next to her son, arms across her chest as if to ward off a blow. 'Please answer the sheriff's questions,' she said to him. Bet had expected Mrs Crew to request Sandy come back right away, but she wasn't going to jeopardize her opportunity to learn something now that she hadn't.

'Hi, Jeremy,' Bet said to the teen. 'Sorry to wake you up. I know this has been a tough couple of days.'

'S'OK.' He raked his fingers through his hair. 'I wasn't really asleep.'

'I wanted to ask you about the building where Jeb keeps his crossbows and arrows.' Bet guessed his mother already told him why she was here, but she was still curious to see his reaction.

His non-reaction was just as interesting as anything he might have said. She could see by his body language that he'd braced himself for the question, and his response felt practiced. 'Why would you ask about that?'

'I want to know if you went in there by yourself. After you went in with Jeb.'

'How could I? The door is locked.'

'How do you know the door is locked?' It was a simple question – Jeb locked up all his outbuildings. But Jeremy might hesitate if he thought about how he'd broken in and didn't want to give that away.

The boy paused, glancing at his mother. Her face took on an expression of concern. She leaned forward as if willing him to give the right response.

'How did I know the door was locked?'

Anyone who repeated back a simple question was usually lying. They used the extra time to form an answer. Jeremy was not looking innocent about the break-in.

'I saw Jeb unlock it and lock it again when we went in there.' Jeremy looked at his mother, as if gauging her acceptance of his response. Julia smiled at him, but Bet could see something in her eyes.

Julia didn't believe him either.

The kid could just be nervous around authority figures. Except he'd answered Bet's question as if relieved he'd come up with something plausible.

'And you never went back into the room without Jeb?'

'He's already told you that.' Julie might regret giving Bet permission to ask questions without Mark or Sandy present.

'Your husband is a heavy sleeper,' Bet said.

'What?'

'Your husband. You said he was taking a nap, but our voices haven't woken him?'

Julia and Jeremy exchanged a look of confusion. Julia walked over to the other closed door and stuck her head in.

She straightened up, not meeting Bet's eyes. 'He's not here.'

'You didn't know he was gone?' Bet asked. Mrs Crews shook her head, looking unsure. She didn't know her husband had left or what to do about it.

'How did he leave here without you noticing?'

Now Julia looked annoyed. 'I fell asleep reading. Your knock woke me up. He probably went out quietly so he wouldn't disturb me.' Mark didn't strike Bet as the kind of man who tiptoed around a room, no matter whose sleep he might disturb. 'With the noise of the storm I wouldn't have heard much anyway.'

'He went out without telling you, knowing that we'd be back to question all of you further?' There wasn't a legal reason for him to remain available, but if a person was ready to prove their innocence, it was an odd choice in the middle of a storm.

'Maybe he's over at the main building?' Julia sounded hopeful.

Bet asked Kane to check there and around back where the family parked their car. 'If the car is gone, Jeb might know where Mark went.' Bet thought Jeb would have called her if he knew Mark left the premises, but maybe Mark just ran to the store or something equally benign. As noisy as the storm was, Jeb wouldn't hear a vehicle leave if he was in his office in the back of the roundhouse.

'While Deputy Stand is doing that, would you mind if I looked in your room?' Bet asked Jeremy.

At the same time Jeremy said 'sure', his mother said 'no'.

Jeremy looked at his mother. 'I don't have anything to hide in there,' he said to her with a reassuring tone. As if whatever he might want to hide from Bet wasn't in the room.

Julia gave her son a long stare before she finally turned to Bet and nodded her permission. 'I'm calling Sandy.'

Bet didn't reply as Julia pulled out her phone; she just followed Jeremy to his door.

She stopped him at the entrance and asked that he wait while she walked into the room. With a quick glance around, she checked inside the closet and under the bed. No sign of the missing arrows. She ran her fingers under the mattress but felt nothing. The bump keys could be hidden somewhere, but Jeremy might have also ditched them once he broke one off in the lock. If he had done the break-in, he must have been aware Jeb would notice the broken key even if he didn't notice the missing set of arrows.

When she was done, she thanked Jeremy, who stood in the doorway watching. Bet came back out into the main room of the cabin. 'Can I look in your room as well?' she asked Julia, though she didn't expect permission.

'I think I should say no until Sandy gets here.'

Before Bet could say anything further, Kane returned.

'Mark appears to have left.'

'What?' Julia said. 'What do you mean left?' The panic in her voice was loud and clear.

'I mean your car is gone and Jeb didn't know anything about Mark's plans to leave. Where would he go in this weather?'

Julia looked at her son, who shrugged. Both their expressions changed. They knew something about his disappearance, and whatever it was, it scared them.

THIRTY-ONE

Bet took a deep breath. She wished for Clayton to be back in Collier. She'd made a mistake letting him leave in the middle of all this. She wished her dad were alive to tell her what to do. She vowed never to be short-handed again, though in a town that rarely had serious crimes, how was she to know she'd face something like this during the worst storm they'd ever experienced? She also knew she would never have felt OK keeping Clayton from his wife and baby. Putting in a call to Maggie for advice crossed her mind, but how could her sergeant in LA advise her about being the lone law enforcement officer in a mountain valley buried in snow?

Bet expected the homicide in the fall to be the only homicide she'd face in her first year as sheriff, yet here she was dealing with something even more challenging. At least the homicide in the fall was clearly a homicide. Right now, she didn't know what she had. Grant's death could still be an accident, and the crime scene at the rental house could be nothing more than a simple squatter with a nonfatal injury. Or she had two unrelated homicides committed by two different perpetrators.

Everyone watched her, waiting for her to make a move.

'Kane, come outside with me for a moment, would you?'

Her new deputy stepped outside as Bet told the Crews she wouldn't be long.

Once out of earshot of the Crews, Bet paused to get her thoughts in order, but before she could, her phone buzzed. Alma's number popped up on her screen. She asked Kane to hold on.

'Gordon Dupree is Wanda's son,' Alma said without preamble.

That was interesting.

'Does he have a record?'

Kane could only hear Bet's side of the conversation, and he looked at her with curiosity as she said those words.

'Nothing. Looks like his parents divorced several years ago. I think he might have lived with his dad. I didn't find evidence of him in Collier.'

'Let's dig further into his background.'

Kane cocked his head, listening intently.

'On it.'

'Where does he live now?'

'His last known is Spokane.' Spokane was the largest town on the eastern side of the state, not far from the Idaho border. Bet thanked her and hung up before updating Kane with Alma's findings. 'Here's what I want to do,' she said to the taciturn man beside her, 'we are going to split up. I'm going to take you back to the station to get the other SUV. I am going to go talk to Wanda Dupree about her son Gordon and you are going to come back here and try to find Mark Crews. Are you good with that?'

'Sure.'

'One more thing.'

Kane looked at her expectantly.

'Do you own a handgun?'

'SIG Sauer M17.'

'Legal?'

'The license is in my wallet.'

Bet didn't ask where the gun was. She didn't want to know if he'd carried it into the station with him.

Kane appeared to read her mind. 'The gun is locked up at George's place.'

Bet appreciated he'd left it behind this morning. 'I have no reason to believe the Crews are dangerous. But I would feel better if you were armed.'

Kane smiled broadly for the first time since she'd met him. 'So would I.'

THIRTY-TWO

Bet parked her SUV at the rental house and walked over to Wanda's. She didn't want to tip the woman off by pulling up in her driveway and give her too much time to think – or Gordon too much time to hide.

Wanda hadn't necessarily lied to Bet when she said she lived alone. Gordon didn't technically live there if he was only visiting, and Bet hadn't specifically asked if she had family in town. But something felt off about it. Why wouldn't Wanda have told Bet her son was staying with her when Bet expressed concern about her being alone in the storm?

They could be estranged, and he was staying somewhere else. If they weren't in communication, why else would he be in

Collier? Alma thought he didn't grow up here. Though he knew Skeet and Larry well enough to have breakfast with them.

Contemplating her strategy, Bet pushed her way through the snow. One light was on upstairs, and another shone from downstairs, both on the back side of the house. It could signal that more than one person was home.

Arriving at the front door, Bet rang the bell and waited. Nothing. She rang the bell again. Still nothing. She rang the bell and knocked loudly. Wanda wouldn't have left the house. She was adamant about staying away from people and the weather was too poor to be out for a walk.

It wasn't much after six, but she could be sleeping; her health condition must impact her energy levels. Bet felt bad asking a sick woman to come to the door, but not enough to leave without getting a response.

She leaned back to look up at the front of the house. A curtain twitched and she knocked again.

The front door finally cracked open. Wanda peered out. Her earlier friendliness had vanished.

'I was taking a nap, Sheriff.'

'I'm sorry to disturb you, Mrs Dupree.'

'Ms,' she corrected her. No prompt to call her Wanda.

'Ms Dupree. I'm here to talk to Gordon.'

A look crossed Wanda's face that Bet couldn't decipher. Before Wanda could respond, Bet continued. 'I know he's here.' She didn't think Wanda would argue about it in the face of Bet's certainty.

'Why do you want to speak to him?'

'He witnessed a violent altercation earlier today. I need to ask him a few questions as a witness.'

Wanda's face telegraphed surprise. She had thought Bet arrived at her door with another reason to look for Gordon. Wanda's surprise quickly changed to relief.

'I'll get him.'

Bet hoped she'd gotten back into the woman's good graces. 'Can I come in out of the storm?'

'No.' Wanda closed the door behind her, leaving Bet on the step in the snow. So much for a return to her favor. Bet guessed now was not the time to ask the woman how she thought she was doing in her new role as sheriff elect.

With nothing to do but wait, Bet started to count. She'd reached one hundred and ninety-two when the door opened, and Bet faced a man fitting Kane's description of Gordon, though he stood shadowed by the partially closed door, making it hard to get a clear look.

'Gordon Dupree?'

'Yes, ma'am.' There was that pesky 'ma'am' again. Had she suddenly started looking old?

'I'd like to ask you a few questions about events at the Tavern earlier today.'

'Yes, ma'am.' She fought the urge to tell him to stop with the ma'ams, but at least he hadn't refused to talk to her.

'Care to explain why you left the Tavern so abruptly?'

'I'd finished eating.' His voice was soft, almost as if he had an impediment of some kind.

He wasn't surly, but he clearly wasn't going to make this any easier. Bet heard a muffled cough, as if Wanda stood just out of sight behind the door.

'But first you witnessed the fight.' Bet didn't pose it as a question. People had more trouble lying when things were stated to them as facts.

'I did. But it didn't concern me. Seemed like a good time to leave.' He paused, and Bet waited for him to finish his thought. 'I'm a peaceful man.'

'I'd like to hear your version of events.'

Gordon relaxed. Perhaps he felt on safer ground as a witness, convinced he wasn't in any trouble himself.

'Larry and Skeet got into something, and Skeet got all Richard Roundtree on him and went after him with a broken bottle. I took that as a cue for me to leave.'

'When were you last at the house next door?'

'I . . .'

Bet waited. Gordon struggled. She'd thrown him off guard by changing topics, but she couldn't guess what he'd started to say. Panic appeared in his eyes, and he didn't finish the sentence.

What did that mean?

'I've got fingerprints.' Bet could lie and say they were his. The police didn't have to tell suspects the truth in the course of an investigation, but the truth might be enough to keep him off-kilter. She let her tone indicate they were his without actually saying the words.

'We live next door.' His voice grew louder as some emotion played out.

It wasn't an admission, but Bet could see he was scrambling for a way to explain if she had found his prints inside the house. It was tough to come up with a lie in a high-pressure situation – like talking to a cop – that wouldn't fall apart later when the lie was investigated.

'Whose blood is all over the house?'

Wanda made a noise from behind the door. A quiet word Bet couldn't hear.

'My mother doesn't feel well. I need to take care of her.'

'I'm almost done.'

'She's my priority.' Gordon finally met Bet's eye, though she still couldn't get a good look at his face. 'My only priority.'

Gordon stepped backward and closed the door.

That was interesting. Whatever was going on, Wanda knew something too. Enough to want her son to stop talking to the sheriff.

The sound of Gordon's voice stayed with Bet as she walked back to her SUV. Could the muffled way he spoke come from a fat lip? As if he'd gotten into a fight, which broke his tooth? Something he didn't want the sheriff to see.

THIRTY-THREE

Gordon wasn't under arrest, but she could request he come in to answer questions. It wasn't illegal to refuse to answer questions from the authorities, but if he refused, she could detain him or even arrest him, except, she needed probable cause. She had nothing but her instincts that he was involved in the events next door, and a hunch wasn't good enough. Even if he did have a swollen lip from a fight, she didn't have any proof he had a broken tooth or that it would match the one found at the rental house. And she would definitely need a warrant to look at Gordon's teeth.

But why else would he be so nervous about talking to her? Why else would Wanda telegraph that she had expected different questions than about what happened at the Tavern?

Stay methodical, she reminded herself. She was just gathering evidence. It could be that Wanda had needed his help, and he told Bet the truth. Bet didn't hear Wanda's words. For all Bet knew, she could have said, 'I'm going to faint.'

Gordon could also have other problems, a warrant out on him for another crime or some other kind of legal issues Alma hadn't found yet. There were a variety of reasons why people might not want to speak to law enforcement. Bet hoped it wasn't a race issue, but she couldn't discount his anxiety talking to a White officer of the law.

Bet got back in her SUV and checked in with Alma.

'Still nothing,' Alma said when Bet inquired about Clayton. 'I'm starting to get worried.'

Bet understood her fears. But at least they knew he'd gotten to the hospital in E'burg in time.

'I wish there was something I could do for them.' Alma let out a breath and changed the subject. 'I found an address for Gordon's father. He lives in Federal Way. I've got a search started on Gordon's background, social media, the usual places. What else do you need from me?'

Bet wished sometimes for a whole room of assistants. Alma was only one person. But she was thorough and wouldn't miss anything. It just took time.

'Check him for outstanding warrants in other jurisdictions. Go statewide but also check with Idaho and Montana.' If Gordon lived in Spokane, the other two states were a quick drive from his home. 'Do a background search on Wanda Dupree as well.'

Wanda didn't really present herself as a criminal mastermind, but Bet couldn't let the woman's cancer keep her from seeing Wanda as a potential participant in whatever happened next door.

'How is the paperwork coming on Kane Stand?'

'I've got his application paperwork together. He passed the background check. Did you know he earned a Distinguished Service Cross and a Purple Heart?'

'He was injured?'

'He also has an oak leaf cluster.'

Service members only got one Purple Heart, for their first injury in combat. Subsequent injuries were honored with an oak leaf cluster, so Kane had been injured twice. Bet wondered what kind of injuries he'd sustained. And how those experiences might impact him long-term.

'What do you know about him?'

Alma knew a little bit about everyone.

'Not much. I remember George's sister, but she left a long time ago.'

'Before I was born,' Bet said.

'Yes.'

'She never visits, does she?'

'Not that I've ever heard,' Alma said. 'But George goes out to Atlanta a couple times a year. He always has.'

'I didn't know that.'

Alma chuckled. 'It gives me job security to keep tabs on everyone in Collier.'

George's visits to Atlanta explained how George knew Kane so well. That led Bet to a new thought. 'Why is Kane's last name Stand if his grandmother is George's sister?'

There was little that went on around Collier without Alma knowing about it, even something that happened more than thirty years ago. 'If I recall, George's sister had a son, but she was a single parent, so she and her descendants are still named Stand.'

The information didn't matter for his background search, but Bet was always curious about other people's lives.

'Who takes care of all the Collier properties when George is gone?' Bet considered the logistics. George was the caretaker for a lot of buildings.

'The Colliers have someone come in for the week. George never leaves for longer than that.'

Bet was surprised she'd never known that, but then the role of sheriff didn't make her privy to people's personal lives any more than anyone else was, unless they needed help or broke the law. As a child she wouldn't have noticed George's activities, then she left the valley for several years for college and police training, then as a patrol officer in LA. She wasn't 'friends' with very many people in her community. She might earn their respect, but that wasn't the same thing.

'Keep me posted if you learn anything else.' Bet hung up the phone.

She reached out to Kane to see what he'd learned about Mark Crews.

'Stand,' Kane said when he answered on the second ring.

'Find him?'

'I was just going to call you. I'm behind him right now. He's driving back toward the Train Yard.'

'Where was he coming from?'

'I thought I'd do a run through the valley after we went our separate ways. I went out the opposite direction on the loop and found Mr Crews entering from a turnoff to one of the campgrounds out at the end of the valley.'

Could Mark have been meeting someone out there? Why else would he be at a closed, snow-covered campground?

'Did it look like he was turning around? Or had he visited the campground?'

'I couldn't tell. I thought about looking for evidence about why he was there, but it was clear no one else was parked there, and the entrance was blocked, so I decided to follow him instead.'

'Let's shake him up a little. Make a Terry stop.'

'What criminal activity do I think he's involved in to legitimize a stop and frisk?'

'Mr Crews and his minor son may have been involved in the suspicious death of Grant Marsden. He left the Train Yard knowing we'd be returning to ask additional questions, in bad weather, going away from town. Someone went back and cleared the scene of the accident, which very few people knew about, so we have legitimate suspicions he's involved in an ongoing crime.'

'Sounds good to me. I'll call when I'm done.' Bet heard the siren from Kane's vehicle over the Bluetooth before he disconnected the call.

Bet decided to drive out to the Train Yard, and if she hadn't heard from Kane before she arrived there, she'd continue out and meet up with him at the stop.

It was a strange time to take a drive, after dark in poor conditions, especially without telling his wife and son where he was going and why. The snow had stopped for the moment, but it wouldn't be long before it fell again, potentially covering up any evidence about what Mark was up to out at the campground. But she and Kane were stretched thin enough as it was. How important was it to go over there and check? Would another piece of evidence disappear before she could get there?

THIRTY-FOUR

As Bet reached the Train Yard, her headlights picked up the sight of Jeb's tractor parked askew near the fence like an exotic orange creature cornered in the yard – with the snowplow attachment still on. Something had crashed through the fence not far away. The boards were scattered and broken, white on white against the snow.

Bet slammed her SUV into park, pointing her headlights toward the damaged fence, and leapt out, slipping on the icy surface of the driveway.

Spots of blood tainted the frozen ground a dusky red.

Had someone driven through the fence? Bet couldn't see any tracks from a snowmobile or four-wheel drive. The snow was churned up, but it didn't look like it had been done by any kind of vehicle. With no one staying on the property except Jeb and the Crews, Bet had to wonder if the Crews were responsible. Had Mark spun out when he left, hitting the fence? Except it hadn't been this way when she and Kane noticed Mark was missing. Whoever broke the fence did so after Bet and Kane had left Pearson's Ranch.

The broken boards looked strange. Bet considered the pattern on the ground and realized the damage came from Jeb's property. As if someone had busted through from inside the pasture.

Bet turned around, scanning the land around her. Everything sat quiet. The pause in the storm showed the intense beauty of a Pacific Northwest winter. The unbroken expanse of white across Jeb's pastures and the fields beyond sparkled in the light of the moon, which peeked out momentarily from a break in the clouds.

Her eyes followed the tracks in the snow, and she could see lights on in the barn.

Jeb kept a pathway from the roundhouse to the barn plowed as well. Was he out feeding the animals? Jeb owned half a dozen horses and Dolly the mini donkey for the boys at his camp. The cross between cowboying and equine therapy sometimes made the difference between a successful treatment and a relapse into addiction.

Jeb always said his horses had saved more young men than he had.

But why leave his tractor out here? What broke the fence? Where did the blood come from? It wasn't a lot of blood, but the spots stood out, black against the snow.

Bet got back into the SUV and parked in front of the round-house. She made her way toward the barn. As she got closer, Jeb's cursing sounded loud and clear through the large rolling door propped partway open.

Reaching the entrance, she looked inside with her hand on her weapon, unsure of what she'd find.

'Jeb?' she called out when she couldn't see him in the brightly lit barn.

'That you, Bet?' His voice came from a stall in the back.

'What are you doing out here?'

'It's Cyd.'

Bet felt a bolt of anxiety. Cyd was Jeb's pregnant mare.

Bet edged her way around the open door. The snow had piled up against it, locking it in place. She rushed down the center aisle of the barn.

Arriving at the stall door, she found Jeb kneeling next to Cyd, who lay on the ground chuffing her distress.

'What's going on?'

'She's in labor and the foal is a breech.'

Bet didn't know much about horses, but she knew a breech – a foal coming butt first into the world – was a dangerous situation in the best of circumstances.

'Where's the vet?'

'Not coming.'

Bet didn't need to follow up. The weather and road conditions were keeping a lot of people out of the valley. If there was any way the vet could make it through, she would have. Not to mention she could be at another emergency. Bet pulled out her phone and sent a text to Kane. *Meet me at Jeb's barn when you're done.* She would have to trust Kane to deal with whatever he discovered from the Terry stop with Mark Crews.

She turned back to Jeb. 'What do you need me to do?'

Jeb looked up from the black and white mare and met Bet's eyes.

'This could be ugly.'

Bet took off her bulky outer coat and started to roll up her sleeves.

Cyd had a knack for unlatching stall doors and could even manage a carabineer with enough time, using her nimble lips and teeth. In physical distress, she'd gotten out through the back gate of her paddock, then crossed the pasture and broke through the fence, stumbling in front of Jeb on the tractor. The blood on the snow was from a minor scratch on her flank.

'She knew it was her time and that she needed help, so she came and found me.'

Jeb stroked her where she lay on her bedding, her black neck damp with sweat, while Bet got ready to help. Bet pulled on the elbow-length plastic gloves Jeb provided and nodded she was ready.

'The foal is backwards and starting down the canal. We're going to have to shove the foal back into her uterus and turn it around.'

Bet considered how big a foal was and how long a horse's uterus might be. She took a deep breath. She might be in the middle of multiple investigations but Jeb and Cyd needed her now. If she was going to have Kane on as her deputy, she had to trust him to do his job. She couldn't walk out on Jeb or Cyd.

'I'm ready.'

They got Cyd into a standing position, then it took Jeb twenty minutes to get the foal turned around. Bet spent most of her time at Cyd's head, calming the horse while Jeb worked at her hind-quarters, but she helped enough at the other end to be terrified by what Jeb was doing. The mare seemed to know that the people were trying to help her, and other than one warning kick when Jeb did something especially painful, she stood quiet.

But her eyes glazed over, and Bet could feel her start to tremble before Jeb finished. The horse finally lay down in the clean bedding, too exhausted to stand. Bet stroked the horse's beautiful and unique face. A bright white blaze split her face in half, white on one side, black on the other. A yin and yang running the length of her nose.

'She doesn't look good,' Bet said. 'Why is she so still?'

'She's exhausted,' Jeb said. 'We're going to have to help get this foal out.'

Bet didn't like the sound of that.

The words had no more come out of Jeb's mouth when Kane appeared at the door.

'Everything OK in here?' He walked down the aisle, eyes on Bet. Bet gave him a quick rundown and asked what happened with Mark.

'He said he was out for a drive.'

Bet snorted her laughter. It wasn't the weather or the time for that.

'He did consent to a search,' Kane said. 'I didn't find any weapons, arrows or drugs on him or in the truck. It was a quick search, but I think I would have found anything bigger than a quarter.'

Bet believed that nothing much got past Kane. She looked over at Jeb, who sat on the ground next to Cyd. Jeb caught her eye. 'It's OK, Bet. Cyd and I need another minute to recover and get ready for the birth.'

'What do you want to do next?' she asked Kane.

'I want to go back out to the campground where Mark was coming from and see if there's any evidence of another person there or why he might have visited. I followed Mark back here to the ranch and watched him go inside the cabin. I don't think he's going anywhere.'

'Sounds good.'

'Are you sure you don't need me here?' Kane asked. Bet wondered what he thought about the sheriff taking a pause in her own investigations to help birth a horse, but whatever he was thinking, he kept to himself.

'I'm going to wrap a chain around the foal's front feet.' Jeb stood up ready for the next part of the ordeal. 'Those come out first, then the head, neck and shoulders, followed by the rest. I

can't get enough traction with just my hands. She should start
to push again once I get started.'

'We got this,' Bet said to Kane. 'You keep doing what you're
doing, check in with me when you're done.'

Bet's phone went off before Kane turned to leave. When Alma's
number popped up on the screen, she asked Kane to wait.

'We've got a couple cars piled up downtown. Some out-of-
towner slid into a parked car and his buddy slid into him. I've
got the wrecker coming, but this is going to take a while, and
we need someone to deal with the detour. I can do it—'

'I'll send Kane,' Bet said before Alma marched out into the
storm to direct traffic.

Bet explained the situation to her deputy and told him the
campground would have to wait.

Kane went out the door, and Bet fetched more hot water and
alcohol while Jeb got the chain, which he cleaned as best he could.

'Infection is a serious risk, even if we get this foal out alive.'

Once they had their materials at hand, Jeb got behind Cyd
again, and Bet kneeled next to her head. Cyd looked at Bet with
a soulful eye. The black half of her face rested against the bedding
in the stall. With only the white side visible, her eye stood out
even more, a black jewel in the overhead lights of the barn. She
nickered softly and nuzzled Bet's hand.

'Let's get her up,' Jeb said.

'Come on, old girl,' Bet said into her fuzzy ear. 'We can do this.'

Bet wished for more confidence. Even her father's advice had
never covered this particular situation.

Then things started to move too fast for her to think about her
own shortcomings. Cyd's life depended on her.

THIRTY-FIVE

The foal stumbled, stork-like on his long legs, his dark red
coat, mane and tail still wet from the birth canal. Bet and
Jeb leaned against the stall door and watched the fragile
creature make his way around the stall. A white blaze painted

the right side of his face, just like his mother's. It started at his forelock and ended at his chin.

'I can't believe he's already up and walking.' Bet marveled at the tiny horse in front of her.

'Horses are born to run away from trouble.'

'I guess that comes in handy when wolves are on the prowl.'

Jeb nodded, too tired to reply. The labor had taken its toll on the man. The foal had been a challenge to move around inside the mare. Jeb and Cyd were both exhausted from their physical exertions. Bet had only experienced the last hour of her labor. Jeb and Cyd had been at it for more than four before she arrived.

'You look like you might drop where you stand.' Bet patted her friend on the back. 'Do you think it's safe to leave them alone?'

The foal started to suckle at his mother. 'Yep. Cyd and Sire will be just fine.'

'Sire?'

'I learned most everything I know about horses from my grandmother. She had a gelding with that name, years ago. First horse I ever rode.'

'Did she have him a long time?'

'Over thirty years.' Jeb straightened up, leaned back to stretch the crick in his back, and headed out of the barn. 'I'll check on them again in an hour or so. I don't think I could have done that without your help, Rivers.'

Bet watched the mother and baby. 'I'm still so amazed Cyd knew she needed your help and how to get it.'

Jeb laughed. 'The maternal instinct is the strongest compulsion on earth.'

Bet's thoughts turned to Wanda Dupree and her belief that Gordon had gotten Wanda into trouble.

Maybe Bet had read the entire situation wrong.

The lights in the barn flickered, and the sound of Jeb's generator kicked on.

'Power's out again,' Jeb said. 'Storm must have geared back up.'

Bet got on the phone to Alma only to learn the power was out all over town.

Maybe the outage would give her a legit excuse to go visit Wanda Dupree again. She'd told the woman she was planning to check on her throughout the storm. Just because her son was with her didn't mean Bet had relinquished her duty to protect a citizen of Collier.

It was her role – no, her mission – to keep everyone safe.

She also had the photos of Doug and Ruby to show her. Maybe Wanda's maternal instinct would make her more willing to help Bet find a missing child.

THIRTY-SIX

J ust as she had before, Bet parked next door at the rental house and walked over to Wanda's. As she got closer, she couldn't hear the generator running in the backyard. The storm had kicked back up again, but not loud enough to drown out that sound.

It was possible Wanda was already asleep and didn't know the power was out, but what about Gordon? Didn't he notice the generator hadn't kicked on when it should have? She found it hard to believe he was asleep. It wasn't much past nine o'clock.

Bet went up the icy steps and knocked on the door. No one answered. She got out her flashlight and began a walk around the house. She peeked through the windows, but found shades drawn on many of them, giving her little access to check out the interior. Arriving at the back door, Bet leaned her ear against the glass. She didn't expect to hear anything, but she wasn't sure what else to do.

A faint metallic clanging sound tapped its way through the house. Bet held her breath and waited, unsure if her imagination played tricks on her or there was a reasonable explanation.

It came again, a steady clang, clang, clang. Three beats, then silence. A moment later it happened again, only faster.

It was too repetitive to be caused by the wind getting in some-where. But what could make that noise? It sounded like an SOS.

Bet went back to the front door again and knocked louder. She couldn't hear the doorbell buzz when she leaned on it. It must not have a backup battery for when the power went out.

Was Wanda signaling for help? Could she have gotten stuck somehow? Fallen and become too weakened to stand?

Exigent circumstances meant a law enforcement officer could enter a building without a warrant if they believed someone's life was in danger.

Not wanting to break down a door, Bet went back around the side of the house, checking for an unlocked window. She stepped in her own tracks, making the path a little easier the second time around. Home security was haphazard in the valley; people tended to either overdo it, barricading their homes as if to ward off the zombie apocalypse, or forget to lock their doors at night. Bet hoped Wanda fell in the latter category.

A window in the back of the house yielded under her touch. She'd found a way to get in.

But should she take it?

Leaning against the glass, she could hear the sound again. Clang . . . clang . . . clang. Quieter, as if whoever made it was getting weaker.

The thought Wanda could be in trouble propelled Bet into action. She pushed the window open and pulled herself through, landing in a heap on the kitchen floor.

Shining her flashlight around, Bet wished for Schweitzer's company, but the big dog was back at the station. Kane's calm face rose in her mind. She might not know him yet, but she felt she could trust him. She could call him in for backup, except he was still dealing with the traffic accident, and she didn't want anyone getting hurt there either. At least Alma knew where she was.

Now that she was in the house, it had that empty feeling, like no one was home. At least no one alive.

And the clanging had stopped.

She closed the window, conscious that her footsteps went only halfway around the house. If Gordon and Wanda had left together and came home now, Bet hoped the darkness would keep them from noticing someone had walked halfway around. But where would Wanda go in this weather? And who made the noise that had brought her into the house in the first place?

Gordon had said his mother needed his help. Perhaps that had been true, and she'd had a medical emergency that sent them out of the valley.

Clang . . . clang . . . clang.

Like someone banging on a pipe.

Bet shined her flashlight around, trying to identify which direction the sound came from.

Under her feet.

The basement.

Bet struggled to keep her breath steady and her heart pounded in her ears. Playing her light around the kitchen, she soon found another door. It looked too sturdy to be a pantry door and it had a deadbolt thrown. If anyone was down there, they were locked in.

The deadbolt twisted easily, and the door swung open without a sound. A steep flight of stairs disappeared into the dark. Easing the door closed behind her, she hoped no one in the house showed up and locked her in.

Step by careful step, she edged her way into the basement. With each step, she stopped and held her breath, ears straining to discern if someone waited for her in the dark.

The banging came again, a rhythmic reverberation, like someone calling for help. Bet hoped it was that, and not someone luring her downstairs to do her harm.

Reaching the bottom, the sound repeated, softer this time, but faster, as if someone saw her light and wanted her attention.

Bet swung her light around the space. A cot lay upended on the concrete floor, with a blanket strewn out behind it as if someone had dragged it after flipping over. Movement started back up and the noise came again.

Bet scanned the rest of the space before rushing over to the cot. The last thing she wanted was to turn her back on the pitch-black room only to discover she wasn't alone and whatever was going on was a subterfuge to keep her off-guard to an attack. Seeing no other signs of life, she made her way to the cot and found an arm stretched out from beneath it, a wrench grasped in a pale white fist. The hand reached out to tap against the hot water heater in the corner of the room.

That explained what she'd heard. She knelt next to the prone figure and carefully peered underneath the cot.

Doug Marsden's face looked out at her. Deathly pale, a bead of sweat across his forehead. A smudge of blood on his cheek.

Tape across his mouth kept him from words, but his eyes spoke volumes.

Help me, they called out, as loud as if he yelled at her. Bet set the flashlight down on the floor, the glow giving her just enough light to see by.

Using all her strength, she wrestled the cot upright. Doug was duct-taped down, one arm and both legs pinned to his sides. She couldn't imagine the strength it had taken to turn himself over and drag his body weight and the cot with just one hand and his toes across the room. Taking in the tangle of tubes and an over-turned metal stand, she realized one arm was free because he was hooked up to an IV. Someone had tended to him, even if he was locked up down here. Or was he getting fed a steady stream of drugs to keep him unconscious? A drip could have run out and he'd regained consciousness long enough to signal for help.

She tore the tape off his face, apologizing for the sting. 'How badly are you hurt?'

Silence.

The floor where Doug had been lying was slick and red with blood.

Bet got out her Leatherman from its case on her utility belt and opened up the knife. She carefully cut away at the tape holding Doug on the cot. He had yet to utter a word since she'd turned him over, his forehead burning to the touch. He appeared barely conscious. She thought again of how much strength it had taken to get over to the hot water heater. How long had the man been banging on the metal case of the tank?

And where was Ruby? Did the Duprees have her somewhere else in the house?

Once she'd freed Doug from the restraints, she was able to assess the rest of him. She found a large bandage on his abdomen and chest. Blood had seeped through the bandages, and an odor wafting from the gauze made her gag. Afraid she would make his situation worse, she left the bandages in place and considered her next move.

She couldn't get him out of the basement by herself.

Her first thought was calling Addie to bring over the ambulance, but she had to secure the scene. She couldn't bring Addie in until she knew the location was safe.

Kane. It had to be Kane. Bet needed someone strong enough to help her get Doug out of the basement, then Addie could meet them as soon as possible.

Bet pulled out her phone but couldn't get any bars. The concrete walls of the basement no doubt blocked her signal. She wasn't even sure Doug heard her as she said she'd be right back and sprinted up the stairs for better reception. She reached the top of the stairs and had just gone into the kitchen when she heard the front door open and the sound of voices.

Gordon and Wanda were home.

THIRTY-SEVEN

Trapped in the kitchen, Bet considered the best choice for her next move. She could slip out the back door, then go around to the front and ask to come in, but what would she do if they said no? She could also admit her presence in the house. She could still argue exigent circumstances – that she'd entered concerned about Wanda and then discovered Doug.

She also needed to contact Kane. She could send him a text, but what did she want him to do? Show up as a diversion? Arrive with lights and siren blazing? Approach with stealth?

Heart still pounding, Bet waited to learn what the Duprees' intentions were.

'You know this isn't what I planned.' Gordon's voice was tense, as if they were mid-argument. Bet strained to hear Wanda's response.

'It doesn't matter what you planned. I have a dying man down in my basement. What are we going to do about that?'

'He's not going to die. You took excellent care of him.'

'He has a serious infection. That man needs more antibiotics. You can't steal meds off that ambulance again. We have to get him to a hospital.'

That explained the break-in on Addie's bus.

'It's not my fault the road out has been blocked.'

Wanda made a noise of frustration and Bet heard a loud slam, as if Wanda had thrown something against the wall.

'You sound like your father. Nothing was ever his fault either. You didn't bring the storm or block the roads, but you still did this. You. All by yourself. We wouldn't be in this mess if you hadn't thought you could be some kinda tough guy selling poison for—'

'I did this for you.'

'Don't kid yourself. You did this for *you*. My cancer was just a convenient problem you could blame all this on.'

'I'm trying to help you keep this house.'

'At what cost? You have us driving out to some campground where your "guy" was supposed to leave that crap you're going to sell, and we found *nothing*. Just another dead end and a waste of my time. I can't believe I went out there with you.'

'You wanted to go.'

'I wanted to see you weren't lying to me and that this really was almost over. Look how that turned out.'

Campground. Guy. Was Mark supposed to leave something for Gordon? Why go there if he didn't do as he promised and leave what Gordon expected?

Bet heard a rustling sound.

'What are you going to do?' Gordon's voice had quieted, and if Bet had to guess, he'd been shamed.

'I'm going to hang up my coat and go down and check on that man. Then, depending on what I find, I'm either going to call 9-1-1 or get a shovel and bury his corpse in the ground.'

Bet started to edge back behind the kitchen island, knowing Wanda would be coming her way, when Gordon's voice stopped her.

'What if I can get him out of here and leave him in E'burg? You know, anonymously, at the hospital?'

'He could die just by you driving him down there. Plus, how do I know you aren't going to ditch him in the woods somewhere, and lie to me about it? I'd have to go with you.'

'Is that really what you think of me?' Gordon's voice had taken on a new tone. 'Your own son?'

'What else should I think? Look what you did to that man. Over what? Money? I didn't ask you to take care of me. I didn't ask you to fix my medical bills. I was doing just fine without you.'

'No, Mom. You weren't. Where are you going to go if you lose this house? And we both know your care was compromised in the first place because your insurance sucks.'

Bet held her breath, waiting to hear what Wanda would say.

'I would rather die alone in this house than know someone else died because of me. I spent my entire career saving lives. How could you possibly think I want this to be how I end mine?'

'Exactly! You were a nurse, and you still couldn't get decent healthcare. How is that fair?'

Wanda made a noise of disgust. 'This isn't about fair. This is about that man in the basement. It was one thing when the valley was blocked off and we couldn't get him out anyway, but I never thought that infection would get so bad so fast. But the road is open now, and we have options. If he isn't already dead, he needs to be transported in an ambulance, not the back seat of your car.'

Bet considered what to do. She had to assume Gordon was armed, and she didn't want to risk any kind of gunfight with Wanda in the middle. But she had to get Doug out of the house.

'Two strikes or not, we can't let that man die.'

Two strikes? Alma hadn't found a record for Gordon Dupree. Had she missed something?

'Now go outside and see if you can figure out why the damn generator didn't kick on.'

Wanda's willingness to shield her son from a third strike apparently ended with Doug's worsening condition.

Making a choice, Bet slipped back downstairs and waited. Her plan might work as long as Wanda came downstairs alone. She hoped the woman didn't think too much of the unlocked deadbolt in the kitchen, and that Gordon's trip to the generator wasn't on the side of the house where Bet had left footprints.

Either of those would give her presence away and blow up her chances for a successful outcome.

THIRTY-EIGHT

B et tucked herself behind the steps leading into the basement. She looked over at Doug's motionless form and hoped he was still alive. It didn't look like he had moved at all since she left him to go upstairs.

Bet didn't have to wait long before she heard the door open at the top of the stairs. The beam of a flashlight lit up the steps in front of her eyes and a pair of legs appeared. She could hear Wanda crying as she descended into the basement.

At least she'd arrived alone and didn't appear suspicious of the deadbolt left undone. She probably didn't always use it and was upset enough about Gordon that she didn't think about it twice. There wouldn't be any need to lock it most of the time with no exit or entrance to the outside from the basement.

Wanda slowly made her way over to the cot. Bet wondered at her physical condition. The stress of this couldn't be good for her weakened state, and she'd been out on a drive in the cold. It sounded like Gordon caused the situation, even if Wanda had helped after Doug was injured. Bet wondered at what point the woman knew what her son was up to and whether she knew anything about Ruby.

'I'm just going to check on your bandages.' Wanda slid Doug's blanket back. 'What—'

Wanda had discovered the tape that bound Doug to the cot had been cut free. Bet knew she must time her actions perfectly. She needed Wanda to stay quiet so Gordon wouldn't hear them if he came back inside before they were done.

'We need to get him to a hospital.'

Wanda spun around at the sound of Bet's voice.

'How did you get in my house?' Anger and fear warred in Wanda's voice. Her body tensed as she took on a fighting stance. Was a cancer victim really going to launch a physical attack against her? Bet braced herself, not wanting to injure the woman.

'I don't think that's really the most important issue here, do you?'

Bet held her breath. Wanda could go either way; help Bet or scream for Gordon.

Wanda's form sagged.

'He's my son.' Wanda turned back to look down at Doug. 'It's my job to protect him.'

'And it's my job to protect all of you. Help me keep you safe, too.'

'What do you want from me?'

Bet explained to Wanda that she just wanted to get Doug to

the hospital. She told Wanda that Doug had children and they needed their father back. The plea for his children might help. Wanda's confused expression at the mention of Doug's kids probably meant they didn't have Ruby stashed somewhere in the house or that the little girl had already died by their hands. She honestly didn't know that Doug had kids.

'Is your son armed?'

Wanda looked at Bet with such sorrow in her eyes, Bet felt it in her own heart.

'I think so.'

'OK. We need to get you and Doug out of the house without Gordon interfering.'

A fleeting expression crossed Wanda's face – so fast that Bet couldn't read it.

'My son would never hurt me.'

Maybe that micro expression had been anger at Bet for hinting that he would.

'I know he wouldn't hurt you on purpose, but if Gordon tries to stop us, you could get hurt by accident.'

'By accident? Or because you might shoot me trying to get at him?' Bet wasn't sure how to respond to that. Sometimes civilians did get in the way of an arrest, and sometimes suspects got shot. It wasn't something Bet wanted to do, but if Gordon was also armed, it was a real possibility.

Wanda looked back down at Doug. 'I patched him up, you know.'

'I know. You did a good job, too, but we both know he's not going to survive much longer down here in your basement.'

Wanda nodded, though she'd started to look dazed. Bet worried that Wanda's condition could worsen as well. Then she'd have two dying people to get out of the house.

'We have a couple options.' Bet thought through the best scenario for everyone's sake. Now that she knew Gordon was responsible for Doug's situation, she could always go after him later. He was unlikely to get very far. Maybe the best thing to do was get Gordon out of the way.

'What do you want to do?'

Bet outlined a simple plan. She would hide in the kitchen while Wanda asked Gordon to run an errand for her. As soon as he left, Bet would contact Addie and have her bring the ambulance over. They would get Doug out of the basement and down to the hospital in E'burg. 'This is going to be so much worse for Gordon if Doug dies.'

'I know. And I . . . I can't let this man die,' Wanda agreed. 'All right, I'll do it. I'll ask him to run to the store for eggs. It's the food I keep down the best.' Bet started to follow her up the stairs when she heard a commotion from the other side of the room.

Bet rushed over to the cot to find Doug having a seizure. She did her best to hold him still so he didn't hurt himself thrashing around. A moment later, as his convulsions stopped, she looked behind her, alarmed that Wanda hadn't come over to help.

Wanda was gone.

Bet went up the steps to the door to the kitchen. She turned the knob, but the door was locked.

Wanda had thrown the deadbolt.

Bet pounded on the door, calling out to Wanda to let her out.

Wanda's voice came back from the other side. 'I'll let you out, Sheriff. I will. I promise. We'll get that man to the hospital. But not before my son has time to leave the valley.'

'You were going to call 9-1-1 yourself, Wanda. The only thing different is that now you're guilty of kidnapping an officer of the law.'

There was a pause on the other side of the door. Bet guessed that Wanda didn't know she'd overheard that part of the conversation.

'This makes you an accomplice to whatever happens to Doug, Wanda.'

Wanda laughed, a deep belly laugh that ended in her gasping for breath.

'What do you think you can do to me? I'm dying, Sheriff. Are you going to throw me in jail? So what?'

'But what about Doug? And his children?'

'Gordon is my child. I'm why that man is in the basement, not Gordon. I will turn myself in. And there's not a damn thing you can do to prove otherwise. My call to 9-1-1 was never going to be about my son.'

Bet found the light switch on the wall, and clicked it off and on a couple times, but the electricity was still out. Gordon hadn't

gotten the generator restarted. She went back down and checked
on Doug, who was still breathing, though his pulse was thready
and his respiration was fast and shallow. His fever raged. She
had to get him out before he had another convulsion that killed
him. Now. She couldn't wait however long Wanda thought Gordon
needed to get away.

Shining her flashlight around, she methodically checked the
basement for something she could use on the door. The wrench
Doug used to bang on the water heater was no use.

She'd almost given up when she saw a toolbox underneath a
bench along one wall. It was shoved behind a box of old rags.
Bet would have missed it, but the silver handle on top glinted in
the beam of her flashlight. Bet dug the toolbox out and dumped
everything out on to the floor. She found screwdrivers, which
might help her get the doorknob off, but that wouldn't help. The
deadbolt on the other side would keep the door in place.

But she also found a hammer.

Picking up the biggest Phillips screwdriver she could find, she
went back up the stairs and, clutching the flashlight in her teeth,
began to pound the pins out of the hinges.

It took her a few minutes on each of the three hinges, but she
finally pounded the last pin out of the top hinge. Using the claw
of the hammer, she wedged it inside the frame and pulled the
door loose. It swung sideways and pulled the deadbolt open with
a screech of splintering wood. She grabbed the door and set it
aside before it crushed her. She stepped into the kitchen, intending
to call Kane and have him escort Addie and her ambulance to
the house.

Wanda leaned against the counter, waiting.

Bet stared at Wanda's hand. 'I guess your son isn't the only
one who owns a gun.' The woman's aim was remarkably steady
given the situation.

'And I know how to use it. I'm not coming back from this
cancer, Sheriff. All I have left to do in this life is protect my son.
You are the only one who knows Gordon was involved.'

Bet wasn't sure whether to be impressed or scared. She also
realized it was the first time she'd ever stared someone down
who had nothing left to lose.

THIRTY-NINE

Shooting another person was harder than most people think. Even individuals without a conscience had a hard time pulling the trigger. Bet knew that Wanda was by nature dedicated to saving lives, not ending them.

Bet stepped farther into the room.

'I'm going to need help getting Doug out of the basement. If you put the gun down on the counter, I'll call my deputy. We'll get Addie to drive him to E'burg.'

'If I put this gun down, you're going after Gordon. I want him to have time—'

'Time to what? Get away? That's what you want for him? A lifetime of looking over his shoulder? Unable to visit you as you succumb to your cancer? That's not saving him. Besides, I'm too shorthanded to go after Gordon. It will take all my resources just to get Doug safely out of the valley.'

Wanda looked troubled. She hadn't had time to think through her actions and was working on pure instinct. Maternal instinct. Just like Jeb said, the strongest force in the world.

Bet tried again. 'Look, if he gives himself up and comes in quietly, I can protect him. Doug isn't dead. It's not murder yet. If this turns into a manhunt outside our valley for a murder suspect, Gordon could get killed.'

'I can't think.' Wanda closed her eyes, but opened them again immediately, her gun hand never wavering.

'Did Doug punch Gordon during a fight? Is that how he broke his tooth?'

Wanda's face showed her shock. 'How do you know about that?'

Bet let Wanda consider the fact that law enforcement might have more evidence against her son than just Doug in her basement. Proof that would put him behind bars no matter what she claimed she had done by herself, or whether Bet was alive to tell anyone what she knew.

'Do you know where Ruby is?'

Wanda's eyes dodged away. 'Who are you talking about?'

'Doug has a little girl. Ruby. He told you about her, didn't he?'

'No. I never spoke to him. Gordon . . . I kept his mouth taped.' Wanda's face creased in concern. 'How old is his little girl?'

'She's ten. And she's been missing for days. If you don't have her, then she's been missing since before you grabbed Doug. That means a little girl is lost in this storm.'

Wanda moaned, low in her chest. A sound of utter grief. 'I don't know how this happened.'

Bet knew. It was how a lot of bad things happened. One choice leading to another. What felt like the best move turned out to be the worst until a person couldn't see their way clear of the disaster falling on top of them. People always thought they had only one option if they felt backed into a corner. They rarely noticed there was no 'corner' behind them. There were multiple choices available, they just hadn't thought of them yet.

Wanda set the gun on the counter, but Bet wasn't taking any chances.

'Please step away from the weapon.'

Wanda moved back until she hit the edge of the sink behind her. Then she began to cry.

Bet reached out and grabbed Wanda's gun. She released the magazine and racked the slide to eject the round in the chamber. After tucking the gun into the back of her duty belt, she pulled out her phone and put a call in to Kane. Once she knew he was on the way, she called Addie. She explained the situation in the barest of terms, eyes on Wanda the entire time.

'But we've got a problem about getting someone to E'burg,' Addie said. 'The power is out because more trees fell. Looks like heavy rains earlier this winter made the hillsides along the road unstable.'

'OK.' Bet didn't want Wanda to hear the road to the hospital was blocked, along with Gordon's only way out of the valley. She wanted this to go one step at a time. Get Doug out of the basement and into Addie's care, then deal with Gordon.

Addie reported she was on her way.

Ending the call, Bet stood a moment watching the dying woman. Wanda had aged since Bet had first met her.

'What are you going to do with me?' Wanda asked.

'Right now, I'm going to read you your rights and secure you in my SUV. I'll let the engine run so you don't get cold, but I can't risk you interfering again. You've proven yourself untrustworthy.'

Wanda didn't put up a fight as Bet stopped at the front door and patted her down, then made her put her heavy winter coat back on. Then she led her out the door and down the plowed road to the rental house where she could put Wanda into her SUV. Once in the back seat, she was contained between metal screens and back doors that couldn't be opened from inside. Bet hopped in the driver's seat and started the engine, cranking up the heat. She drove the vehicle over to Wanda's driveway and made sure her prisoner was comfortable. Gordon must have shoveled the driveway, because it was clear of snow. If Bet had asked the woman who did it for her, maybe she would have known about Gordon sooner.

'I won't be long,' Bet said.

She called Alma to update her on the situation and asked her to do a search for Gordon using his father's last name. Maybe that was how his criminal record didn't pop. Kane arrived, lights and siren rising over the sound of the storm, which had come back with a vengeance while Bet was stuck in the basement. She wondered how far Gordon had gotten.

Wherever he was, he hadn't left the valley. The blocked road would keep her suspect in, but it also meant they couldn't get the ambulance out. Alma was running Gordon's car info to get make, model and license. They could track the man down later; saving Doug's life was more important. In this day and age, people rarely hid from law enforcement for long. Between tracking his vehicle, credit cards and digital trails, Gordon couldn't stay out of sight forever.

Bet explained to Kane that Gordon had left. 'I don't think he'll come back here, but we need to protect Addie while we get Doug out.'

Addie arrived a few moments later, and the three of them went back down into the basement. Bet and Kane carried the backboard, while Addie brought up the rear, hauling her trauma bag. With the electricity still out, Bet and Kane held flashlights and Addie had a light clipped to her hat. They carefully made their way down the stairs.

Bet and Kane set the backboard down while Addie rushed over to Doug's side. She pulled on gloves and Bet moved over to provide additional light as Addie took his vitals. Bet sent Kane up to keep an eye on Wanda and watch for Gordon. Though she doubted Gordon would return with the flashing lights of the emergency vehicles filling the driveway.

Addie put her fingers on Doug's wrist, then his neck.

'Are you getting a pulse?' Bet asked. Addie shook her head and bent over, putting her ear next to his mouth.

'I'm not getting anything.'

'He was still alive when I came downstairs. That was less than half an hour ago, but he also had a terrible seizure.'

'Help me get him on to the spinal board.' Addie moved to Doug's head, grasping the man by his armpits while Bet went to his feet. Together, they got Doug secured in place.

Addie straddled Doug and began chest compressions. 'If he stopped breathing in the last five minutes, we might be able to bring him back.' She gave Bet instructions to get a defibrillator out of her trauma bag. Once Bet had it out and set up next to Doug, Addie stopped compressions and reached once more for a pulse.

Finding none, she shocked Doug, his body jerking against the backboard.

Addie reached for his neck again but shook her head. 'Come on, damnit,' she said. For the next thirty minutes, she administered drugs, inserted an airway, and attached an ampoule bag – which Bet squeezed on command – and administered CPR.

Nothing.

'I'm sorry, Bet,' Addie said after she failed to get a positive result. 'He's been down too long. There's nothing more we can do.'

Bet thought of Bodhi, waiting to hear from her about his father and little sister. She wished she had better news. At some point, she'd have to tell him his father was dead, and his sister remained missing.

'We'll need to get him to the morgue.' Bet pictured Grant Marsden, still out in Jeb's walk-in. 'Are you up for doing a run with both bodies?'

Addie would take them both down to E'burg as soon as the

road cleared. 'I've got chains on,' she reminded Bet. 'I'll be OK once the trees are removed.'

Bet's thoughts turned to Gordon as she and Addie carried Doug up to the ambulance. Kane came over to assist as the two women reached the front room.

As Bet walked past the SUV carrying her end of the stretcher, she caught Wanda's eye. The woman looked at Doug's covered form and let out a wail that Bet could hear even over the strength of the rising storm.

Wanda couldn't help her son now.

FORTY

Addie gave Bet the two-day supply of drugs to take as a preventative from exposure to Larry's blood. She promised to hand his sample over to the lab tech for testing. Then she headed out to Jeb's ranch to pick up Grant's body while Bet checked in with Alma. The road would be open soon.

Kane could man a roadblock to stop Gordon from trying to leave, but that would mean she was on her own to track Gordon down. She thought back over all the evidence that led her to him. His appearance in Collier. The broken tooth, which she had no doubt would fit a matching hole in Gordon's mouth, and easy access to the rental house. What could help her find him?

The bar fight. He was there with Skeet and Larry, and Skeet was still locked up in her jail cell.

'Meet me at the station,' Bet said to Kane. 'We don't have a lot of time before the road down to the highway opens up again.'

Kane hopped into the other SUV and pulled out in front of her. Bet got into her own vehicle and eyed Wanda in the back seat. 'Do you need any medications that I should get before we leave your house?'

'I'll be fine.'

Bet thought that might not be true, but there wasn't much she could do if Wanda wouldn't help herself. She followed Kane.

After a few minutes of driving in silence Bet asked, 'Are you doing all right back there?' She thought at first that Wanda wouldn't answer.

'That man died, didn't he?'

'That man's name was Doug.'

As a nurse, Wanda wasn't squeamish, but it was clear that Doug's death had impacted her. Either because of the unnecessary nature of it, or because her own son was now in a lot more trouble. Not to mention her own role in the situation.

Wanda remained tight-lipped the rest of the drive.

Bet parked in front to find a welcome sight. Clayton's Trooper sat in its regular spot on the side of the station house. She went to the back door of her SUV and helped Wanda from the vehicle. Kane joined her to help Wanda cross the icy ground and manage the front steps. Bet wondered how he felt about her locking up a woman who was so clearly ill. Bet didn't feel great about it either, but she could hardly leave the woman at the crime scene, especially with Gordon at large. It wasn't Bet's decision what to do with Wanda. The district attorney would make the choice about how to charge her and a judge would determine if she could remain at home.

As they walked in through the front door, Bet asked Kane to settle Wanda in a cell in the back. She was glad she'd given him the nickel tour earlier, so he knew where everything was. As soon as Kane and his prisoner disappeared behind the locking door to the cells, Bet turned to Clayton.

'Am I glad to see you,' she said. 'But I thought the road was still closed.'

'Good to see you, too,' said the new father. 'The road isn't officially open, but the Stenleys helped me get through. Sorry you were so much on your own.'

Clayton always thought of others before himself. Bet wanted to ask about his family but decided to reassure him first. 'That's all right, it looks like we have a new part-time deputy. Nice to have a little backup for both of us.'

'Alma filled me in,' Clayton said with a genuine smile on his face. 'Great to have another deputy on board.'

Bet took Clayton at his word. He wouldn't deceive Bet. He could be cagey talking to a suspect if he needed to, but he was hopelessly honest in the rest of his life. If he were unhappy about the situation, he'd tell her about it, backing up his observations with well-thought-out concerns. 'Everything OK at home?'

'Things were a little harder than we anticipated, but Kathy is doing great.' Clayton held out his phone. 'Meet Rose Marie.'

Bet looked down, expecting a misshapen head or some other oddity of a newborn, but found instead a photo that could have appeared on a Gerber ad. She should have known an All-American farm boy like Clayton and his wife, equally gorgeous, would produce the perfect child.

'That's the cutest baby I've ever seen.'

Clayton laughed as he tucked his phone back into his pocket. 'And you didn't even have to lie about it.'

Bet pulled Clayton to her and hugged him hard. She felt tears come to her eyes, an unexpected emotion.

'I'm just so glad everyone is OK.' Her voice was fierce, but she didn't care. Maybe it was OK to tell people how she felt once in a while.

She released Clayton as Kane came through the door from the cells. His glance was inquisitive at her show of emotion. Did it matter? Why did she second-guess everything Kane might wonder about her? He worked for her, not the other way around.

But he was a combat vet like her father, and that made her feel like she wouldn't measure up. The thought hit her like an unexpected wave.

'Suck it up, princess,' she could hear Maggie say. There was a time and place for self-reflection and now wasn't it.

'Clayton, Kane. Kane, Clayton.' It would have to do for introductions as there was no time for anything more formal. The two men traded a quick handshake and sized each other up. Kane tipped his head toward Clayton, his body language showing he would defer to the senior man, even if he was younger.

So far, so good.

'What are we going to do with Wanda Dupree?' Alma asked.

Bet returned to business. 'I'll get to that. When did the Stenleys say the road would be open to regular traffic?'

'About an hour,' Clayton said.

'Good. That gives us time.' Bet caught everyone up on the events that landed Wanda at the station and Gordon under suspicion. 'Addie is going over to Jeb's to load up Grant. Once the road clears, she'll get both Doug and Grant down to Carolyn at the morgue. Our job is to locate Gordon before he leaves the valley and ends up in the wind. Gordon may be the only person left alive who knows where Ruby is, so I really want to track him down. She is officially a missing person.'

The other three watched her expectantly. If only she had a crystal ball to locate Ruby and Gordon.

'Kane, you're going to set up a roadblock just past the turnoff to George's house. Stop anyone coming in or out. It's possible Gordon contacted someone outside the valley to come and get him. Check IDs and license plates of anyone coming in. I don't know that anyone will try to drive into the valley, but at least that will give us information if we need to follow up. Gordon won't automatically assume there's a manhunt going on. He may think I'm still locked in the basement if his mother gave him any information while I was helping Doug.'

Kane nodded his understanding.

'Then, no one goes out of the valley without a vehicle search. Gordon could try to sneak out in someone else's car. Clayton will help you load up our temporary barriers in the SUV. We have a couple behind the station. We are going to make it look like we have the road down to only one lane because of road conditions. Anyone coming in from the highway below will know both lanes are open, but the ruse might work if Gordon is only checking from this end.'

'What are you going to do?' Clayton asked.

'While you're helping Kane, I'm going to go wake up Skeet and ask him a few questions. He's friends with Gordon. Maybe he knows where he's hiding or something about the situation with Ruby. You and I will go check out anything he reports. We can also follow up with Larry. He was at the table having break-fast with Gordon before the bar fight. He must know something about the man.'

Clayton looked puzzled and Bet realized he didn't know anything about the bar fight. 'I'll catch you up later.'

Clayton and Kane headed out the door to get the barricades loaded into Kane's SUV, and Alma sat back down at her desk.

'What about me, boss?'

Bet chuckled at the endearment. They both knew Alma didn't

really think of Bet as 'the boss' any more than she had the other two sheriffs she'd worked with. She considered herself in more of a parallel position.

'I want you to get searching for more about Gordon. I know you checked out of state for warrants, but let's see if he owns any houses or property where he might go. Then check out his father. If Gordon does get out of the valley, his father might know where he is. I don't want to wait until he's already escaped to start figuring out where he could hole up. I want that information ready if we need it. I can send Federal Way PD out to visit his father if Gordon gets out of the valley.'

'On it.' Alma turned to her computer.

Another text from Bodhi popped up on her phone. *Any news?*

She couldn't dodge his questions for long. 'And at some point, I have to go tell Bodhi his father is dead and his sister is still missing.'

Alma looked at the phone in Bet's hand. She didn't have to ask who sent her a text.

'I can go with you.'

'That would be very helpful. Hopefully we'll have a line on Ruby soon, so I can give him some good news.'

Alma went back to her computer. Bet texted Bodhi that she was following a lead and hoped to have more information soon.

Then she punched the code into the door leading to the cells. Skeet must have sobered up by now and despite the time closing in on midnight, he probably woke up when Kane brought Wanda in. If Bet promised to help him with his current situation, maybe he would give up his friend for the 'greater good'.

'Before you go back to talk to Skeet,' Alma said, without looking up from her screen. 'There's fresh coffee and a sandwich in the break room.'

'OK.'

'I mean it. I used to have to make your father stop to eat too. Don't think I can't.'

'Yes, ma'am,' Bet said, amused at Alma's mothering.

But it wouldn't hurt to be fortified either. There was still a lot to do.

FORTY-ONE

The sheriff station had four cells. One held the bloody sleeping bag, which Bet needed to take down and seal up if it was dry. In the cell next door, Skeet lay on the cot, humming to himself. Across from him, Kane had put Wanda in the first cell, so she couldn't see Skeet and he couldn't see her. They didn't appear to be communicating.

Wanda sat with her back against the wall, eyes closed. No matter what she'd done, her cancer treatment and her claim that she was dying worried Bet. Donna should come over first thing in the morning and check on her.

At least the sheriff station was warm and dry with working electricity. The generator had not yet given up the ghost, and Wanda wasn't going to be exposed to anyone with a cold or flu. Other than her own house, it was probably the safest place she could be.

Bet saw Wanda twitch, reacting to the sound of her footsteps. The woman only feigned sleep. Bet paused at the cell door. 'Can I get you anything?'

Skeet stopped humming and Bet heard him moving around in his cell. 'What about me?' he called out. 'What if I want something?'

'Be with you in a minute.' Bet looked down the aisle at her other prisoner. Skeet stood with his fingers wrapped around the bars of his cell. His fingers tightened and his knuckles turned white, his anger just under the surface. Clearly sobering up hadn't helped his mood.

'I need to know that you aren't having any physical issues.'

Wanda opened her eyes. Her expression was puzzled.

'You're worried about me?'

'It's my job, ma'am.'

'I pointed a gun at you. I locked you up in the basement and—'

'Whoa, wait, what?' Skeet's voice sounded incredulous. 'You did what? That's—'

'Skeet.' Bet cut off what was no doubt going to be a compliment. 'Sit. Down.'

She heard the cot creak under his weight and turned her attention back to Wanda.

'Your well-being is my responsibility as long as you're in my custody.'

Wanda laughed. 'Once I'm in prison, the state has to pay for my health care, doesn't it?' Wanda closed her eyes again. 'I guess my son got what he wanted after all.'

That was ironic.

'We don't know yet what kind of trouble you're in.'

Wanda didn't respond.

'You never heard a snowmobile over at the rental house, did you?'

Wanda shook her head. 'Nope.'

'Why did you tell me that?'

The woman sighed. 'I knew I made a mistake when I said I heard a car. Your face showed you had already figured out I couldn't hear a car with the windows closed. It had to be something loud, right? It was the first thing I thought of.'

Wanda looked terrible. Her skin was ashen. Maybe Donna should come out and do a check on Wanda now. The last thing Bet wanted was for the woman to become sicker during her time in lockup. She also needed to find out what medications Wanda required and arrange to have them on hand at the station. Just because Wanda said she didn't need anything didn't mean that was true.

Bet turned and walked over to Skeet's cell. He sat on the edge of his bunk, clearly enjoying the conversation taking place across the aisle.

'What did you do to make her point a gun at you?' he asked.

'Let's talk about you,' Bet said. 'Come over here where I can put the handcuffs on. We're going to go have a little chat.'

'Good,' he said. 'I'm getting bored.'

Bet sat Skeet in one of the straight-backed chairs in their only interrogation room and put the bag of his belongings that she'd confiscated during his arrest on the table in front of him. She had already confirmed with Alma that Kane had left to set up the roadblock. Clayton stood in the doorway, listening in.

Bet was relieved that her deputy didn't look too exhausted from his first twenty-four hours as a father. She felt bad he was here instead of with his family, but until Gordon was apprehended, she was glad to have the person she trusted most back at her side.

Schweitzer squeezed past Clayton and sat down to one side of Skeet, pinning him with his fierce gaze. Bet watched Skeet shift uncomfortably under the big dog's scrutiny.

'That dog is bigger than a pony. Are you sure he's safe?'

Bet gave Schweitzer the hand signal to drop down, which he promptly did, but his gaze never wavered.

'Perfectly safe,' Bet said. 'As long as you don't make any sudden moves.'

This, of course, was a lie. Schweitzer wasn't trained as an attack dog. He'd only react physically if Skeet launched himself directly at Bet.

'Skeet. I want to talk about your friend Gordon.'

The expression on Skeet's face turned guarded. He might help himself out of his predicament with a little information and Bet didn't doubt he'd throw his own mother under the bus if it would lessen any jail time.

'What makes you think I know this . . . Gordon?'

Bet sighed. There was nothing worse than a two-bit criminal trying to pretend they were a genius at negotiations.

'Everyone at the Tavern saw you having breakfast with him before the fight.'

Skeet's body deflated. 'Oh, right. That.' Score one for Bet.

'Yes, Skeet. That. How do you know Gordon?'

It didn't really matter to Bet if he told the truth or not. She was more interested in getting Skeet talking. It made it possible he would slip up and give her something useful.

'We go way back. He didn't grow up here, but he visited his mom a lot. I knew him then.'

'You can't have known him that well. You didn't even recognize his mother when we walked past her cell.'

Skeet looked puzzled. When he put it together, Bet could swear she heard a click.

'That's Gordon's mom in there? Holy crap . . . I mean . . . Gordon's mom pulled a gun on you?'

'But you'd never met her, right? So, you two were never really tight.'

'We were! I've known Gordon for years.'

It always amazed Bet that human nature often meant a person couldn't bear to be told they were wrong, even if it was to their advantage to be misunderstood.

'We just didn't hang out at each other's houses. We weren't that kind of friends. Not when we were kids.'

'But it's different now?'

'Oh sure, Gordon has been crashing at my house since—' Skeet paused, then tried to cover his tracks. 'Why are you asking about Gordon?'

'You have a wife and kids, don't you Skeet?'

'Why are you asking about . . .'

Skeet's voice trailed off, and his eyes went scared. 'What does my family have to do with anything?'

Bet wondered what Gordon would do if he were cornered. Had he returned to Skeet's house and holed up with Skeet's wife and kids? The last thing Bet wanted to do was arrive at Skeet's house and end up with Gordon drawing them into some kind of siege. But Gordon didn't know that Doug had died, so maybe she could salvage the situation without any more civilians getting hurt. And somewhere in all of this was Ruby.

'Is Ruby at your house too?'

'Who's Ruby?' Bet could see honest confusion on Skeet's face. There was no way he was faking the fact he didn't know that name. 'You don't have someone else's kid staying with you?'

It was possible he didn't know her name.

'What kid?'

'Doug's daughter?'

'Who's Doug?'

No way that was an act either. Skeet didn't have those kinds of skills.

'Here's what I'd like you to do,' Bet said rather than acknowledge his questions. 'Tomorrow morning, we are going to text from your phone that you have been released and that you want Gordon to pick you up at Iron Horse Park. He's the kind of friend you would reach out to for that, right? Since you've been putting him up?'

Iron Horse Park sat not too far from the sheriff's station, but far enough away that Gordon might think he could remain unseen. The weather dictated an indoor meeting spot far away from any civilians. If Gordon was willing to come, Bet and Clayton could get into position to grab him in the parking lot near the restrooms. If he wasn't, maybe he would at least admit to Skeet where he was.

'Sure, sure. Paula is going to be really pissed off at me for getting into so much trouble. It would make sense I'd ask him to pick me up. But we don't have to text. I can call him.'

'Text is fine.'

'Sure, just give me my phone.'

'No. You are going to tell me the code to get into your phone and I will send the text.' Bet pulled the phone out of the bag and held it up. 'Do I have permission to access your phone?'

Skeet squirmed in his chair. He clearly didn't know what to do. 'Gordon would never hurt my family.'

'You want to bet their safety on that?' Bet demanded. Skeet's face turned green. 'How long had it been since you'd last seen him when he showed up in town?'

'A couple years. We'd been in touch, you know, over social media like, but not in person. He's been out in Spokane you know. He said . . . he said he needed to see his mom . . . but he couldn't stay at her house because . . .' Skeet's voice trailed off again, and Bet thought he might have started to consider the ramifications of a man who arrived to visit his mom but didn't stay at her house. A woman who had apparently also threatened a police officer and now sat in the jail cell across from his own.

'She was sick so . . .' His voice trailed off as if he no longer believed what he was saying. 'He wouldn't hurt my family.'

'Let's make sure that's true,' Bet said. 'Do I have permission to access your phone?'

Skeet nodded. He walked her through his code to access the phone, and she checked on the battery life. There would be plenty left to send a text in the morning. Gordon would never believe Skeet had been released at midnight, so they couldn't do it now. Bet would wait until eight, then try to get him to come to the park.

Tonight, she would do a drive-by at Skeet's house to check for any signs of Gordon at the property or endangering Skeet's family.

'Does any of this have to do with that bloody sleeping bag hanging in the other cell?'

Bet stared impassively at Skeet. She channeled the expression Kane had used when he looked at people. She managed to keep up the neutral face and let Skeet sit a moment, picturing what might be happening with his family.

Skeet telegraphed his anxiety when he didn't ask how much his help was worth.

Bet scrolled through his texts until she found one that said Gordon. She asked how he would phrase the text and wrote it out to send in the morning.

Then she set the phone down on the table and looked back at Skeet.

'Now what?' he asked.

'Now I go over and check on your family, and you go back to your cell.'

FORTY-TWO

The following morning, Bet and Clayton parked not far from the entrance to Iron Horse Park, each in their own vehicle. Connected through their phones via Bluetooth, they could be in two different locations, with eyes on the restrooms. Clayton was in his Trooper, which Gordon wouldn't ID as a police vehicle. Bet sat farther away in her SUV.

Last night, after sorting out the text with Skeet, Bet had checked on Skeet's family while Clayton did a circuit of town to look for Gordon's car. Both came up empty. Bet found unblemished snow all around Skeet's house. No one had been in or out of the property for the last several hours. Gordon couldn't have arrived in his car or on foot.

Bet and Clayton both got a little sleep, but she'd have to figure out a time to relieve Kane. He'd been up all night at the roadblock. She tried to keep overtime shifts at eighteen hours max, but extraordinary circumstances required sacrifice. She had to trust Kane knew what he could handle. He reported no one trying to get in or out of the valley, and George had brought his great-nephew food and hot coffee partway through the shift.

At least when morning came, they knew Gordon was still in the area. Before she sent the text from Skeet's phone, Bet ran coffee and breakfast over to Kane, who reported that everything had been quiet and he was OK to continue his watch.

Hopefully, Gordon wanted help from Skeet just as much as Skeet claimed to want help from Gordon, which would make him more likely to meet his friend. Gordon, or at least someone with Gordon's phone, texted back to say he'd be there to pick Skeet up, so she and Clayton were in place to meet him.

Bet anticipated Gordon would want Skeet to use his own car to drive Gordon out of town. No one had come into the valley yet to expose their sham one-lane-road explanation for the road-block and, for all Gordon knew, Bet was still locked in the basement. She hoped that was enough to keep him from knowing they were looking for him. Bet had Wanda's phone, so she knew Gordon hadn't tried to reach his mother and wasn't expecting her to return a call.

It turned out Skeet drove a big old Cadillac, perfect for transporting someone in the trunk. Skeet reported it was currently outfitted with studded snow tires and wouldn't have any trouble getting down to the highway.

Bet and Clayton waited for Gordon to show up and enter the empty restroom; they planned to drive into the lot behind his vehicle – blocking his escape – and arrest him in the park. Skeet, meanwhile, was back in his jail cell, waiting to hear if his assistance paid off. Bet wondered what conversations might be going on between Wanda and Skeet right about now.

'What's our plan if he doesn't show?' Clayton asked.

'We know he's still somewhere close by. We'll catch up with him eventually. Hopefully he can tell us where Ruby is.'

Clayton sat quiet again.

'How does it feel to be a father?' Bet asked. She unzipped her coat. It was warm in her Kevlar vest, even without the SUV's heater running.

'Amazing. Terrifying.' Bet could feel Clayton's smile through his words even though she couldn't see his face.

'You must be looking forward to that paternity leave we planned on. With Kane in place, I can give you the full six weeks we talked about.'

'After the storm damage is cleared and Gordon is in custody.'

Bet chuckled. 'I hope Kathy forgives me for keeping you that long.'

'She knows I'll be back as soon as I can. Her parents are with her, so she's not alone. Because of the C-section, she'll be in the hospital another couple of days anyway. If we nab Gordon now, I'd like to head back to E'burg tonight. I'll come back tomorrow to help with the storm fallout.'

'Deal.' Bet looked at the clock on her dash. Gordon should arrive any minute.

'Do you feel good about Kane?' Clayton asked.

Bet thought about the man she'd met so recently. He'd shown good instincts. He clearly had her back in the fight. And she'd known George Stand her entire life. He was one of the most trustworthy people she knew. It didn't mean his nephew was, but at least he came from a strong foundation.

'I do. I think he's going to do an excellent job as your temporary replacement, but you're still my number one.'

Bet held her breath, wondering if Clayton had started to change his mind about his employment situation. Before he had a chance to reply, a burgundy Cadillac the size of a boat appeared.

'Isn't that Skeet's car?' Clayton's voice held confusion.

Bet hunched forward to get a better look. The weather had let up somewhat, but there was still a light snow falling, obscuring her view.

The vehicle turned into the lot, with two figures in the front seat.

'He's got someone with him,' Clayton said.

'Yep. Hold where you are. Let's see how this plays out.'

Bet watched as the driver put the car into park and shut off the engine. The two figures sat without moving. Bet peered through her binoculars.

'It looks like a woman is driving and Gordon is in the passenger seat,' she said.

'Is that Skeet's wife?' Clayton asked.

'It is. Her name is Paula. I met her at the Tavern after the fight.'

Gordon must have gone to Skeet's house this morning and gotten Skeet's car so he wouldn't be seen in his own.

It also provided him with a hostage. Did he not trust Skeet?

Bet thought about her response to Wanda's situation. One decision after another. Had she made bad choices the whole time she searched for Doug and Ruby? She'd accused Wanda of the flaw, but was she guilty too?

Clayton remained quiet. They both understood the dangers of having an innocent person in the middle of this kind of situation, though maybe Paula was involved in ways they didn't know about yet.

'You are a peace officer first and foremost,' Maggie liked to remind the new patrol officers. 'Do your best to keep it.'

Gordon got out of the car, gesturing to Paula.

As she got out of the car, Gordon straightened up.

'He's got a gun,' Clayton said at the same time Bet identified the object in his hand. 'What now, Sheriff?'

Once Gordon walked into the restroom with Paula and realized that Skeet wasn't there, he'd know it was a setup.

'Wait,' Bet said to Clayton as she typed into Skeet's phone, which she'd brought with her.

She just hoped her new message to Gordon worked.

FORTY-THREE

A moment after Bet sent the text, Gordon twitched and reached into his pocket, pulling out his phone. He said something to Paula, who walked over and put both hands on the hood of the car. He read the text and glanced around the park. Bet held her breath, but his eyes swept over the spot where she parked, the SUV camouflaged by bushes and trees.

Gordon gestured for Paula to get back into the Caddy. Once inside, Paula started the car up and pulled out of the parking lot.

'What just happened?' Clayton asked as he started his engine. Bet explained she'd sent Gordon to Wanda's house.

'I texted him from Skeet's phone saying Skeet would catch a ride to Wanda's house and meet him there. I also texted "we have to talk". I'm hoping he's concerned about his mother's welfare and doesn't think too much about why Skeet made that choice. I'd rather have a standoff with him at that house than inside that tiny restroom. Far too easy for Paula to get shot in there.' Bet adjusted her seat and pulled on her seatbelt. 'I'm going to drop out of sight so he doesn't see my SUV. You can follow closer in your Trooper to make sure he goes straight to Wanda's.'

Clayton pulled out first, leaving lots of space behind the Cadillac. With almost no other traffic, it wasn't hard to keep an eye on the giant burgundy boat of a car. Bet got behind Clayton but stayed far enough back to be out of sight if Gordon looked in his rearview mirror.

They made a strange slow-motion chase through town and out past the cemetery. Gordon could realize he was being followed, but with the Trooper, a civilian vehicle, and the loop road the only main road in the area, Bet felt it was safe.

Bet and Clayton made a quick plan as they approached Wanda's place. Their priority was getting Paula to safety.

'If she's out of the car and he sees running as his best option, he might leave her behind,' Bet said. 'So, we'll let him think he can escape in the Cadillac. If he doesn't get her out of the car, but he gets out, we can grab him by himself. If he does bolt in the car and Paula is safe, we can follow him and pull him over. He can't get out of the valley with the roadblock there.'

There was no guarantee Gordon would leave his hostage behind, but it was the best they could do in the current circumstances. Saving civilian life always came first. They knew who their suspect was. He could be tracked down later.

Gordon parked in the driveway at Wanda's house. The generator was likely still out, so he couldn't use the remote to open the garage. He may have also wanted to be ready for a fast getaway.

Clayton reported that he had parked next door at the rental to assess the situation and provide Gordon the chance to escape in the Cadillac, potentially leaving Paula behind. Bet met him there.

They trudged through the snow between the houses.

The Cadillac sat empty in the driveway. Gordon had cut through the crime scene tape she'd left on the front door before leaving last night. It confirmed that Bet had gotten out of the basement, and that Wanda was likely in custody, but he'd also think the house now sat empty and Skeet was on his way.

Bet told Clayton she would enter the house through the back and directed him to double-check the car and take the front.

Arriving at the back door, Bet could see a light on toward the front of the house.

Clayton would test the front door. If it was open, he would slip inside and come around and let her in so they could enter quietly.

If it was locked, they would wait and see what Gordon did next.

Bet barely had time to get to the back door when she heard a loud argument between a man and a woman upstairs. The argument escalated to screaming. Waiting to see what happened next no longer felt like the best option. 'I'm going in,' she said to Clayton over the radio mic strapped to her shoulder.

Bet pulled out her Maglite with the Bust a Cap – the same tool she'd used on Doug's car – and slammed it against the sliding glass door.

The door exploded in a web of lines. The shatterproof glass didn't break out as Bet thought it might, but the Bust a Cap still made a big hole. Bet reached through to the latch and unlocked the door.

The door slid open, and Bet maneuvered herself into the kitchen. Seeing no one in the kitchen or dining room, she stepped toward the front of the house. Heavy footfalls echoed from over her head. The situation was bad for Paula, but Bet didn't see an alternative. She would do her best to talk Gordon down. Maybe knowing his mother was gone would prove to him the jig was up and ending the showdown without violence was the smartest course of action.

Clayton burst through the front door at the same time, and she gestured for him to follow her.

At the top of the stairs, she found a hallway with a series of doors on either side. All of them were open except the one at the end. Bet and Clayton made their way down the hall, clearing each room as they came to it, until they reached the last.

Bet reached out and shoved the door open, using the wall to block her body in case Gordon started firing. With her own weapon in hand, she expected to see Gordon with a gun on Paula. Instead she found the woman tied up on the bed and an emergency rope ladder, the kind used in case of fire, hanging out an open window. Bet looked around the room for any place Gordon could have hidden, using the rope ladder as a diversion, but it was quickly apparent that Paula was alone. Bet rushed to her side, calling to Clayton to go after Gordon.

Paula had been bound with a belt around her feet and hands and gagged with a scarf. She appeared unharmed. Clayton would either reach Gordon before he got to the car or go after him in pursuit. He had a portable warning light in the Trooper, which turned his own vehicle into an unmarked.

She texted Kane that Gordon might show up at the blockade in the burgundy Cadillac. At least Gordon would be alone when the confrontation happened, without civilians caught in the middle.

Something had finally gone right.

Bet pulled the gag off Paula, who immediately began to cry and speak so fast Bet couldn't understand a word she was saying. Bet got her hands and feet unbound and reassured her that she was fine, and that Gordon was gone.

Paula finally got her breathing under control.

'What about my kids?' Bet managed to finally understand her words. 'Where are Ricky and Darrell?'

'Your kids?' Had Gordon managed to get Paula *and* her kids into the house before she and Clayton arrived? 'He brought your kids in the house?'

'No. In the car.'

'They were in the back seat?'

From a distance the car had looked empty. Clayton probably hadn't had time for a full check before Bet's voice came over the radio telling him she was going in. The two kids could have been lying down in the back seat.

'Not the back seat, you idiot. In the trunk.'

FORTY-FOUR

Bet froze. Everything had happened so fast once they arrived at Wanda's house. Had they just handed two tiny hostages over to the man who'd killed Doug?

Bet felt like an accomplice too. It was her fault those kids were in that trunk and Gordon was on the run. Bet called Clayton immediately to find out if he'd checked the trunk before coming into the house.

'I heard you going in, so I came through the front door. I only had time to glance in the back seat.'

There was nothing to be done about it now. Bet told Clayton about the kids, then she hung up the phone so he could concentrate on following Gordon.

Clayton would never forgive himself if anything happened to those kids, even if it wasn't his fault.

But they didn't put those kids in the trunk – Gordon did. Bet didn't meet up with Gordon and invite him into Paula's house – Skeet did. Clayton didn't have more time to check out the car because Paula started screaming, and they could only respond to each situation in the moment.

Her job was to get those kids back safe and apprehend Gordon. The rest didn't matter now. She could agonize over their actions later. She returned her attention to Paula.

'Did Gordon indicate what he planned to do? After he met up with Skeet?' Paula sat on the edge of the bed, sobbing. 'Paula, I need you to focus here. Help me get your kids back. What did Gordon say to you?'

Paula hiccupped and rubbed her nose on her sleeve, but she regained enough control to answer Bet.

'He said he wanted Skeet to drive him out of town. Once Skeet was there to pick him up, he would release me and one kid, but he'd hold the other hostage until Skeet took him where he wanted to go.'

'Did he say where he planned to have Skeet take him?'
'No.'

Bet weighed her options. Gordon was trapped in the valley now. She had to find out if Clayton had him in his sights.

'I'll be right back.' Bet stepped out of the room. 'Wait here.'
'Where are you—'
'Wait here, please.'

Bet closed the door behind her. She didn't think Paula would go out the window on the rope ladder into the snow. Without a vehicle, she had nowhere to go. But Bet didn't want her to hear her conversations about Gordon in case any of the news was bad.

Kane answered on the first ring.

Bet explained about the kids in the trunk of the Cadillac.

'I'll approach with caution if I see the car.'

Kane's voice held no emotion. No sense of whether he thought Bet had botched the situation not blocking the car in at Wanda's house. If he thought working for her had been a mistake. She couldn't blame him if he did. She wished she'd done things differently.

She put in the call to Clayton.

'I still can't find the Cadillac.' Bet could hear the self-recrimination in his voice.

'There was no way to know those kids were in the trunk. You had to back me up when I entered the house. I'm the one who made the choice not to block Gordon in, thinking we'd have a better chance to get Paula out of the situation safely.'

The only sound was Clayton's heavy breathing over the Bluetooth.

'I made a guess which way he went from the house and headed into town.' Clearly Clayton wasn't going to talk about fault. Bet didn't blame him for staying focused on the search. 'I figured you'd already been on the phone with Kane, and he'd let us know if Gordon went to the roadblock, so I'm heading toward Skeet's place. I know where he lives.'

Bet confirmed it was the best choice. 'I wish we could get a chopper up,' she said. 'But there's no way to fly one in this weather.' The storm was heating up again.

What could they do besides search the valley?

Gordon's cell phone.

With a kidnapping taking place, she didn't need a warrant. She could apply for one after the fact, and have his cell traced immediately. Giving Clayton a heads-up on her plan, she ended the call.

Then she called Alma with the information and made sure she had Gordon's cell number. 'As long as he doesn't ditch it, we can locate him.'

Alma promised to call as soon as she had anything.

Bet updated both her deputies and returned to the bedroom

where Paula remained in the same spot on the bed, her face slack, her body still. Bet knew what overwhelming fear looked like.

'Paula,' Bet reached out and took the woman's hand, 'we're going to do everything we can to get your kids back. What I'd like to do is take you to the station where you can be updated as things progress.'

What Bet really wanted to do was keep an eye on her. Bet didn't want her out in the community with Gordon at large. Paula's house was now a crime scene, as the original kidnapping occurred there, and Bet didn't know yet what Paula's involvement was in any of this. Leaving her at the station where Alma could watch her was the best place she could be.

Paula didn't move.

'Paula,' Bet said again, a little louder. 'I need you to be strong for me, OK?'

The woman shook her head, an abrupt gesture that appeared to snap her out of her catatonic state.

'Fine. Whatever will get my kids home safe.'

The two women left the house and walked back along the road to get to Bet's vehicle.

'I have to pat you down, OK? Standard procedure for anyone riding in my car.'

Paula barely responded but held her arms out at her sides. A quick pat down turned up nothing, so Paula sat in the back while Bet drove them to the station.

Bet would need to take a full report after things slowed down, but for now, she kept Paula talking. She asked how long Gordon had stayed with them and how well she knew him, trying to get a general picture of the man.

'He's just an old friend of Skeet's come to visit. I never thought he could do something like this,' Paula said, 'threaten my children this way. Who does that?'

Bet didn't have the heart to answer her, but in her mind she knew.

A very desperate man.

FORTY-FIVE

Bet and Paula arrived at the station to find Alma on the phone. Bet had already confiscated Paula's phone, telling her she needed it in case Gordon tried to contact her – she wasn't going to tell the woman that she didn't trust her. At this point she only had Paula's word and her apparent distress that there really were kids in the trunk. Paula could have thrown that out as a reason not to shoot at Gordon or to throw suspicion off her own involvement in whatever was going on.

As they walked in the station, Paula asked to use the restroom, giving Bet a moment alone with Alma.

'What do we know?' Bet asked.

Alma handed over a slip of paper. 'Here's the coordinates from the provider. Good thing his phone has GPS.'

'That was fast.'

'Kidnapping-in-progress tends to get results.'

Bet asked Alma to keep Paula in the front room with her. 'She's currently a victim, not a prisoner, so we can't force her to stay here, but do the best you can. I don't trust any of the people close to Skeet right now.'

Alma said that as long as Paula thought staying at the station would help get her kids back safe and sound, she wouldn't be going anywhere. 'I'll call over to Sandy and get something hot to drink sent over, along with something to eat.'

Bet expressed her approval.

'One other thing,' Alma said. 'I don't know if this is useful, but I got a call back from one of the cashiers at the Polaris dealership.'

Bet had forgotten about Alma's inquiry into Doug's trip out to Federal Way.

'She recognized Doug from the photo I sent over. She said he was there having an aftermarket rack and gas can put on the snowmobile.'

The gas can now missing from the wrecked sled? Why would

a guy in serious financial trouble make that kind of purchase?

'It seems a little odd, doesn't it?' Alma cocked her head at Bet as if she could explain Doug's actions.

'It does.'

'Why go all the way to Federal Way when he could have gone to E'burg instead for the same thing?'

An excellent question that Bet couldn't answer.

'Good work, Alma. I'm not sure what it means yet. Keep digging into Doug and Gordon and write up the warrant for the GPS location on the cell.'

Bet called to Schweitzer, and the two went out to the SUV. Bet didn't know if they'd have to track either Gordon or the kids, but she wanted Schweitzer's nose if the situation arose.

Schweitzer hopped into the back, and Bet fired up the SUV. She typed in the GPS coordinates from Alma and hoped Gordon wasn't on the move.

The blue pin popped up on the digital map. There wasn't a county-maintained road on the image, but Bet knew a forest service road ran there.

Behind Jeb's property.

Coincidence? Or were Jeremy and the rest of the Crews somehow more involved in this mess than they'd let on? She thought again about Gordon's remark to Wanda about the camp-ground. And Mark's odd drive last night where he turned around at a campground.

Bet called Jeb. The last thing she wanted was for Gordon to add to his list of hostages, though Jeb wouldn't be as easy to grab as an unarmed woman with kids.

Jeb's phone rolled over to voicemail. Cursing, Bet waited for the beep and gave a quick rundown of events, then requested Jeb call her ASAP. Next she put in a call to Sandy.

'Coffee and tea are on the way to the station, or are you going to go talk to my clients again?' Bet heard amusement in Sandy's voice.

'I wish it was that simple. Have you communicated with the Crews today?'

'Nope. I'm making drinks for Alma. *Should* I be in touch with them?'

'I'm afraid they may be in danger.' Bet thought it might be

better to go with that lead rather than her speculation they might be aiding and abetting a killer. 'I don't have their numbers in my cell to access while I'm driving, and I can't reach Jeb.'

'Sit tight.' Sandy's voice turned clipped and serious. 'I'll call them.'

Bet waited for an eternity. As a patrol officer, she would have raced out to respond to a crisis. Events on the street happened fast, she had to stay responsive. Every sense had been heightened as she made constant threat assessments and chose the best move in every situation.

But on patrol, someone else took charge when a complex crime unfolded. Bet had no one to look to for answers now. She couldn't just run into a room with guns blazing. She'd made the call that got Paula's kids taken by Gordon. The last thing she wanted was to make a choice that also got them killed. Her confidence had taken a hit at the worst possible time. She cycled through advice from her father and Maggie, but nothing stood out as helpful. She was on her own.

Sandy's number popped up on the Bluetooth screen. 'The Crews are at their cabin at Jeb's. I've told them to remain inside and not answer any knock except yours or Jeb's.'

Bet waited but Sandy fell quiet. Something had spiked her friend's anxiety.

'What aren't you telling me?'

'I don't know. I'm reporting what they said to me, but I know when a client is lying. Something is wrong out there. I just don't know what it is.'

Sandy promised to call Bet if she learned anything new, and Bet assured Sandy that she would contact her as soon as she had answers.

Bet reached out to Clayton and gave him the coordinates as well. 'I don't want us to announce our presence.'

They agreed to meet near the spot where the forest service road split from the loop that ringed the valley floor. It was a different road than the one that Bet and Jeb traveled to get to the ridge and retrieve Grant's body, but it was part of the same system.

With lights flashing, Bet continued driving as fast as road conditions allowed. The storm was ramping back up, and the kids would be exposed to severe cold if they were left in the trunk for long. She had no idea how well dressed they were for the weather. It would be even worse if Gordon had the kids out of the car and into the elements. They could all end up freezing to death in the snow.

FORTY-SIX

B et arrived to find Clayton's vehicle at a wide spot on the forest service road. He climbed out and met her at the driver's side window.

'What's the plan?' he asked as she rolled her own window down, snow swirling in with his words. The storm was back for what Bet hoped was one final wallop, keeping the sky dark, despite it not yet being noon. With other storms following this one, however, the valley might stay fully encased in winter for the foreseeable future.

'I don't want to spook Gordon into doing something stupid. If he's trying to get help from the Crews, we don't want him to add to his hostage list.'

'We can walk in from here.'

Bet eyed the road in front of them. The storm had wound up with an explosive punch. 'He's not going to hear or see us,' Bet said. 'As long as we don't get too close. Let's drive a little farther in.'

Gordon might not be in the same place as his phone, or the phone might have moved since the cell company got the coordinates, but Bet had nothing else to go on.

'Park across the road here to block him in and keep anyone else from getting past. If I remember right, this road dead-ends. We'll drive mine in but stop before we get in sight of the Cadillac. That way we can assess the situation and make a plan but have the SUV for cover if we need it.' Bet would never forgive herself if either kid was hurt or killed in this mess.

Clayton moved his Trooper and came around to the passenger side. The vehicle dipped as he climbed in.

Turning off her headlights and flashers, Bet started to creep forward while Clayton kept his eyes on the pin marking the coordinates on the screen. GPS was accurate enough to be within a few feet. Schweitzer sat on high alert in the back, eyes on the woods around them.

'Stop,' Clayton said after a few minutes. The forest closed in around, but snow still found its way to them. Evergreens blocked a lot of the wind, but the frozen drift on the ground came up to the bottom of the SUV's doors. 'The phone should be just around this bend.'

Bet parked and the two got out, pausing to listen. The only sound was the roar of the wind that bent the tops of the trees. Bet let Schweitzer out, giving him the command to heel, and the three began to make their way down the road. They could see the fresh tracks left by a vehicle with studded snow tires. Not needing Schweitzer to scent, she kept him at her side.

They had only trudged forward for a few minutes when a form took shape on the road in front of them.

A burgundy Cadillac.

The car sat dark and still. The vehicle wasn't running. No lights, no exhaust, no movement of any kind.

After a whispered conversation, they split up. Bet and Schweitzer tucked into the trees on the driver's side, while Clayton did the same on the opposite. They moved carefully, their approach hidden from anyone in the car by the thick trunks and the falling snow.

Reaching the vehicle, Bet tried to see inside. A thin layer of snow had covered the entire vehicle, turning the bright paint job into a pastel shade of its former color and making it impossible to see into the interior. Despite being close to midday, it was dark under the dense cover of trees and stormy sky.

Bet held her breath and waited for any sign of movement, but the car sat frozen on its springs. Footprints skirted the vehicle, including near the trunk, but she couldn't tell how many people had left marks behind.

She put her hand on her Glock as she drew up alongside the driver's side window. Schweitzer knew what the gesture meant, and he stepped forward on high alert, pinned to her other side. Clayton must have seen her come out of the trees, because he sidled up to the passenger side.

The snow brushed easily from the window. The vehicle was empty. The door was unlocked. At least she didn't have to break another window.

She dropped down to search for a trunk latch and Schweitzer began to circle the car. He placed his front paws on the trunk lid and whined. Something was inside.

Clayton opened the door on the other side. Bet found the trunk release and pulled on the button, but nothing happened.

'I found his phone, but I can't get the trunk latch to pop,' she said as Clayton leaned inside.

'There should be an emergency release in the back seat.'

The two moved to the rear doors, and Bet helped Clayton tug on the back seat. It unsnapped away from the frame with a satisfying pop. Bet leaned over and shined her flashlight inside. Two faces looked back at her. She could see duct tape over their mouths, and both boys blinked, their eyes sleepy. Was hypothermia starting to kick in?

'Let's get them out.' Bet reached in and, with Clayton's help, pulled them through the back seat, untangling their limbs from the blankets they were wrapped in.

'It's going to be OK.' Bet carefully removed the tape from the younger boy's mouth. He cried out at the sting but took a deep breath, tears in his eyes. Bet opened her knife and cut through the tape on his hands and legs while Clayton did the same with the older boy.

'Are you cold?' she asked the younger one, but the older boy answered for both.

'The blankets kept us warm. It wasn't so bad.'

'Were you sleeping?' She wondered if they had been lulled by the movement of the car.

'Benadryl always makes us sleepy.'

Bet started to ask more questions when she stopped herself. There was time to sort all that out later. First they had to get the kids somewhere safe and track down Gordon.

She looked over at Clayton, who had finished removing the tape from the older boy and was helping him stand up in the snow.

Taking the boys back to the station was their priority, which meant Bet would be following Gordon alone.

FORTY-SEVEN

While Bet and Clayton conferred about their next course of action, Schweitzer stood next to the boys. He leaned against first one and then the other to show them he was there to keep them safe. The boys looked dazed, but both responded to the big dog, putting their arms around him. The younger boy buried his face in Schweitzer's neck, earning him a lick on the side of his cheek.

Surrounded by cold, dark woods, a set of footprints led off through the trees. There were no tracks from another vehicle; Gordon had left on foot. At least he didn't have the hostages anymore. Bet assumed it was Gordon who left the car.

She leaned over to talk to the boys again. 'Do you know the person who left you here?'

'His name is Gordon,' said the older boy, who had introduced himself as Ricky.

'Did he say why he left you here?' She was glad Gordon didn't keep the hostages, but it did make her wonder what he planned to do next.

Both boys shook their heads. 'But he was crying,' said Darrell, the younger child.

Clayton looked as puzzled as Bet felt. That wasn't the emotional state Bet expected.

'Do you know why?'

'He was sad?' Darrell said. 'That's why I cry.' It was as good an explanation as any.

'He said someone would find us eventually because he left his phone.' Ricky looked at Bet as if this explained the entire situation. The boys were remarkably calm given what they'd endured, though some of that could be the residual effects of the medication. They didn't appear traumatized, which was a relief. With a little luck, they would never know how much danger they had been in.

'Why would he do that?' Clayton asked Bet. She shrugged that she didn't know either.

'Did he say anything else?'

The two boys looked to each other.

'Oh yeah,' Ricky said, as if a thought just occurred to him. 'He said he didn't know what else to do.'

Bet didn't know how this information would help her, but it did give her some insights into the man's mind. It was possible he realized trekking through the snow hauling one or two drugged young boys with him would just slow him down, and he had several new potential hostages not far away at Jeb's place.

'We need to get the boys back to the station,' she said to Clayton.

'And we need to follow those tracks.' Clayton gestured toward Gordon's footsteps where they disappeared into the trees.

'Right.'

She thought of Kane down at the roadblock. She could use his help but didn't want to leave the only road out unmanned.

'You're wishing for one more person.' Clayton had assessed the situation right along with her.

Bet got out her phone to bring up a map and confirm the direction the tracks led.

Straight to Jeb's place.

She tried calling Jeb again, only to find no cell coverage. Calling the station over her radio, she told Alma they had found the kids safe and that Paula should wait for them there.

Then she asked Alma to try calling Jeb. 'I'll wait,' Bet said. The sound of Alma picking up the landline was followed by silence. She waited until Alma came back on the radio.

'No answer. Straight to voicemail.'

'We'll have the kids back soon.'

Bet looked at Clayton, weighing her options.

'I can follow those tracks while you take the kids back to their mother,' Clayton said.

Bet appreciated the offer, but she wasn't sending her deputy to do her job.

'Let's do this. You take the kids back to the station. Schweitzer and I are going to follow the tracks and do recon. When you're back, we'll formulate a plan to get Gordon arrested safely. We've managed not to have any casualties from our actions so far. Let's see if we can keep it that way.'

'He's gone to Jeb's.'

'I think so.'

'He could have a new set of hostages.'

'He could. And we can't reach Jeb, which might indicate he already has, but I don't think he wants to hurt anyone. Why else would he leave the kids behind?'

Clayton looked troubled. He struggled between needing to get the boys warmed up and back to safety and leaving Bet alone in a forest with an armed, desperate man on the run. 'Just because he hasn't shot at us before, and he left Paula and the boys unharmed, doesn't mean it's going to stay that way.'

'I'll be careful, Clayton. It's just recon.'

Clayton kneeled next to the two boys. 'Hi, guys, my name is Clayton. I'm going to take you back to your mom now, OK?'

'We just want to go home,' Ricky said.

'Can he go with us?' Darrell asked, his arm still around Schweitzer.

Much as Bet knew how comforting Schweitzer could be, she had other plans for him.

'Schweitzer is going to help me do my job,' Bet said. 'But Clayton will take good care of you.'

Darrell gave Schweitzer one last hug, and he reached out to let Clayton pick him up out of the snow.

With one look back at Bet, Clayton started down the road to where they'd left his Trooper. Clayton couldn't carry both kids, so he had Ricky by the hand. His progress through the deep snow would be slow. It was going to be quite some time before she had backup again.

Kane.

Maybe she should get him to come out to meet her, but that would take time too, and Gordon was no doubt doing his best to get out of the valley. The roadblock was still a possible spot to apprehend him. Gordon could have grabbed a car at Jeb's with or without a hostage.

Clayton and the boys disappeared as the forest and the falling snow swallowed them.

Bet asked Schweitzer to get a scent from the driver's seat and the footsteps leading from the car. Then she followed her dog as he followed the tracks, picking up speed into the trees.

FORTY-EIGHT

The forest grew darker and darker, and the snow continued to fall. Schweitzer kept his nose pinned to the footprints. Bet kept her eyes out for motion, knowing Schweitzer would keep her on Gordon's trail. It grew pointless trying to identify anyone advancing on her through the woods as the trees danced wildly under the onslaught of the wind.

After several minutes of trudging through the snow, they arrived at the edge of Jeb's pasture. She could barely make out the outlines of the buildings in front of her because of the raging storm. She also didn't see signs of anyone slogging across the open expanse between her and the buildings, which continued to fade from view as the storm took on blizzard conditions.

Bet had to assume Gordon had reached the buildings and held Jeb and the Crews at gunpoint to help him get out of town. Jeb would be smart about things, but he would also look for any opportunity to fight his way out. Bet had no idea what the Crews would do in the situation. Julia would probably fight like a mama bear for her son's safety, but Mark and Jeremy were wild cards.

Maybe Sandy was wrong about them lying to her and they really were safely locked into their cabin, and Gordon hadn't put them in danger.

But that still left Jeb.

Bet called in over her radio while she stood at the edge of the trees. She hoped it would still work despite the distance between her and Clayton and the radio's base in her SUV. At least she knew Gordon couldn't hear her over the storm.

Clayton was just turning in to the station with the kids. Bet described what she'd found and told him she planned to get over to the buildings and see what she could suss out.

'I'm silencing my radio and cell,' she told him. 'I'll get back on when I have something to tell you.'

'Where do you want me?' he asked.

Bet described a turnout on the loop not far from Jeb's that

couldn't be seen from his buildings, especially with the weather. 'Wait there until I have something to report.'

Clayton agreed, and Bet silenced her radio. She double-checked her phone – it still had no bars. She wasn't surprised, but she hoped it would come into range as she got closer to Jeb's. Maybe she could send a text to Jeb from there. She silenced it as well. Then she signaled to Schweitzer to lead them across the open expanse of snow. She was relieved to have the big dog with her, as she could imagine getting turned around in the storm and walking in circles until she froze to death. Schweitzer wouldn't let that happen.

She tried to shield her eyes from the flying ice particles as the two of them made their way out from the relative safety of the trees and faced the full brunt of the storm – and whatever lay waiting for them at the ranch.

FORTY-NINE

B et struggled to cross the pasture while Schweitzer bounded along beside her in huge strides. At times he almost disappeared in the deep snow. With the whiteout conditions, she plunged up to her hips in the fresh powder. The wind tried to push her off course, but Schweitzer constantly looked up to make sure she was still there, as if he knew she couldn't find her way without him. Despite the weather, halfway across the field she started sweating under her heavy winter clothes and Kevlar vest.

She had started to think even Schweitzer's excellent nose had led them astray, when the barn showed up as a darker patch in front of her. She flexed her fingers to keep them from stiffening up. She wore her Mechanix gloves, but they weren't very thick, as she needed dexterity to reach the tools of her trade. At her fingertips were a TASER, handcuffs, Maglite, and of course her Glock 21. She couldn't fire her weapon if she wore thicker gloves, but she also wouldn't be much of a shot if her fingers turned into icicles.

Bet worked her way to the barn, getting her heavy breathing under control.

Arriving at the side farthest from the road and the roundhouse, she tucked herself against the wall, blocking any view of her from the other buildings. Schweitzer whined, communicating that the tracks didn't approach the barn – his nose wanted to continue toward the roundhouse – but she gestured him to her side.

Testing the rolling door, she found she could edge her way inside, despite the fresh snow piled up on the ground. She wanted to get out of the weather and find out if she had cell reception and any more information from Clayton or Alma.

As she and Schweitzer squeezed through the door, she heard a nicker from the far end of the barn. She could just make out the bright white blaze on Cyd's face as she leaned over her stall door. Pulling out her phone, a few bars appeared on the screen. Relieved, she put a call in to Alma first, to find out if she'd had any luck reaching Jeb.

'Still straight to voicemail,' Alma said. 'I've left another message, but he's not picking up.'

Bet wandered down to Cyd's stall as she spoke on the phone, confident no one was going to show up at the barn. Gordon wasn't going to try to flee on horseback. The horses and Dolly the mini donkey all peered over their stall doors at her, but Schweitzer walked straight back to Cyd. The beautiful American Paint Horse let Bet stroke her forehead, as Sire suckled contentedly at her side. Cyd reached out and touched her nose to Schweitzer's. The two knew each other, and he wagged his tail at the sight of his friend.

'Life's pretty good out here in the barn, isn't it,' Bet said to Cyd as she hit speed-dial for her deputy. Maybe in her next life she could come back as a horse.

Clayton had dropped off the kids at the station and headed toward the turnout. 'I'll be ready to come in lights blazing or covert in about five minutes – whatever you want.'

Bet explained she could barely even see the main buildings yet, so she didn't have any answers, but would continue with her recon.

After hanging up with Clayton, Bet put a call in to Kane. He told her that no one had come in or out of the valley while he'd been there, other than the Stenleys keeping the road open.

'Should I stay put?' he asked after Bet filled him in on the latest developments. Kane had been at the roadblock for a very long time, and up a lot longer than Bet's eighteen-hour max, but she couldn't afford to pull him.

'We still need someone at the blockade. If Gordon makes a run for it, it's his only escape. For all I know, he's taken a vehicle from here and he's already on his way to you. If you're doing OK, I can guarantee you'll be getting a lot of overtime.'

Kane confirmed he was doing fine, though Bet could guess he'd rather play a more active role. Taking orders from her without complaint made him rise in her estimation. Maybe he would work out. She had the next six weeks to find out while Clayton was home with his wife and baby.

Before heading back out into the storm, Bet called Sandy for a report on whether she'd had any further conversation with the Crews.

'I've called both Julia and Mark's phones again to check in,' Sandy said. 'No one is picking up now. How worried should I be?'

Bet reassured Sandy she was on Jeb's property and would contact her as soon as she had any information. Sandy promised not to drive over to check on her clients. The last thing Bet wanted was for her friend to get caught in the middle of whatever scenario unfolded at the ranch.

Bet slipped her phone back into the inner pocket of her coat, which she left unzipped. With her bulletproof vest on, she had the extra warmth, but that and her heavy coat made it harder for her to move easily. Signaling to Schweitzer to heel, she went back to the rolling door and slid it on its tracks just enough to slip outside again.

She made her way toward the cabin the Crews rented, the path much easier now that she crossed an area Jeb kept plowed. From the angle she approached the building, she could see their car parked in back.

The Crews were likely all on the premises, and Gordon hadn't taken their vehicle for his own escape. Maybe she'd find one of Jeb's vehicles missing.

This would be so much easier if Gordon just stole a car and got caught at the roadblock, preferably without taking any more hostages.

The windows in the back of the cabin were dark. Bet reached

the building and leaned against the wall to catch her breath. The march through the snow was more of a workout than any ten-mile run.

She peered into the windows, but the bedrooms were empty, so she edged her way around the corner of the building. She signaled to Schweitzer to stay behind her, as she didn't need his nose to chart their course.

The front door stood open, light spilling from the front room out on to the ground as the wind sent snow inside. Bet waited, but no one came out and, from the snowfall around the door, she could tell it had been that way for a while. She crept up to the opening and looked inside, but the cabin sat empty. She searched both bedrooms and the bathroom to confirm no one was home.

That didn't bode well for the Crews.

The roundhouse was barely visible through the storm. Lights shone out through the tall front windows, but Bet couldn't see clearly enough to identify anyone inside.

The Train Yard felt like a ghost town. Snow blew between the buildings, and the wind howled in her ears. The empty cabin felt desolate behind her. Was she about to stumble on a mass killing? Had Gordon finally snapped from the pressure, getting rid of whomever he didn't need to facilitate his escape?

Tracks between the cabin and the roundhouse were now filling with snow, as if Gordon had herded everyone in front of him into the main building.

Jeb wouldn't go down without a fight.

But he would also have called her at the first sign of trouble. Since he hadn't called, she feared that he never saw Gordon coming.

FIFTY

Despite the heavy snowfall, crossing the space between the cabin and the roundhouse would expose Bet to anyone looking out of the windows. She clicked her radio on, so Clayton could hear her if anything went sideways. She preferred to stay off a channel that could be heard by anyone with a police scanner, such as Jeb had because of his role with search-and-rescue, but she also didn't want to go into the round-house without Clayton having ears on her.

She edged around the door of the cabin and leaned against the wall, preparing to make her way to the other building. Images of what she might find there rose in her mind. But she had to stay in the present and react accordingly, not get caught up in a spiral of 'what if'.

The storm had begun to lessen again. The space between the roundhouse and the cabin was clearer than it had been when she arrived. The sky was still heavy with clouds, but the snowfall was lighter. She was a moving target for anyone inside.

Signaling to Schweitzer, she crossed the plowed area between the buildings to get to the side of the roundhouse that faced the road. She leaned against the building, her breath coming out in clouds as she panted from the exertion and the spike of adrena-line. Her chest hurt from the cold air even as the wind dropped, and the world turned still.

Schweitzer looked up at her, his own breath coming out in heavy pants, his eyes glistening at the chance to work with his person. She put her hand on his neck, grateful to have him at her side.

Maggie and her father had both told her, a solid partner was the best thing a law enforcement officer could hope for.

Schweitzer was that partner.

No sounds came from the roundhouse, though she doubted she'd hear anything quieter than a gunshot through the brick walls. No sound from vehicles on the loop reached her ears. She glanced in the direction of the turnout, but it wasn't visible from her location. Clayton could hear her breathing over the radio though, so she did her best to slow her respirations. In addition to the hard work of walking through the snow, her heart rate had bumped up again as she prepared to cross the space, exposed to Gordon and any gun he might have trained on her.

Maggie always reminded her that adrenaline could be a good thing or a bad thing. 'Use the energy and the focus it gives you,' she would say before they went into a dangerous situation. 'Don't let it overwhelm you. Focus on keeping your breath steady and monitor everything around you. Tunnel vision is real, don't miss the bigger picture.'

At least that advice was useful in her current situation.

Bet peered around the corner of the building and checked out the entranceway. The front of the roundhouse was a series of six tall doors. They were glassed-in from top to bottom, except the third door from the right. Jeb had converted that thirty-foot-high door into his front entrance. He had framed a regular-sized door into one that once allowed a train engine to fit through. It created the only opaque surface where she could hide.

Bet looked through the window closest to her. Then she gave Schweitzer the hand signal to stay, knowing he wasn't going to like her leaving him behind, but if someone came out of the round-house firing a weapon, she wanted him out of the line of fire.

She raced across the glass front as fast as she could and tucked up against the solid door in the middle. She leaned against it, ear to the wood.

'At the front door,' she whispered, so Clayton would know her progress.

Hearing nothing from inside, she peeked carefully around the edge of the front door.

No movement. No sign of anyone. Her eyes carefully swept the room, searching for any glimpse of Gordon, Jeb or the others.

A light shone out from the back of the roundhouse. It fell through the archway that led into Jeb's office and his living quarters, as well as a game room in the back. Bet tried the front door and the knob turned in her hand. Should she slip inside or make her way around the building on the outside to better evaluate the situation? She'd already made choices throughout this inves-tigation she'd later regretted. If she had time to think things through now, she should take it. Maybe she'd make wiser deci-sions moving forward.

Clayton could walk over from where he had parked, so no one would hear a vehicle arrive. But they might need his Trooper to block Gordon in or for a fast pursuit. The sky lightened further as the clouds began to part, her ability to use the weather as a shield slowly dissipating.

The roundhouse was exposed on all sides. No trees or bushes blocked the view, and anyone looking out through a window would also see Clayton as he made his way to her. She couldn't risk it without knowing what was going on inside.

'I'm going to circle the building on the outside,' she told him. 'Sit tight.'

The rest of the roundhouse was primarily solid brick, making her traverse of the exterior easier than crossing between the cabin and the front door. The hardest part would be this first moment as she returned to Schweitzer at the side of the building by racing past the tall floor-to-ceiling glass. She steadied her breathing and bolted back to the corner, hoping no one saw her from the front room as she made her escape.

Reaching the corner where Schweitzer sat, she looked down the shorter wall in front of her. It had three large windows, but she would be able to see into the rooms and confirm they were empty before she crossed in front of them. The snow was deep, as Jeb didn't plow here.

Bet made her way to the first window on the side of the building that paralleled the loop road. The going was much harder in the deep drifts of snow. She knew from her time with Jeb that the windows on this wall looked into the kitchen. She reached the first and found the space empty. Light streamed through the windows as the clouds began to lift, giving her a clear view.

She could see the door to the walk-in freezers, including the one where she and Jeb laid Grant's body to wait for Addie and her bus to take him to the coroner.

Looking down at Schweitzer, Bet's mind went to Grizzly. Where was Jeb's Newfie? If Gordon was indeed holding the Crews and Jeb hostage, what had he done to the dog?

It did her no good to invent worst-case scenarios as she did her reconnaissance, so she continued her course around the building.

The snow made her work hard for every step. Her breath was heavy and ragged over the radio, but she wasn't going to cut off her only link to the outside world. Fighting her way through, she made it to the corner of the building. The back curve was a long expanse of brick with only clerestory windows tucked up under the eaves.

There were three doors in the back. Each door had glass in the top half. One led into the kitchen Bet had just cleared. The one in the middle led to Jeb's living quarters, and the last led into a hall near his office, the one they'd used to check his outbuilding when they discovered the missing crossbow. Knowing she couldn't be seen by anyone through the high windows under the eaves, Bet picked up her speed to reach the second door.

The room was dark, but the clerestory windows shed enough light that she could see no one waited in the dark. She tried the knob, but this door was locked.

That left the doorway into the hall. The window in the door glowed with light from inside. She plunged through the snow to reach it, hoping it would provide more than one entrance that she could breach without making a sound.

Reaching the door, Bet eased her way up to look through the glass.

Then the snow around her exploded, and Bet was knocked to the ground.

FIFTY-ONE

At least she'd found Grizzly.

She'd managed not to scream when the big dog launched himself, taking her down into the snow. Schweitzer had immediately grabbed Grizzly by the neck, but they both recognized each other before either one got hurt. The two dogs began to greet each other like long-lost friends. In any other circumstance, she would have enjoyed seeing the two romping in the snow, but there was work to be done. At least they were all on the backside of the roundhouse and virtually invisible to anyone inside.

'Jeb must have let Grizzly out,' Bet whispered into her radio, wondering what Clayton had heard when the one-hundred-fifty-pound dog slammed her into a drift. Her heart pounded with the rush from the ambush. 'That likely means Jeb is still inside.'

Jeb would have wanted to protect Grizzly from Gordon if Gordon brandished a gun. Grizzly was an excellent guard dog but no match for a bullet.

Bet brushed off the snow and gestured both dogs to her side. She and Jeb spent enough time together that she knew what signals Grizzly responded to, and now both dogs sat at her feet waiting for their next command.

She peered through the window in the final door. Bet couldn't see anyone down the hall but found this door unlocked as well.

'We currently have two unlocked doors, the front entrance and the door into the back hall.' Bet described the details, not knowing how familiar Clayton was with the building. 'Acknowledge.'

The mic clicked twice.

With the storm diminishing, she felt far more vulnerable than when the weather had obscured the sight and sound of her movements.

She gestured for the dogs to fall in behind her. 'I'm going to head around to the last wall, the one farthest from the road.'

She edged up to the corner, though she didn't expect to find anyone standing around in the snow even with the storm ending. The last section of wall had the same three windows as the side facing the road, along with one last door into the game room.

Working her way to the first window, she peered into the room Jeb had set up as an all-purpose room. There were a variety of mismatched but comfortable chairs. A Ping-Pong table took up one corner, and a few folding tables were stacked against another wall.

Bet used those tables when she taught the boys how to tie flies. Her father had volunteered for a number of years, and she'd started helping him when she was still a young girl, teaching the basics of fly-fishing. After his death, she took over his role there too.

Movement caught Bet's eye. Mark, Julia and Jeb sat in a row of folding chairs. Jeremy was wrapping duct tape around Julia, as Gordon stood nearby with his gun pointed at Mark's head.

Mark looked terrified, his eyes wide as he watched his son finish securing his wife. Bet couldn't imagine what it felt like to be taped helplessly to a chair while someone forced your son to tie up his mother.

She took a closer look at Jeb. He looked still, but his hands moved ever so slightly. He was trying to work his way out of the duct tape. It was a futile exercise, but no doubt the attempt gave him a sense of agency in a situation where he had no control. Bet wondered how he managed to get Grizzly to safety yet couldn't escape himself.

Jeremy turned sideways, allowing her a partial glimpse of his face. His eyes looked glazed. She wondered if he was going into shock. He didn't appear to be injured, but she didn't like how pale he was.

Gordon had his back to her. His body language was rigid and tense, but that wasn't a surprise. No one spoke as Jeremy finished securing Julia.

Bet tucked back against the wall as he finished, not wanting to be seen. Even if Gordon didn't see her, Jeremy was too likely to accidentally give her presence away.

What brought Gordon here to the ranch? Some connection to the Crews? Was Grant involved in whatever brought Doug and Gordon into conflict? Was Jeremy an innocent bystander? Jeremy was from Seattle. Gordon lived in Spokane. They were twenty years apart in age. Jeremy had no prior connection to Collier that Bet or Alma had found. Was it pure coincidence he went out with Grant on the snowmobile?

What was she missing here?

'Done?' The voice probably belonged to Gordon, though it was muffled through the door. She pressed her ear against the wood, hoping to hear something useful. Like what Gordon planned to do next. The fact that he had the adults taped up was better than nothing. At least he hadn't killed them outright.

'Done.' Bet recognized Jeremy's shaky voice.

'Now get me that gas can.'

'This is about a gas can?' Jeb's voice came through the door as clear as if Bet was in the room. 'You've got us held at gunpoint over a gas can? You can have all the gas cans you want—'

'Ask my dad about that gas can. He can fill you in.' Jeremy's voice held anger now, not fear.

'Shut up.' Gordon's voice had an edge that Bet didn't like. What did Mark have to do with the gas can? It must be the one Doug bought in Federal Way.

'What's he talking about, Mark?' Jeb asked.

'All of you shut up unless I ask you a question.' Gordon's voice was stressed.

Bet waited to see what else she might hear, hoping for something that could be used to de-escalate the situation before Gordon changed his tack and harmed his hostages.

FIFTY-TWO

After a moment of silence, Gordon's voice broke through again.

'I tried to make this easy, *Mark*,' his emphasis on the name carried disgust. 'All you had to do was put that stupid can in the dumpster at the campsite. But no. You had to play the bigshot, thinking you were clever. Holding my product hostage for your safe passage. What did I tell you would happen if you didn't play straight with me?'

'You said you'd grab my son.' Mark's voice sounded strangled. He wasn't used to not getting his way.

'Exactly. So that's what I'm going to do. I'm going to hang—'

Julia's voice broke through. 'I know where the gas can is. Take me, leave my son.'

'See, Mark? Your wife is much better at this than you are. OK, *Mom*, where is it?'

Julia's voice grew stronger. 'Jeremy stays here. I'll take you to it.'

Mark's voice grew stronger. 'Julia, stop it. As soon as he—'

Whatever Mark planned to say was cut off by a shout from Jeremy and a loud crash, followed by Julia's panicked voice. 'What did you do?'

'I just hit him on a pressure point,' Gordon said. 'He'll be fine.'

'At least sit him upright,' Jeb said, indicating the sound of crashing had been Mark's chair tipping over. 'He could choke or—'

'Do you want to be next?'

Jeb answered with silence.

'Don't hurt anyone else.' Jeremy sounded terrified. 'I'll get the gas can for you.'

'Jeremy, no—'

Gordon cut Julia off. 'Don't do anything stupid, son. Just get the can. Once I have it, I'll be on my way.'

Bet had a split second to make a decision. Once Jeremy left the room, she could grab him and try to negotiate for the safe release of the others. Or she could let it play out and hope Gordon spoke the truth. He hadn't killed any of the other hostages except for Doug, whose death appeared accidental, and who had likely been involved in whatever scheme was going down.

Grabbing Grizzly by the collar, she hauled him around the corner with Schweitzer on her heels, making her way as quickly as possible to the unlocked door into the hall.

Slipping inside, she took the dogs into Jeb's quarters and quieted them. She whispered her plan to Clayton. She'd wait until Gordon got his gas can and left the roundhouse with it, then Clayton would arrive to block the entrance to Jeb's while Bet went into the game room. She'd lock the door, liberate Jeb to help Julia and Mark, then go out and help Clayton secure Gordon.

She slipped out through the other rooms to lock the other doors in the roundhouse. That should slow Gordon down if he tried to come back in. She caught a glimpse of Jeremy hauling the red gas can from behind the cabin. It must have been in the car or on their trailer.

Bet got into position to race into the rec room as soon as Gordon left.

The sound of Julia's scream was the first sign things wouldn't go as planned.

FIFTY-THREE

It was the scream of a mother fearing for her child. Bet felt it in her bones. Julia wouldn't scream like that for anyone's safety except Jeremy's.

Bet traversed the distance down the hall between the front room and the rec room in the back.

She couldn't race into the room firing off her weapon with four civilians in there, so she stopped short of the door. Because it was a hallway, she couldn't hide, but she also wasn't visible to anyone not in her direct line of sight.

The adults were still duct-taped to their chairs. Bet couldn't see either Jeremy or Gordon. But Julia continued sobbing, 'Please don't take my son.'

'I'm sorry.' Gordon's voice came through to where Bet stood. 'I'm sorry for all of this.'

Gordon came into view as he pushed his way out through the door, red gas can in one hand and the other shoving Jeremy out in front of him with a gun jammed into his back.

Rushing into the room, she found Mark still as a corpse on the floor. Julia rocked dangerously from side to side, threatening to throw herself over on to the ground, her eyes pinned on the prostrate form of her husband. 'Help him,' she said, her voice no longer a scream but urgent and low.

Bet ran to the doorway after Gordon and Jeremy. If Gordon had heard her enter, he might return. She peered out carefully to keep anyone from seeing her. Gordon's retreating figure slipped around the back of the Crews' cabin.

'Go, go, go,' she said into her radio to Clayton. She locked the door and rushed to Mark's side.

'Not him.' Julia's voice rose. 'Don't help him, help my son.'

Mark was unconscious but breathing. Bet checked him over as fast as she could but saw no obvious signs of trauma. Jeb made noises in his throat, unable to speak from the tape Gordon had used to cover his mouth while Jeremy went out for the gas can.

Bet went to Jeb and ripped the tape off in one fast movement. He grunted against the pain but kept his eyes on Mark. 'Carotid strike.' Jeb gestured toward Mark with his chin. 'If he doesn't wake up fast, we have to worry about a blood clot or other complication.'

Jeb knew a lot about fighting, his black belt and combat experience making him the expert in the room. Bet needed to get Addie or Donna over to tend to Mark, but she couldn't do that until she secured the scene.

With sufficient time to move his Trooper across the entrance to Jeb's driveway, Clayton could use it as a shield and block Gordon from leaving in the Crews' car. It shouldn't take long now, unless Gordon tried to shoot it out with her deputy.

Julia continued weeping and calling out for her son, which was understandable, but not helpful.

'Julia, please be quiet! We are doing everything we can as fast as we can.'

Bet was impressed when the woman fell silent. Bet pulled out her knife to free Jeb; he could tend to Mark and cut Julia loose.

'I'm going to lock this door behind me,' Bet said to Jeb. 'That should slow anyone down trying to get back inside.' Gordon could break the door down if he had to, but hopefully it would be enough of a hurdle to keep him from trying.

'Please, get my son back,' Julia begged one last time.

Bet set the lock in the doorknob and pulled the door closed as she stepped out into the cold. With her back against the building, she was momentarily blinded by the brightness of the snow. She searched for signs of Gordon and Jeremy and warned Clayton over the radio she was coming around the edge of the building so he wouldn't mistake her for their quarry.

Then she heard a sound.

A snowmobile.

Gordon must have pulled one of the Crews' sleds off the trailer. If he'd seen the Trooper across the driveway, he'd know it was his best chance for escape.

A moment later, a sled careened past her on course for the road, the gas can strapped to the rack. Jeremy drove with Gordon hanging on behind. Jeremy tipped up on one track, and for a moment Bet thought he might crash, which would keep Gordon from escaping, but the kid righted the machine, and they picked up speed. She didn't dare shoot at the fleeing figures as she would just as likely hit Jeremy as Gordon.

Bet yelled for Clayton to follow the sled, though she knew it would be futile if Gordon forced Jeremy to drive off-road where the SUV couldn't follow.

Gordon could even get out of the valley without going through the blockade if they went down the right forest service road, leaving him free to escape into the wider world, armed and dangerous – Jeremy's help no longer needed – turning the teenager into a loose end.

Bet made her way up the ramp of the Crews' trailer, which Jeremy and Gordon had left open, and inspected the sled closest to the back. She recognized it as the one Julia rode. The key was in the ignition and Julia's helmet was stashed nearby. Bet started the engine of the sled and slid the helmet on. It fit well enough, and she told Clayton her plan before she flipped down the face shield.

'Do not shoot Gordon. He may be the only person who knows where Ruby is.'

Relieved Julia's snowmobile had reverse capabilities, Bet carefully backed down the ramp and got herself turned around on the unfamiliar rig.

As she came around the corner of the building, she could just see Gordon's sled heading toward the far end of the valley with Clayton on his tail.

She could try to get a helicopter up to search for Gordon, too. But the weather was worsening again, and helicopters would still be grounded for the duration of the storm.

She gunned the engine and shot out of Jeb's driveway. She might be Jeremy's only chance at survival.

FIFTY-FOUR

It didn't take Bet long to adjust to Julia's snowmobile. It was a trail style, lightweight and easy to maneuver, but it couldn't handle the deeper snow or challenging conditions like the heavier sleds. Jeb owned the bigger, sturdier snowmobiles, which was what Bet was used to. She'd have to be careful not to get stuck or flip herself over in her hurry to overtake Gordon and Jeremy.

Accelerating, she shot down the road in pursuit. The air was freezing as it filled her jacket. The bulletproof vest would keep her core warm, but the air chilled her neck and ran down the arms of her coat. Unzipped, the coat flapped behind her like wings.

Glancing down at her dashboard, she could see Julia's gas tank was mostly full. They had probably planned a much longer ride the day they went back for Grant, and they hadn't ridden again since. The other sled was also unlikely to run out of gas anytime soon.

Jeremy and Gordon reached the forest service road on which Jeb and Bet had ridden up to the accident on Iron Horse Ridge.

Even if they stuck to forest service roads, the two could easily get lost in the wilderness and freeze to death before making their way out. And any information Gordon had on Ruby would disappear with him.

Clayton stopped at the turnoff, unable to follow in the deep snow. Bet raced up next to him. She yelled over the noise of the sled for him to go back and help Jeb with Mark while she went in pursuit.

It was possible Gordon hadn't seen her follow and would think he was in the clear.

'Update Kane,' she called out before she turned on to the service road.

The road grew dark under the trees. The afternoon light was shifting toward dusk, and the curve ahead blocked her view. The thought of an ambush from behind a turn or a group of trees circled in her mind, but Gordon was clearly in flight mode.

With one deep breath, she followed Gordon and his hostage.

Maggie and her father had helped her develop the tools she needed to be a good cop, but they couldn't do anything more now. She had to trust her own gut.

She just hoped it wouldn't let her down.

FIFTY-FIVE

The first hundred feet were a straight line up the road, with daylight still filtering through dense evergreens. After that, the road curved to the right, and the woods blocked what little ambient light remained at almost five o'clock at this time of year. In addition to the season, the peaks rising around her to the west brought early dusk down on the valley. But at least Bet could clearly see Jeremy's tracks in the snow.

She paused at the turn and shut her engine off, straining to hear the sound of his snowmobile. A low, groaning whine sounded above Bet. They were on the way up Iron Horse Ridge, where all this had started. Bet hadn't been farther up the road than where they'd found Grant and Julia, but she guessed that it might drop over the other side and meet up with a trail that led out of the mountains and over to Ingalls Creek Road to the north.

She'd had reason to be on that trail back in September, so she knew it could take Gordon all the way out of the valley, Jeremy vanishing with him.

Once Gordon made it out of there, he could disappear into the rest of Washington State or leave the area altogether, even getting into Canada where he might never be found.

Running with his mysterious gas can, filled with whatever everyone found so valuable.

And Ruby might stay lost forever.

Bet zipped up her coat and started her engine back up, falling in behind the other sled. She wondered how long he would keep Jeremy. Would he take him all the way out of the mountains? Or ditch the kid along the way? If Gordon didn't know how to drive a snowmobile, at least Jeremy was safe until they got back to civilization, as long as he didn't wreck like Grant had.

As she headed up the trail, she tried to imagine a spot where she could maneuver around and get in front of them. She could try to contact Kane and have him get in front of Jeremy where the trail passed the back side of the Collier residence. If Kane didn't know the trail, George certainly would, and he could direct his nephew.

But it was also possible that Gordon would double back around to town in some way and still try to get out down the main road in another car. Better that Kane stay at the roadblock. Bet wondered if he regretted signing up with her and getting stuck waiting at a roadblock that might not see a single vehicle.

With her phone out of range, Bet kept her focus on the trail in front of her. She couldn't let Gordon disappear with Jeremy.

During the drive, her mind contemplated possible scenarios to explain the ongoing situation. Doug could have purchased the gas can as a cover for transporting something illegal. Drugs? Gordon must have expected to meet Doug with the can on the road behind the cemetery. But for some reason, Doug didn't bring the can. A fight ensued. Gordon stabbed Doug, which ended up killing him after infection set in.

The question was, how did Gordon know the can was on the sled Grant wrecked on a ride with Jeremy?

She occasionally stopped on the drive to listen until she caught the sound of the other machine. At least she was keeping the same distance. The fact Jeremy wasn't picking up speed made her think Gordon wasn't aware she followed. As long as they stayed on the trail, she would be able to track them without difficulty.

She rode forward again, her mind returning to the puzzle. If Gordon knew Doug hid the can, the first place he would look would likely be Doug's house. Doug might have even told Gordon where to find it, in exchange for his freedom. Easy enough to sneak into the yard and look for it. Once Gordon realized the sled and the gas can were gone, it wasn't a huge leap to know Grant took it out without his father's permission, one look at Bodhi and his leg brace showed he wasn't out riding around. But how did Gordon know that Grant had ridden out with Jeremy?

Thirty minutes in, she reached the ridge. The trees thinned as she approached the scene of Grant's accident. The sun was down now, and the storm proved it had a little more juice. The wind blew snow across her line of vision. She wasn't sure she would be able to hear Jeremy's vehicle anymore, even if they weren't very far in front of her.

The ridge was a long way from help. If Clayton took one of Jeb's snowmobiles to follow her, he couldn't be gaining very fast. He was smart enough to know getting in a wreck wouldn't help anyone.

Bet passed the location of the accident – at least, she thought that's where she was. With the heavy snowfall since rescuing Grant's body, his snowmobile was no longer visible. Despite the fact someone dug it out not long after the accident, it had since been fully buried.

Gordon must have threatened the Crews, who went up to retrieve the can. Mark was supposed to hand it over at the camp-ground, but he tried to be clever and hold it hostage in exchange for their safety, but that plan had backfired, bringing them to the situation they were in now.

Julia's sled labored in the deeper snow on the exposed ridge-line. The trail narrowed, with sharp drop-offs on either side as she scaled the ridge toward a summit. In front of her, she could just make out where the service road ran across a saddle between two peaks. Wind rocked her from both sides as the storm swirled around her. The blowing snow was soon joined by falling snow as she approached another round of whiteout conditions. Full dark fell, and she struggled to see.

Her headlights lit up nothing but a wall of white in front of her. She slowed to a crawl to keep the tracks in view and not drive off the trail. Jeremy's driving skills impressed her. To stay on the trail in these conditions while a passenger threatened his life with a gun would be a challenge for anyone.

Gripping the handlebars to keep control of the sled, Bet ignored the mental images of pitching off the side of the ridge and tumbling to her death. Even landing in the snow wasn't going to help with a five-hundred-pound sled on top of her or slamming her against a tree. Not to mention the likelihood that even if she did survive an accident, no one would find her before she froze.

How had she gotten herself here? Chasing after a killer alone. Was saving Jeremy really worth giving her own life? The first unwritten rule of law enforcement was getting home safe after a shift. Had she just blown that particular edict?

Maggie would tell her to come home in one piece.

Her father would tell her she'd signed up to protect the community.

Right now, their advice was in opposition, but turning back held danger for her too, so she might as well move forward.

Bet shook off her rising anxiety and focused on the road in front of her. She'd reached the saddle and ducked between the two peaks on either side of her. The wind stopped fighting her for the moment and shifted to her back as she drove into the venturi created by the gap between the mountains.

Snowfall had increased, keeping her visibility at zero. She plunged forward, her sled laboring in the deepening snow. Rounding another curve, the steep mountainside hemmed her in on her right while the drop-off on her left narrowed the trail. She continued to fight her way through the extreme conditions. She couldn't see all the way to the bottom of the drop-off, and she tried not to imagine the weightlessness of a fall from that height.

Her father had died from a fall off a trail. Granted, his fall might have been to end the suffering his cancer caused, not chasing a kidnapper and his victim, but was she about to follow in his footsteps again?

The road tucked back into the trees. Relieved to have some respite from the storm, Bet accelerated. She had no idea how far behind she was at this point.

Then the road diverged.

Jeremy's sled left visible tracks despite the wind and snowfall. Jeremy and Gordon went to the right. Their choice to take the road to the right meant they were heading back toward town, not down toward Ingalls Creek Road. Maybe Gordon didn't know the road came out there and had just been looking for a way around Jeb's place that kept him off the main road. He might think no one had come after him and he was home free.

Bet shut her engine off for a moment but heard nothing outside the roar of the storm. At least she hadn't seen any sign of Jeremy dumped on the side of the trail. It made sense that Gordon couldn't drive a snowmobile, which would protect Jeremy as long as Gordon needed a driver.

All she could do now was move forward. She had just reached out to start her engine again when a rumble started all around her, the sound echoing off the surrounding peaks.

She waited in the dark as the avalanche bore down. With no idea of its direction, any move she made might drive her straight into the path of the torrent.

FIFTY-SIX

The thunder of the collapsing snow filled Bet's ears, and the ground shook under the sled. Bet sat hunched over, desperately hoping she wasn't in the path of the slide.

When the noise finally abated, she regained her composure enough to look around. Her Maglite revealed the path behind her was blocked. No help could follow her, and she couldn't return the way she'd come. She refused to let herself think that Clayton could have been caught up in the deadly wave of snow.

She started forward on Gordon and Jeremy's trail. It was the only path for her to follow.

Twenty minutes later, after heading mostly downhill, Bet faced the end of the trail. The service road stopped with nothing but forest in front of her. Tracks crisscrossed the ground at the base of the trees, as if Jeremy had struggled to find a way through. Shutting off her engine didn't help. No sound of another snowmobile came back to her. No signal on her phone or her radio. No help from the outside world.

Bet climbed down off the sled and shone her Maglite on the tracks in front of her. A single set of tracks disappeared at a slightly wider spot between the trees.

As they got closer to town, her anxiety about what Gordon planned to do with Jeremy grew. At some point, the teen would become expendable. Bet continued to reject the thought she might have missed Jeremy, dumped somewhere behind her in the snow.

Focused on finding him, Bet got back on her sled and carefully entered the trees.

It was slow going. The snow wasn't as thick on the forest floor, but the path left behind wasn't as obvious either. Fallen logs and rocks were buried just under the frozen surface, waiting to pitch her from the sled. She could make out the tracks some of the time but lost them at others with the poor visibility. Despite the dense trees, snow still blasted around her, obscuring her vision.

She was exhausted. Riding a snowmobile was hard work in the best conditions. The time she'd already been out had been grueling. Keeping the sled upright on the ridge and dealing with the heavy drifts were starting to take a toll. Not to mention she'd had barely any rest in the last three days.

'Buck up, buttercup,' she said to herself. She couldn't afford to start taking stock of her aches and pains.

'Focus on the things you can control,' said Maggie's voice.

Something bright flashed in the beam of her headlight. The red and gray paint job of Mark's snowmobile.

The sled wasn't moving. Bet stopped in her own tracks to listen, shutting off the sled and turning off the headlight.

The natural sounds of the forest surrounded her. Had Jeremy's sled run out of gas? Was Gordon tucked in behind the snowmobile or a nearby tree, a gun trained in her direction?

Bet slipped off Julia's snowmobile and melted into the trees. The last thing she wanted was to be a sitting duck if Gordon crept around in the woods. Angling around to the left, Bet made her way forward. She didn't turn on her flashlight. Hands in front of her, she took step by careful step.

Her strong sense of direction held her in good stead when Mark's snowmobile appeared in front of her. Carefully, she circled the machine, finding no sign of anyone waiting nearby.

She couldn't stand there in the cold all night just because Gordon might be hiding in the trees. She sped up her approach to the vehicle, where she reached out and put her hands on the engine. It was rapidly cooling in the cold night air.

Gordon and Jeremy were gone.

It made far more sense that Gordon had left the area. He had nothing to gain by waiting around to see if anyone showed up after him. So even though it made her feel like a bright white target, she popped her flashlight on and started looking for tracks in the snow. The ones she found led off through the woods, but she couldn't tell if they were made by one person or two.

Before she started following, Bet pulled out her phone. She could use her compass, even if she didn't have coverage.

The tracks led in a northeasterly direction. She guessed Gordon hoped to reach town, cell service, and help.

He couldn't call his mother or Skeet, but he must know someone else who would be willing to smuggle him out of the valley. Or maybe he was going to reach out to someone in Spokane, which would take time.

Falling into his tracks, Bet went through the list in her head of the people Gordon had breakfast with the morning of the fight at the tavern.

There was Larry, who had been injured by Skeet's broken bottle. His girlfriend Tammy. Plus, there were three other people who had been at the table, individuals Bet only knew by name.

The snow fell away from underneath Bet's foot as she stepped into a hole. She stumbled forward, pitching herself headlong into a tree. She barely caught herself against the trunk before smacking into it face first, arms heavy with fatigue.

'Crap,' she said as she leaned against a big Doug fir. She pressed her forehead against the rough trunk, slowing her breathing and taking stock. She'd felt something pop in her ankle when she fell with such sharp force, and she waited to see if delayed pain would hit. The last thing she could afford was to get injured out here.

If she couldn't walk, the outcome would be turning into a giant frozen popsicle no one found until spring.

She breathed slow and steady, filling her lungs with the icy air to clear her head. Leaning there against the tree, she felt a vibration.

Her phone had come back into range.

Pulling off a glove, she reached inside her coat pocket. Messages popped up on the screen, the most recent a voicemail from Rob Collier. Bet almost laughed with relief. She didn't realize how isolated she'd felt ever since she'd turned off the loop road.

She scrolled through her messages. Nothing from Clayton. If he'd tried to follow her, he would be stopped by the avalanche and he'd have to go all the way back down the way he'd come. She refused to consider anything else. Alma had left several messages asking her to check in with the station. One text from Kane stated he had nothing to report and was just checking in.

Bet texted Kane to sit tight, that Gordon may still be trying to get out of the valley past the roadblock, and she'd call soon. Then she called Alma and gave her a rundown of the situation.

'Where exactly are you?' Alma asked.

Bet looked around the dark forest.

'I have no idea. Let me check.'

Bet put Alma on speaker and popped up Google maps.

The pin showed her location as halfway up the valley between town and Jeb's place, not far from a cluster of houses on a side street off the loop road. She had to assume Gordon also had a map on his phone and could figure out how close he was to civilization.

Bet told Alma she planned to continue following the tracks.

Hanging up, she pulled her gloves back on and trained her flashlight on the footprints in the snow. She was relieved to find two sets diverged around a rock in front of her. Jeremy was still with Gordon.

Better a living hostage than the boy dying alone in the wild.

FIFTY-SEVEN

Fifteen minutes later, Bet saw a light through the trees. If Gordon hadn't turned the light on himself, he would have seen it as well. It was possible that rather than call anyone for help, he planned to steal a car or force someone else to help him as he'd done with Jeremy. As Bet approached the houses, which were tucked into a cul-de-sac at the edge of the valley, she unsnapped the keeper on her Glock.

The tracks made it to the edge of the trees, then made an arc around the back of the closest house.

If Gordon's intention was to continue past these houses and call someone to pick him up, he wouldn't sneak around the back of this one. Bet hoped he was just looking for an empty house to hole up in – not another hostage.

The light shining through the trees was an exterior light on the front of the closest house. No lights were on in the house itself. With a little luck, no one was home.

Bet moved farther back into the trees again and put a call into Alma with the addresses of the three houses, asking for information about the people who lived there.

Alma came back with names for the owners. One was a summer rental owned by Robert Collier. One was up for sale and sat empty. The third was a retired couple who Alma played bridge with.

'Should I contact them?' Bet could hear the concern in Alma's voice. 'To see if they're all right?'

'Yes. I'll wait. Tell them there is a potential break-in in progress on their street and to make sure their doors and windows are locked and to stay inside.'

Bet listened to the click as Alma put her on hold. She hoped Alma's friends weren't just like Alma, who would no doubt get out one of her many legally registered firearms and wander out in the snow to 'help' law enforcement.

Alma came back on, her voice tight. 'They've double-checked all their doors and windows. They'll lock themselves into their master bathroom until we call back and let them know they're safe.'

'Thank you, Alma. I hope we didn't scare them too much.'

'They're Lakers.'

A person couldn't live out here in the valley for their entire life and be timid. Lakers were hearty stock who could take care of themselves. Knowing the couple was probably armed as well, Bet figured Gordon was in more danger than they were if he tried breaking into the room where they hid.

If he broke into one of the two empty houses, it would put him in an enclosed location and make it harder to run.

Stuffing her phone back into her pocket and sliding her Maglite into her utility belt, Bet made her way toward the first house – the house for sale with the exterior light on – and followed the footsteps around back.

She reached the back door as snow fell more heavily again. She was confident in her ability to remain unseen in the yard. But it also dropped the temperature and made it harder for her to see very far in front of her.

Would she ever be warm again? Her teeth had begun to chatter. The cold had sunk into her bones like an unwanted visitor who didn't know it was time to go home.

No electric lights on this side of the house, no help from the moon or stars with the storm back in force. The darkness was now complete. She leaned against the back of the house and felt for the door. Unlocked.

She cracked the door, easing it open, then stopped it from slamming with the force of the wind. For a brief moment she wished for the backup and warm weather of Southern California. In Los Angeles she'd been part of a huge team, with fellow officers around her and someone else in charge. And she never had to chase a suspect across a mountain range on a snowmobile in a winter storm.

Gritting her teeth against the cold, she leaned into the gap, hoping to hear something useful.

Nothing. No voices. No movement. But there was a light on at the front of the house. A glow came down the hall in front of her, providing just enough light to see inside the room. On the right, she could see a sofa and two chairs, both facing a fireplace. A set of shelves lined another wall, with what looked like books, puzzles and board games. A table sat to her left, with four chairs around it. The items were sparse enough for Bet to guess the house was staged rather than fully furnished.

'God damn it!' The voice that came down the hall was low, male. Gordon. It was not the voice of a teenager. 'That hurts like a bitch.'

'Pain is a good sign.' The woman's voice was vaguely familiar. 'At least you don't have frostbite. I'd better not—'

The last of the dialogue was blocked as the storm continued to pick up around her.

Who had met Gordon at this empty house? And where was Jeremy?

She tried to guess what Gordon would do, but she didn't know the man. She didn't know what he was afraid of or what would talk him down.

She couldn't second-guess someone she didn't understand.

Maggie would tell her right now, 'Don't make assumptions based on your own logic. You'll be wrong every time.'

Bet thought back to the tactical training she'd received. She knew how to storm a building by force.

Then Maggie's voice came through again loud and clear. 'The best thing you can do in an explosive situation is diffuse it. It's great if you can hold your own in a fight, but it's always, always better if you don't have to.'

Just because her attempts to end things without violence before had failed, didn't mean they would fail now.

One more chance to get this under control without starting a gun battle. Bet's own voice was finally the loudest in her mind. *You got this, Rivers.*

First things first – she had to know what she was up against.

Carefully pulling the door shut, she tucked herself down against the far side of the house. She called Clayton, but he didn't answer. Kane picked up immediately. She outlined the situation and gave him the address. She requested he pull his car across the mouth of the cul-de-sac and send her a text when he arrived.

Waiting for Kane, she would suss more out about the situation in the house. Who was helping Gordon? Where was Jeremy? What kind of firepower did she and Kane have to face?

She'd held it together through the events of the last couple hours. She'd dealt with the mess at Jeb's place, the crazy drive across the ridge, the challenge of dodging trees through the forest, even an avalanche. Only now did she feel panic rise.

She couldn't remember who said fatigue makes cowards of us all, but she understood the statement in her bones. It made everything harder.

She bit down on her lip. Pain coursed through her, focused her. She felt her breath calm. Her mind cleared.

'Visualize a successful resolution,' she said to herself. 'One step at a time.'

She edged her way around the building with her hand on the wall for guidance. Turning on her flashlight would make her too easy to spot.

Her head leaned into the wind as she fought the strength of a full-force gale. She pushed her way through the deep snow and made it to the corner of the house.

A light shone through a window at the far end. The glow of the exterior light pointed toward the driveway where a four-wheel-drive pickup truck with a camper shell sat parked. With the vehicle mostly barren of snow, it couldn't have been parked there for long.

Bet shuffled forward until her feet hit something hard and she fell, getting her hands out just in time to break her fall. The shock sent the last of her anxiety fleeing as she struggled to regain her footing. It was the front porch, the snow thinner under the overhang. She made her way up the steps through the unbroken snow.

Whoever met Gordon at the house must have gone through the garage. Could it be the owners of the property?

The front door had an arched window inset at the top. Even though it was beveled, it was clear enough for her to look inside. A living room sat to her right. She could just make out a sofa in an otherwise empty room.

To the left was a dining room, with a kitchen beyond. That was the room with the light on.

Two people stood leaning against a kitchen island, facing a third. The third was Gordon, but Bet couldn't make out the identity of the other two. Body type showed neither was Jeremy.

Her phone vibrated against her chest.

The screen felt impossibly bright in the dark.

Kane had arrived. Bet gave him instructions on how to make

his way through the woods to the left of the house, where the trees would shield them from view.

They would plan their next move from there.

At least she was no longer alone in the dark.

FIFTY-EIGHT

Kane crept out of the woods like a ninja. 'What's the plan?' His voice, though pitched low, still carried through the storm.

Bet filled him in on what she knew, and what she didn't. 'We have to assume everyone is armed.'

Kane nodded as snow dusted his eyelashes. He still had that gaze that made Bet feel like he could read everything about her on a cellular level. She felt strangely exposed, despite being bundled up in multiple layers. Something about Kane continued to nag at her. Like they'd had a past together she couldn't quite remember.

'Did we know each other? Before I mean?' she asked.

He cocked his head, his expression one of curiosity. 'We've never met. I'd remember.'

Bet felt a little foolish. She hadn't meant to ask the question out loud. Especially in the middle of everything going on.

'You must remind me of George.'

Kane smiled at that, his teeth bright against his dark skin and the darker night. 'I get that a lot.'

Bet returned to their current situation. 'From what I can tell, there's only one vehicle here, in the driveway. I don't see anyone else parked out front.'

Kane confirmed he'd seen no other vehicles either. Bet described the layout of the building that she'd been able to assess so far.

'What I'd like to do is enter the house through the back and see what we can determine inside without being seen. Jeremy was Gordon's hostage, and I didn't see any evidence of Gordon dumping him in the snow, so we have to assume he's still got him. The storm is to our advantage. It's loud enough to cover any sound we make.'

Kane agreed and the two made their way over to the back door. Bet eased it open. They stepped inside the house and closed the door behind them.

No sounds indicated anyone heard their breach of the house.

Murmuring came through from the other room, but no one came their way.

With a gesture to Kane, Bet crossed toward the hallway. She leaned against the wall and listened.

'It's not my fault Doug tried to change the rules.' That was definitely Gordon's voice.

'What happened exactly?' The woman's voice started muffled, but became clearer, as if she had turned and faced the hallway mid-sentence.

'Doug got this bright idea that he should be fronted his money because he was taking a bigger risk than the rest of you.'

'We're all taking a risk here,' the woman said.

'And our risk just got a lot bigger,' another male voice said. 'Doug is on the sheriff's radar now. I heard she's looking for him.'

'Relax. I have Doug taken care of,' Gordon said. Bet wondered how much the others knew about Doug. 'Taken care of' could mean so many different things. 'And I've got our product back. Now I just have to get out of this damn valley to deliver it to our buyers in Spokane.'

Bet's speculation about events appeared to be accurate.

'Larry and I have another idea,' came the woman's voice again. Larry. Larry Summers. The man with the stitches in his neck from the barroom brawl. The woman must be Tammy Bishop, the real estate agent. The two at the tavern with Skeet. '*I* take the product to the buyers, and *you* lie low here in the valley until the road is open with no blockade. I read online it's just because of snow on the road, but we can't take the risk it's for something more.'

'No way.' Gordon's voice became agitated. 'The buyers are expecting me to show up, not you two.'

'You can just call them and explain you can't make the drive, but you're sending me in your place.'

'This isn't a yard sale. You can't just switch people around during a million-dollar deal.'

A million dollars? Bet's mind raced over the possibilities of something in a gas can worth a million dollars and landed on a thought prompted from her brief exchange with Jamie Garcia. A surge of drugs in the area. Something liquid.

Liquid methamphetamine was an obvious possibility.

During the time Bet worked in LA, Southern California had seen an uptick of dealers dissolving their meth shipment into water for transport. At the other end, the water was boiled off and the drugs were reconstituted for sale. That could explain what was happening here. But if that was what they were all looking for, how did Ruby fit in? Doug wouldn't have taken her along for a drug buy, so where was she?

'How about we do things my way,' Gordon said. 'You are going to drive me and the product out of the valley right now. And your girlfriend is going to stay with me in the back as collateral until we get to Spokane.'

'What are you—'

The gunshot that cut Larry's question off was even louder than the storm.

FIFTY-NINE

Bet didn't panic. She caught Kane's eye and gestured that she would head toward the kitchen and for him to exit out the back and go around to the front of the house. She slipped up to the edge of the hallway and peered into the kitchen.

All hell was breaking loose.

Gordon writhed on the ground, blood pouring from his arm.

'What have you done? What have you done?' Larry yelled at Tammy like a record caught in a groove. His face turned red, and Bet hoped he didn't pop his stitches. 'What have you done?'

Tammy stood over Gordon, pointing a gun at his head.

'I was protecting myself,' she said. 'Calm down. Both of you. Gordon, you aren't going to die.'

Tammy kicked the gun away from where it had fallen from Gordon's hand.

'Here's what's going to happen. We are going to patch you up, Gordon, and you are going to call your guys in Spokane and explain to them that I am going to make the delivery. Then you are going to wait here with Larry while I take care of business.'

Bet couldn't risk Gordon bleeding out, no matter how much Tammy might think she knew about 'patching him up'. She had to take control of the situation and locate Jeremy and Ruby without anyone else getting shot.

'Everyone, freeze. This is Sheriff Rivers. I have the house surrounded. Drop your weapon. This is the sheriff. Drop your weapons now!'

The kitchen fell silent, except for the sound of Gordon groaning from his spot on the floor.

'Surrounded?' Tammy's voice didn't shake. 'With what? With who? You don't have enough manpower in the valley to have this house surrounded. You're bluffing.'

Before Bet could repeat her command to drop the gun, Kane burst through the front door yelling, 'Down, down, down,' as if he fronted an entire company of officers.

'Drop the gun, Tammy,' Larry begged as he hit the floor, covering his head with his hands.

Tammy swung her arm toward Kane, her first shot wildly inaccurate and embedding itself in the ceiling. Bet grabbed hold of Tammy's arm and spun the gun out of her hand before Tammy had time to fire a second shot. Then she twisted Tammy's arm behind her back, pinning the woman in place.

Kane picked up the guns dropped by Tammy and Gordon, before he snapped handcuffs on Larry, then crossed over to check on Gordon. He rolled the injured man over on to his back and tore through his clothes to find the wound.

'What's his condition?' Bet asked as she handcuffed Tammy, who no longer put up a fight.

'He'll survive.' Kane grabbed a dish towel. 'Hold this on your arm,' he said to Gordon as he stopped to snap a pair of gloves on. 'Where is Jeremy?' he asked Gordon as he put additional pressure on the wound.

Clayton's voice called out from the door. 'I'm coming in. I've got the update from Alma and we've got Addie on standby.'

The cavalry really had arrived. Bet just hoped it wasn't too late.

SIXTY

Kane moved his SUV while Clayton held pressure on Gordon's wound. The sound of a siren poured into the house through the open front door as Addie pulled up outside.

She rushed in with Kane close behind.

'I've got this,' Addie said to Clayton. 'Let me do my job now. You've all done yours.'

'Where is Jeremy?' Bet asked Gordon as Clayton stepped out of Addie's way, returning to the question Clayton's appearance had interrupted.

Gordon looked up at her, his face twisted in pain from the gunshot wound in his arm as Addie tended to him.

'What's in it for me?' he asked.

'I don't think you're a killer, Gordon.' Bet kept her voice soft. 'I don't think you meant for any of this to happen.'

She paused. Like the eye of the storm, the world dimmed down to just her and Gordon. Nothing else mattered. 'He's just a kid, Gordon. You aren't gaining anything by leaving him out there.' Bet would search the house if Gordon didn't tell her anything, but her sense was Jeremy had never made it inside. 'Do the right thing.'

'I've been trying to do the right thing all along.'

Bet pictured Wanda, her son desperate to get her better care and save her house.

'That may be true, but you sure haven't gone about it the right way.'

Gordon said nothing.

'I'll search the house.' Clayton started to leave the kitchen.

'You're not going to find him,' Gordon said. 'There's a shed out back.'

Clayton nodded to Bet that he'd heard and went out the back door.

'And what about Ruby?' Bet asked, now that Gordon was cooperating. 'Where is Ruby?' Surely, he'd tell her that now.

Gordon looked at her, puzzled.

'I have no idea who you're talking about.'

SIXTY-ONE

Addie determined that Gordon's wound was clean, and the bleeding had stopped. It was more of a big scratch than a serious gunshot wound. She left him in Bet's custody for processing at the station, with instructions for Donna to check him out in the morning. Addie had more pressing concerns with Jeremy. He'd been located, unconscious but breathing.

His hypothermia was severe enough that the boy's heart could stop, so they had to get him to the hospital as soon as possible. Bet, Addie and Clayton got Jeremy loaded into the ambulance. Clayton would drive while Addie did her best to raise his core temperature and save his life.

Bet watched the ambulance drive away from the front of the house. Addie and Clayton should have Jeremy down to the hospital in E'burg in about an hour, as long as the storm hadn't blocked the road again.

Addie had been out to E'burg once already, to haul Mark to the hospital. She suspected he'd had a stroke from the carotid strike. Luckily for Jeremy, she'd gotten back in time to take him out of the valley. A wait could have killed him.

The storm had stopped for the time being, and Bet thought it might have finally passed altogether. There was a new feel to the air. It no longer smelled like ice. Instead, the world smelled fresh and clean.

The sky above was clear. The moon was bright and low in the sky. Stars sparkled at the darker reaches of space. Bet felt tiny in the vastness of the universe. Her eyes landed on the house across the cul-de-sac. She called Alma to reach out to her bridge-playing friends.

She had done her job. Collier was safe.

Neither Maggie's voice nor her father's rose in her mind. She was alone with her own thoughts as Sheriff of Collier. But now she knew exactly what she was willing to do to protect her town.

The yoke was still heavy, but at least it fit.

Kane appeared in the window of the kitchen. After running Larry and Tammy over to the station to lock them up in a cell, he'd returned to start recording the crime scene. He'd mark the perimeter, take photos, and begin the report to sort out the charges. Larry, Tammy and Gordon faced prosecutions for their crimes.

Bet didn't know what would happen to Wanda, but that was out of her hands.

She got into the front seat of the SUV and looked at Gordon in the back seat, where she'd had his mother not that long ago. How much damage had all these events done to these families? The Crews, the Duprees? What permanent scars did Paula and her kids have? For what? Gordon said Skeet and Paula weren't involved, he'd just used Skeet for a place to stay. He'd only brought in Larry, Tammy and Doug because he'd needed help with the initial buy, but Bet had no reason to trust him, so she would investigate Skeet and Paula too.

But that could wait until tomorrow.

'I'll be taking you to jail in a few minutes.' He would receive additional medical care from Donna at the station if he needed it, then Bet would transport him to the jail in E'burg in the morning, and he'd receive follow-up care.

'His fingers are also going to hurt like hell,' Addie had said. 'He's got frostnip, which is one stage before frostbite.'

It was still her job to look out for Gordon, no matter what he'd done. 'Do you need any further medical care before we head to the station?' she asked him.

Gordon said nothing.

'Do you understand your rights as Kane read them to you?'

'I gotcha, lawman. Just make sure my mother is taken care of.'

'You can check on her yourself when we get to jail.'

Bet watched his expression, expecting to see anger and resent-ment. His eyes connected with hers in the rearview mirror. It was as if nothing existed beyond the cul-de-sac. With the storm over, the world had become still, the SUV a tiny boat on a quiet black sea.

'Do you have any idea what it costs to survive cancer?' He

paused but didn't break eye contact. 'My mother was going to lose everything.'

'What about all the people you were going to kill putting that poison on the street?'

Gordon had already admitted Bet was right. The gas can was full of liquid crystal meth, picked up by Doug in Federal Way. Gordon was too well known in the area as a small-time dealer, so he needed someone else to act as the mule.

'Addicts aren't my problem. My concern is for me and mine.'

It was a selfish way to live, but Bet understood protecting someone you loved. 'What about Doug or Mark or Jeremy? Doug's dead and Mark and Jeremy both could be.'

'What would you be willing to do to save your own mother?' Gordon's voice was calm, as if sitting in the back of the sheriff's SUV with a gunshot wound and frostnip and discussing an existential question was the most natural thing in the world.

Bet would have given a lot to have been able to save her mom or her dad.

Gordon knew he was going to jail, probably for a very long time, but his expression was serene. As if he'd resigned himself to his fate.

'Why did Doug, Larry and Tammy all get involved?' She might as well see what she could learn about the rest of the group.

'Doug is broke and about to go into bankruptcy. I knew he'd pick up the drugs for me out in Federal Way and do the transport. He was going to be one and done. One job to save his house. Real estate is a mess, so Tammy wanted in. She borrowed against her house to help me with the cost of the original buy.'

'And Larry?'

'Larry is just greedy. He was looking at a whole new career working with me down the road. I was going to expand my enterprise.'

Bet couldn't blame Gordon for wanting to save his mother's life. The problem was how he'd gone about it.

She thought about what she was willing to do. 'I wouldn't kill another person.'

But even as she said the words, she heard the lie. She was trained to kill another person if the need arose. She would do it to protect herself, her deputies, or an innocent bystander if the situation warranted it. She revised her answer. 'I wouldn't kill another person except in defense of myself or another.'

Gordon laughed, the sound loud in the small interior. 'Right. No one with a badge ever makes a mistake. You always know the score before you fire.'

You don't know me. Bet stopped herself. She didn't know him, either. Not really. Not inside. Not what he and his mother had endured. Not what had pushed him to where he was now. He'd been a small-time dealer and thought this one big score would fix his life. She wasn't the judge and jury. That wasn't the role she played.

He fell silent, and Bet knew all she needed to know – except Ruby's whereabouts, which he couldn't help her with. Gordon had brought Doug in as part of the scheme because Larry vouched for him, but he knew little about his personal life. He didn't even know Doug had a daughter.

'Here's what I can't figure out, though. How did you know Grant went out on the snowmobile with Jeremy?'

Gordon let out a heavy breath, and Bet thought he wasn't going to speak, but she waited in case he changed his mind.

'Doug told me the can was in the garage at his house. Once I had him down in the basement, he knew he was beat. He gave me the combination to the lock so I could go get it. I promised to let him go if it was there. I wasn't out to kill the guy.'

Gordon faced three strikes for what he'd done. Life in prison was a likely outcome. Bet couldn't imagine facing that kind of future.

'But the snowmobile was gone. Doug was still conscious, so I had him track Grant down on the phone. One call to some girl named Aimee and I learned he'd gone out with the kid staying out at Pearson's.'

Bet thought back to her conversation with Aimee. She had never asked if the girl had spoken to Doug. That thought never crossed her mind. But what did Bodhi know? It was likely Aimee never told him anything either.

Gordon continued his story. 'I went over to the Train Yard and convinced the father – Mark – that I'd kill his entire family if he didn't do as I asked. You can piece together the rest.'

Gordon must realize he had little to lose by telling the truth now. Tammy and Larry would fall all over themselves to serve Gordon up on a plate and get a better deal for themselves. Skeet wouldn't help after Gordon threatened his wife and kids, even if he wasn't involved in the drug deal. Tammy and Larry would argue they were just investors in the scheme, landing Doug's death and Jeremy's kidnapping squarely on Gordon's head. The group was going to tumble like an ill-balanced stack of dishes, breaking quicker than china on the floor.

Bet went back into the house before she left to make sure Kane would be all right on his own. She'd return after taking Gordon to jail and they would finish securing the premises together.

'But processing can wait for tomorrow,' she said. 'I don't think we have to worry about anyone sneaking in here and sabotaging our crime scene.'

'I'll get as much done as I can before you return,' he said.

Gordon was quiet as Bet got back into the SUV, and they made their way through the snow back to the station. She radioed ahead to Alma to let her know she was coming back with Gordon in custody.

'I'll be here,' Alma said. The woman had been up for days. She'd gotten even less sleep than Bet had, yet her voice sounded as strong as ever. Bet considered what she'd be willing to do to protect Alma, a woman she'd known her entire life. Her thoughts turned to Julia and Mark Crews. They had broken the law to protect their son. Bet didn't have all the details, but Gordon did tell her that Jeremy had fired the crossbow that caused Grant's accident.

'Just doing stupid teenage stuff,' he'd said. 'That's how the kid explained it to us. It's amazing anyone lives to adulthood.'

And even after Mark and Julia learned the truth, that Jeremy stole the crossbow and caused Grant's accident while he was out screwing around, they never would have come clean about what Jeremy had done. The set of bump keys he'd used to open the door to Jeb's outbuilding were most likely disposed of where Bet would never find them, though she guessed a quick look at the boy's internet history would show tutorials on how to make them.

Then there was Julia, who felt responsible enough to make sure Grant was found, letting the sheriff think they were just Good Samaritans. The guilt weighed on her more than it did Mark, but she wasn't going to sacrifice her son for the truth.

Bet rolled up to the station. With the road clear, she could get everyone transported down to E'burg tomorrow. They'd be safe enough in the jail for the time being.

Gordon struggled through the snow to the front door. His hands were cuffed, making balance tricky. 'Can I ask you a favor, Sheriff?'

'What's that?'

'Can you help my mother?'

Wanda had harbored Gordon after he committed serious crimes. She didn't kidnap Doug, but treating him meant she had participated in the events that killed him. Gordon thought he was helping his mother, but his actions would end up having the opposite effect.

Trapped between wanting to save Doug's life and knowing a third strike would send her son to prison for life, Wanda had chosen to do nothing, which was still a choice.

'I look out for everyone in Collier,' Bet said. 'That's the job.'

They had reached the front steps. Alma sat behind the computer, her reading glasses perched on the end of her nose, eyes pinned on the two of them as they came through the front door.

'Thank you, Sheriff,' Gordon said. 'That's all I could ask for.'

Bet opened the door, and the two stepped in out of the cold.

SIXTY-TWO

The next morning, Bet sat in the chair in the small interview room and stared at Bodhi across the table. He faced her, his back to the door. She was alone in the room with him, but the recorder's red eye flashed as it documented their conversation.

'You understand my dilemma, right?' She kept her voice even, not threatening, but hard enough for him to know she was serious.

Bet was in a tricky position where Bodhi was concerned. Now that she had a better understanding of Doug's behavior – transporting the liquid crystal meth from Federal Way to Collier – she couldn't rule out Bodhi's involvement.

He'd said a few things that made her believe he hadn't been totally honest with her.

'Why would I have helped you if I'd known what my father did?'

'You could have believed he'd run into trouble during the deal and hoped I'd track him down without discovering the full nature of his actions.'

Bodhi considered her words. He looked like he might throw up.

But he was also the son of a murder victim and the only remaining family member capable of taking care of Ruby once they found her, so she desperately hoped he wasn't involved.

The police in Cle Elum checked out the hotel that Doug had in his GPS to see if they could find evidence of Ruby's location. With Doug dead, it was all Bet had to go on.

'I knew my father was in financial trouble,' Bodhi said. 'If I seemed less than honest with you before, it was only because I'd just found out how bad things were when I was digging through his stuff. I wasn't sure what he'd be willing to do to try to fix it. He's acted strange the last couple weeks.'

There was a ring of truth to Bodhi's words. He'd clearly not been worried about his father or his brother when Bet arrived at his house the first time. His father's disappearance appeared to be a surprise.

And the way he spoke about Ruby made Bet believe he wouldn't jeopardize his sister's life, but he wasn't telling her everything. Bet could feel it in her gut.

'There's something else.' He hung his head. Bet waited. 'I think it's my fault Ruby's missing.'

He closed his eyes, as if too ashamed of what he was about to say to look Bet in the eye.

'Dad asked me to take care of her for a few days. He usually took her with him when he had jobs out of town. She's home-schooled, you know, so he could do that. I didn't want the respon-sibility. I told him it wasn't fair since I was injured, which was bullshit. I could have watched her. I just didn't want to. We had a stupid fight. He must have left her somewhere because of me—'

Bodhi's tears and guilt were real. Between his clean record, excellent grades at UW, and genuine attempt to help Bet locate his father, she believed he was telling the truth and had no involvement with the scheme.

Further, Gordon, Tammy, and Larry had all said he wasn't involved. Bet found it hard to believe no one in the crew had served Bodhi up if they thought it would help their own case by turning evidence against him.

Things got heated at the cemetery with Gordon and he'd stabbed Doug during their altercation. 'I was defending myself,' Gordon had said. 'He had a gun.'

It was a possible scenario, and it didn't put Bodhi in the middle.

Gordon also admitted to wrapping Doug in a sleeping bag from the trunk of Doug's car to get him to the rental house, then sliding him across the snow from the rental to his mother's house using the missing shower curtain as a sled.

'I really, truly thought the man would survive after my mother treated him,' Gordon said. 'But all I could think about was three strikes, you're out. Once I had that gas can, I swear I would have let him go. I would have even still paid him. I just couldn't do what he asked and pay him before the deal went through.'

Gordon didn't go back and clean up the crime scene fast enough. It didn't occur to him George would check on the empty rental house.

'Getting caught selling drugs would have been three strikes too.' Bet wondered at the stupidity of the criminal mind.

Gordon looked rueful at Bet's remark. 'I know. But I didn't think I'd get caught. Letting Doug go when he was so angry felt like he could blow it for all of us. I just wanted him to cool down first. Then . . . well, you know what happened next.'

All the bits fit together now, from the freak accident with the stolen crossbow that killed Grant to the million-dollar payout Larry, Gordon, Doug and Tammy all thought they would profit from. Doug never imagined Grant would take his sled, so he hid the drugs in plain sight. It was only meant to be for twenty-four hours.

Bet started to reassure Bodhi when she heard a knock on the door. Alma poked her head inside. One look at Alma's face showed the news was good. She followed her out into the hallway.

Ruby had been found.

Alma handed the phone over with Clayton on the line. He'd stopped in Cle Elum on his way back from driving the ambulance to E'burg.

Local police discovered the hotel Doug saved in his GPS was closed down temporarily due to the owner's illness, but a sign on the door recommended another local hotel.

Ruby had been alone in a hotel room for four days, surviving on baloney sandwiches, a bag of potato chips, and water from the tap. She'd been expecting her father back in less than two hours, and just kept waiting when he didn't show. The Cle Elum police had secured Ruby's safety until Clayton arrived to transport her back to Collier.

'I've got her with me right now,' Clayton said. 'She's fine. She said her father told her to wait, so she did. With the do-not-disturb sign on the door and the storm raging, no one had any reason to check the room.' Bet heard the emotion in his voice. 'Should I bring her straight to the station?'

Bet looked at Bodhi through the small glass window in the door. 'Definitely. I've got a young man here who is going to be very, very glad to see her.'

Bet hung up the phone. She looked down the hall toward her office. So much had happened in just a few days. At least Ruby would soon be safely home.

And Bet had survived. Mark and Jeremy would both recover.

And so would Collier. The snow would stop, and winter would end.

Maybe she deserved the job after all.

EPILOGUE

Kane stared back at her with that unflinching stare, though today his eyes were soft and inquisitive. Another round of storms was winding up but hadn't arrived yet. The main road had been fully dug out by the National Guard, and the Stenleys worked on the rest of the roads in the valley. Her community was no longer isolated from the outside world.

'You're sure after everything that happened, you still want to be my deputy?' Bet laughed.

'I do.'

'You're OK taking orders from a woman, not to mention one who's younger than you?'

Kane chuckled. 'It wouldn't be the first time, ma'am.'

'You know you can't keep calling me ma'am.'

'I figured you'd say that.'

'Yet you did it anyway.'

He smiled. 'Yes, Sheriff.'

Bet relaxed back into her chair. 'OK. Six months of probation. You'll be full-time for the next six weeks while Clayton is on paternity leave, then you may have to go to part-time. I'm trying to work the budget to have two full-time deputies, but I can't guarantee anything. That will also give us time to make sure this will work out – for both of us.'

Kane could decide if he actually wanted to put down roots in Collier.

He sat looking at her. It was obvious something was on his mind.

She finally broke the silence. 'Something you wanted to ask me?'

'Have you heard anything about . . . your exposure.' He tapped his own hand at the spot where the cut on her thumb had exposed her to Larry's blood.

'I'm fine.'

Kane took a shaky breath. 'I'm sure glad to hear that. I felt terrible about it.'

His response perplexed her. 'It wasn't your fault.'

'Are you sure?'

'What do you mean?'

'The struggle, with the bottle. If I had just left you alone, let you do your job, maybe you wouldn't have gotten cut.'

It had all happened so fast, the events were a blur. But at no time had Bet considered Kane responsible for what happened. And here she'd been thinking he would think less of her.

'Don't think that for a minute. You did the right thing in the moment, and it all came out fine in the end.' Bet had done the two days of the HIV cocktail Addie gave her as a preventative, but the negative test results came back on Larry's blood before she'd had to take any more.

Kane nodded, though his expression still looked troubled.

Bet decided to admit the truth. 'I thought you might think less of me.'

Kane shook his head. 'You did the best you could every step of the way. No one died on your watch. Doug made his own bed.'

His words made Bet feel lighter.

'All in a day's work, right?'

Kane stood up. 'Guess I'll go make a drive through town.' He clapped the brown hat of his office on his head. Bet had been right. Her father's uniforms fit him like they were made for him. She'd gotten new ones ordered that hadn't arrived yet. But Kane merely said he was honored and wasn't bothered at all to wear the uniform of a dead man.

'He didn't die in this hat, right?' was all he'd said. Her father would have appreciated the man's sense of humor.

Kane left the room. Bet heard the sounds of his voice talking to Alma before the front door opened and closed and the station fell silent.

She leaned her chair back against the wall, looking out through the window. Collier lay quiet under its blanket of snow. The sky was blue, the bright sunlight glinting off the frozen lake in the distance, an unbroken expanse of white hiding the dark water beneath. On the edge of the sky, dark clouds massed again. But they'd survived one round of storms, and Collier could do it again.

Rob Collier's number popped up on her cell and she tried to figure out what time it was in Hanoi as she answered the call.

'What time is it there?' she said in greeting. 'I couldn't do the math fast enough. Or maybe I should ask what day it is.'

Rob's laughter came over the cell, the connection unusually good. 'Same time as you.'

'What do you mean?'

'I mean, I just landed at SeaTac. I'll be home in about two hours, give or take.'

Bet's heart jumped, but a surprising moment of shyness kept her from telling him.

'Why don't you sound happy to hear I'm coming home?'

'I am. I am happy. It's just . . . I didn't expect it.'

'Life is full of surprises, isn't it?' Bet couldn't argue with him there. 'I hope it's a good one.'

'I'm really looking forward to having you home.' She didn't know what they had, but she was ready to find out.

She heard his sharp intake of breath. She'd said the right thing.

'I've missed you.' His voice was filled with something else. A longing.

'I've missed you too.'

It was, after all, the truth. As for the rest, she'd just have to wait and see.